PRAISE FOR

cathy yardley

"Another winner from Yardley."
—*Booklist* on *Couch World*

"This book won't disappoint."
—*The Best Reviews* on *L.A. Woman*

"Yardley provides her audience with a lighthearted romantic romp that balances humor and heat, a difficult undertaking to achieve."
—*The Best Reviews* on *The Driven Snowe*

Dear Reader,

The editors at Harlequin and Silhouette are thrilled to be able to bring you a brand-new featured author program for 2005! Signature Select aims to single out outstanding stories, contemporary themes and oft-requested classics by some of your favorite series authors and present them to you in a variety of formats bound by truly striking covers.

We want to provide several different types of reading experiences in the new Signature Select program. The Spotlight books offer a single "big read" by a talented series author, the Collections present three novellas on a selected theme in one volume, the Sagas contain sprawling, sometimes multi-generational family tales (often related to a favorite family first introduced in series) and the Miniseries feature requested previously published books, with two or, occasionally, three complete stories in one volume. The Signature Select program offers one book in each of these categories per month, and fans of limited continuity series will also find these continuing stories under the Signature Select umbrella.

In addition, these volumes bring you bonus features...different in every single book! You may learn more about the author in an extended interview, more about the setting or inspiration for the book, more about subjects related to the theme and, often, a bonus short read will be included. Authors and editors have been outdoing themselves in originating creative material for our bonus features—we're sure you'll be surprised and pleased with the results!

The Signature Select program strives to bring you a variety of reading experiences by authors you've come to love, as well as by rising stars you'll be glad you've discovered. Watch for new stories from Janelle Denison, Donna Kauffman, Leslie Kelly, Marie Ferrarella, Suzanne Forster, Stephanie Bond, Christine Rimmer and scores more of the brightest talents in romance fiction!

The excitement continues!

Warm wishes for happy reading,

Marsha Zinberg

Marsha Zinberg
Executive Editor
The Signature Select Program

surf girl SCHOOL

cathy yardley

TORONTO • NEW YORK • LONDON
AMSTERDAM • PARIS • SYDNEY • HAMBURG
STOCKHOLM • ATHENS • TOKYO • MILAN • MADRID
PRAGUE • WARSAW • BUDAPEST • AUCKLAND

Lots of thanks to my mom, Yen Yardley, who took up surfing last year and was able to tell me how she learned.

ISBN 0-373-83667-8

SURF GIRL SCHOOL

This edition published by arrangement with Harlequin Books S.A.

www.eHarlequin.com

Printed in U.S.A.

To Joe Wilson II, the hero I finally found.

I love you.

CHAPTER ONE

"WE ARE GOING TO LAND the Kibble Tidbits account, or we are going to die trying!"

Allison Robbins nodded vigorously at her boss Frank's vehement statement. She noticed that everyone else at the conference table at Flashpoint Advertising was also nodding in agreement.

"I don't have to tell you how big this account is," Frank said, pacing around the conference-room table like Patton rallying the troops. "We're talking millions of dollars in media placement, more millions in brand-advertising development and creative development and direct mail. Their parent company? Only one of the largest fast-food restaurant chains in the United States!"

Allison tried not to think about the fact that one of the largest fast-food restaurant chains in the United States also had a dog food product. There wasn't any correlation.

Probably.

Frank continued, undeterred. "And, if we land this part of the account, the Kibble Tidbits dog food product, there's a good chance we could get the whole damn shooting match!"

Frank gestured to Allison, and she stood up. Her heart was beating fast, the usual before she had to make a presentation.

She had enough adrenaline in her bloodstream to bench-press a school bus.

"Frank's asked me to pull together some notes on how we're going to attack the proposal," Allison said. "Gary? You want to run the slides?"

Gary, her assistant, instantly had the laptop and projector running like clockwork. Before they hit the lights, though, she noticed several people rolling their eyes and sneering ever so slightly. She didn't blame them, she supposed…it was the day before Thanksgiving, it was three o'clock and a lot of them hoped to go home early. Beyond that, she knew she didn't have their unswerving support.

It hurt a little, sure, but she knew it.

The fact was, if they managed to land this account, Frank was going to be promoted to vice president. That meant there would be an account supervisor position open for the taking, for one of the very account executives sitting around this table. Every single one of them was aware of it.

And Allison was going to have it, or die trying.

Everyone also knew that Allison was probably first in line for the job, she thought, clicking her laser pointer on, which only added to their resentment. That hurt just a touch more.

Her heart was still dancing wildly in her chest, but she pushed the sensation aside. She was next in line for a damn good reason. She was the best at what she did. Period. End of sentence.

"They've been saturating the market with some feel-good stuff, but more of today's consumers are getting more health conscious—not just for themselves, but for their pets…"

She started to run through the slides, her voice never

wavering. The slides were very convincing, and she noticed lots of people taking notes. The slides ought to be convincing. She and Gary had been here till midnight getting them done.

"In addition to that, we're going to suggest a direct-mail campaign to veterinarians, and maybe a coupon to the consumers themselves..." She paused. "Gary? Could you check the thermostat? It's getting a little hot in here... I'll bet they cranked up the heat again."

That's when she noticed everyone look around at each other. She felt as if she was on fire.

"Not too low," Marianne, one of the other execs, said hastily. "Actually...honestly, I'm a little cold."

"Really?" Allison realized that a couple of people were nodding, and to make matters worse, they were all staring at her. She took a deep breath, or as deep as she could manage, and tried to ignore the heat rushing through her. It was nothing. Probably just a little...well, she was only twenty-nine, so it wasn't a hot flash. Maybe something she ate. "So, to continue. What we're recommending..."

Her heart suddenly pumped faster, demanding her attention. *What the heck...?*

"Allison?" Frank asked when she paused noticeably. "You all right?"

She struggled for focus, reined herself in. "Sure. Anyway, it's all there in the handouts." She wasn't going to be able to continue. The feeling threatened to overwhelm her, and she forced herself to keep her voice steady. "You don't need me to walk you through it. Especially when most of you probably have turkey and pumpkin pie on your minds, not dog biscuits."

She got a polite business-laugh, and she realized that Frank was still staring at her curiously as she went back to her seat. She sat down because she was afraid she'd fall down. It felt about a million degrees in there. Worse, she was starting to find the atmosphere absolutely cloying. It was like breathing fog. She looked longingly out the hermetically sealed window.

Just one deep breath...

"Great job, Allison. Of course, that's what I expect." Frank walked to the front of the room. "I also expect everyone to be putting in overtime on this one. Whatever it takes. So enjoy your turkey or pie or whatever...because come Monday, we go to war. You can go ahead and go home early, if you like."

His eyes said *but not if you want to get the promotion.*

They all thanked him...and then filed out, going to their respective offices. Nobody was leaving, Allison felt quite sure of that.

Allison felt her head start to pound in tempo with her heart.

Frank hung back, staring at her. "What the hell was that about?" he asked as Gary packed up the projector and laptop. "You didn't even go over your presentation, after all that work." He squinted at her. "And you look sort of pale."

"Frank, I *am* sort of pale," she said, laughing it off. Or trying to. All she wanted to do was rush outside and take some gulping breaths, but she forced herself to get up slowly, steadying herself. "I'm in here at six-thirty, don't leave until eight. When do I have time to tan?"

"Well, make sure you're not coming down with a cold," he said with a grumpy note of concern.

"I will," she said. A cold. Maybe that was it. The flu...

"Because I really need you on point for this. We can't afford to screw this up."

"Of course." Like she didn't know that?

He waited a second, just to let her know that he was serious, then he left. She walked slowly back to her office. She felt nauseous.

Gary was putting the laptop away, but he stood up. "What happened?" He repeated Frank's question but, unlike Frank, his voice rang through with real worry.

"Nothing," she said. "Can I ask you for a favor?"

He looked at her, frowning. "Your wish, my command, yadda yadda. What do you need?"

"Did you bring your car?"

He blinked at her from behind his wire-rimmed glasses. "Um, yeah. What, do you need me to pick something up?"

"More like drop something off," she muttered, grabbing her briefcase from behind her desk. "Come on. I'll tell you on the way."

They walked toward the parking lot at a fairly decent pace. She could see some people glancing at her, obviously wondering if she was leaving early. She kept her expression schooled, and ignored the desire to hold Gary's arm for support, letting him talk about her schedule, the upcoming presentations...the works.

When the doors opened to the outside, she took in a deep, explosive breath.

Gary glanced around, then put a steadying arm around her waist. "Whoa. What the hell?"

"Anybody looking?" No matter how hard she breathed, she still felt as if she couldn't get enough air.

"No." Now his voice crackled with worry. "What's going on?"

"You're taking me to the hospital," she whispered. "Slowly. Something's wrong."

If anyone could look casually panicked, it'd be Gary. She almost laughed at the war of emotions on his normally impassive face. "You got it."

She got into his car, barely grinning at the way he sedately pulled out of the parking lot…and then gunned the engine when they were out of sight of the building.

"What is it? What's happening?" Now that they were safely out of earshot, Gary's voice rang out like a very high-pitched trumpet. "You looked awful. I thought you were going to pass out."

"I feel like I can't breathe," she said, finally leaning back against the cushions. "My heart's beating like a wild woman."

"Does it hurt?"

"Well, it's not what I'd call *comfortable,*" she snapped.

"Do you think it's a heart attack?"

"I don't…well. Hmm." She tried to remember what it had been like when her father had his three heart attacks. The problem was, she'd never actually been there when he'd had them. All three times, he'd been in his office at work.

That probably wasn't a good sign, she thought, gnawing her lower lip.

She rolled down the window, tried to take deep breaths as the beginning of rush-hour Los Angeles traffic zoomed around her. They pulled into the emergency room with a squeal of tires. Gary practically carried her to the door.

"I am not completely incapacitated here," she said.

"At least you feel well enough to bitch at me," he said with his usual straight face.

In a shorter amount of time than she would've expected, she was shuttled off by a nurse practitioner. "So? You've got chest pains? What type? What time, exactly, did they start?" the woman asked.

"A little squeezy, and my heart's beating like crazy. They started about an hour ago."

"Have you had any heart problems before? Any heart attacks?" She handed Allison an aspirin, which Allison stared at. "Take this."

Allison did as she was told. "No heart problems personally, but attacks run in the family."

"Feel nauseous? Dizzy?"

"A little of both," Allison admitted.

"Lie down. Breathe this." The nurse put the tubes of oxygen in Allison's nose and then started unbuttoning Allison's shirt, sticking her with EKG pads. "Are you taking Viagra?"

Allison was so surprised, she sat up, strangling herself on the oxygen hose. "Am I taking *what?*"

"Are you taking anything like Viagra?" the nurse repeated impatiently.

Allison couldn't help it. She let out a burst of nervous laughter. "Do I look like I have erectile dysfunction to you?"

"Gotta ask it, whether you're male or female. Okay. Just lie back and let me check this out."

Allison did, focusing on her breathing.

"Ms. Robbins...have you been under any stress lately?"

"Well, sure. Who isn't?" That probably shouldn't have come out as defensively as it did.

"Are you regularly under pressure?"

"Only when I'm awake," she tried to joke, then thought about the last nightmare she had—a client review where she was giving a presentation in nothing but granny panties and a big grin. "Okay. Sometimes when I sleep."

The woman nodded knowingly. "Well, I can't say this conclusively, and the doctor's going to want to talk to you, but from everything I've seen, you aren't having a heart attack."

Allison slumped back against the gurney. "That's a relief."

"But I will say one thing," the nurse added. "You seem to be having the mother of all panic attacks."

"FIVE...FOUR...THREE...TWO...ONE!"

Sean Gilroy watched, amused, as his surf buddies and their families surrounded a vat of boiling peanut oil. His good friend Mike was wearing a big black apron and a welder's mask, and he was slowly lowering the turkey into the oil. There was a ragged cheer when the whole bird was submerged.

"Whooo!" he yelped, stepping back and taking a triumphant, Rockyesque stance. "We have turkey! I repeat, we have turkey!"

"Thank God for that," Sean's sister, Janie, said, holding her baby daughter on her hip. "I was worried that maybe we'd just have French fries for Thanksgiving."

Sean chuckled. "You've been spending too many holidays with that traditional family of your husband's," he pointed out, tugging at her ponytail the way he did when they were kids. "'Bout time you returned to your surf roots."

She smiled. "I know. It's been a while since I hung out

with you and the Hoodlums. Or my big brother, for that matter."

"Graduating from college, getting married, two kids in two years," he said, stroking his niece's face and feeling a little goofy grin cover his face, even as he felt a little pang. "Hell. It's not like you haven't been busy. Besides…I'm always here, kid. You know that."

"You can say that again," his friend Gabe said with feeling.

Sean's eyebrow went up, with a little grin. "Commenting on my lifestyle, buddy?"

"Just saying what everybody else says, bro." Gabe's lightning-flash smile showed that he meant no malice in the statement, but there was still a look of concern in his eyes. "Next year, you might want to think about shaking things up, that's all."

"Shaking things up how?" Janie asked, curious.

"Like maybe a new girlfriend," Sean's friend Ryan interjected, popping the top of a Negra Modelo beer. "Dude, you've been single for the past two years. Guy doesn't have a girl for that long, there's a chance he might, you know, explode." He took a sip of beer. "Just thinking about it freaks me out."

Mike walked up, popping the front of his welder's mask off his face. "Yeah, but you're not Sean," Mike pointed out. "He's a lot more surf-Zen than you are."

"So what, that makes him a monk?"

"No, it just means that he's not ready to hit on every girl who walks into the surf shop," Mike responded, glancing nervously at the turkey. "Of course, if we're voting for what Sean can change next year, I'd say replace that piece-of-crap pickup truck of his. Creaking around in that would make me nuts." He grinned. "But I'm not that Zen, either."

Sean shook his head, listening to them bicker. He walked out toward the surf, taking a sip of his own beer. He was going to eat too much tonight to go for a night surf, which was too bad. He'd been surfing every day for the past month, despite the cold November temperatures. He was just too restless lately. For somebody who people described as Zen, he wasn't feeling serene and calm lately. The problem was, he had absolutely no idea *why* he was feeling so wound up. He'd been going along, perfectly fine, doing the same job, in the same city, and the same apartment, for…he quickly did the math. About sixteen years.

So why was he feeling so restless *now?*

Gabe walked next to him, also looking out at the water, watching as the sun set into the Pacific. "What's going on, buddy?" he asked, and now there was no joking…his voice was all concern.

"The usual," Sean replied. "Been slow down at the surf shop, and Oz is going progressively balder by tearing his hair out." Oz, his boss and the owner of the shop, was not a great businessman. "Otherwise, the surf's been great, if sorta cold. So my life's pretty much normal."

"Are you still happy at the surf shop?"

"I love working at the surf shop," Sean said. "You know me."

"Yeah, I know you." Gabe's voice sounded a little resigned. "If you wanted a new job, or a change, you know…the offer's always open. You could come work for me at Lone Shark Clothing."

Sean shifted uncomfortably, staring at the ocean, watching

the last sliver of the crimson sun disappear into the waves. "I love you like a brother, Gabe," he said in a low voice, "which is why there is no way in hell I'm going to work for you."

Gabe sighed impatiently. "Look, it's not like a handout. It's just…I've known you since high school, and that's how long you've been working at Tubes, for Oz." He shook his head. "Sometimes a guy can get bored, doing the same thing."

Sean took a deep breath. *Or restless.* "I don't know clothes. I know surf stuff. I like helping people choose their gear, talk waves. I like teaching kids in the summer," he explained. "I like the community. And besides, I feel like I owe Oz."

"I know he took you and Janie in when you were kids," Gabe said. "But you're, what, thirty-one now? And he doesn't pay you nearly enough, you know that."

Now Sean felt really uncomfortable. "Yeah. I know that. But he lets me live over the shop. It's a trade-off." Before Gabe could keep going, Sean put his hand up. "I appreciate your worrying about me, man. But, well, it just feels too much like a handout, and I don't need a favor. I can take care of myself."

Gabe looked at him, frowning, then shrugged. "Can't blame a guy for trying."

"Yeah, well…you're acting like your sister." Sean grinned. Gabe's sister, Bella, was a notorious buttinsky. "And your wife would kick your ass if she found out."

"If I found out what?"

Charlotte, Gabe's wife, walked up, her expression curious. Sean had known her for years, too, but it was still amazing to see the two of them together. They'd been married for three years now, and it still seemed as if they were in perpetual honeymoon mode. They got razzed about it by the rest of the Hoodlums, their rowdy bunch of surf friends. But Sean knew better. Gabe and Charlotte were like peanut butter and jelly, a perfect match.

His restlessness shifted a little. Maybe he did need a girlfriend.

"We were just talking, honey," Gabe said, nuzzling her neck. "No biggie."

"Really?" Her voice said she wasn't buying it one bit. Then she glanced at Sean, even as her arms went around her husband's waist. "You okay? Did you eat anything?"

"Waiting for the turkey," he said. "But everything looks great. You guys keep pulling together a great party. Thanks for inviting me."

"You're not just a friend…you're family," she said, sincerity rich in her voice. She'd lost her parents at an early age, so she knew what it felt like to be alone. Sean was grateful he had Janie and her family, but he knew what she meant—the Hoodlums were his family, had been for years. "You sure you're okay? You've seemed a little out of sorts lately."

Sean laughed, even as he wondered just how restless he'd been, if people were starting to comment on it. "What, am I wearing a sign?" he asked, a little embarrassed.

"Oh. That's what Gabe was bugging you about, I get it." She reddened a little. "Well, we just…you know."

"I know," he answered, chucking her under the chin. She was like a little sister, too. "Don't worry about it."

"Uh-oh," Gabe said, noticing that Mike was back at the

vat. "I'd better make sure that they don't maim anybody or start a fire. We'll talk later."

"If we have to," Sean said with a little grin to show he was kidding. Still, as he watched Gabe and Charlotte walk away, and saw his friends all gathered again around the turkey, he realized that he still felt weird. Like all the surfing in the world wasn't going to solve it. He was lucky to have his friends, his job, his place to live. He'd always loved his life. He just wasn't sure what was missing.

He took one last look at the surf, hearing the crash of the waves in the growing darkness. His life wasn't perfect, he admitted. But at times like this, it was pretty darned close. And for now, that'd have to be enough.

"HAPPY THANKSGIVING," Allison said with as much cheer as she could muster.

"Happy Thanksgiving, dear," her mother replied. "I can only speak for a minute—they're going to serve dinner soon."

Allison shifted the phone to her other ear. "That sounds nice," she said, looking down at the remnants of the deli turkey sandwich, sitting on a paper plate by her open laptop. "How's Dad enjoying the Bahamas?"

"He's been thinking of investing down here. You know how he is," her mother said with a tone of tolerant amusement. "Just like your brother, always on the lookout for some kind of deal."

"Once a venture capitalist, always a venture capitalist," Allison said. "I take it Rod never made it down to the islands, then?"

"No. He's in the middle of some deal with a company in…let's see, Norway? Sweden? Someplace cold that doesn't celebrate Thanksgiving." Again, that small laugh, with the boys-will-be-boys-and-businessmen brand of humor.

"And Beth?" Allison asked.

"Are you crazy? She's studying for finals!"

Beth, Allison's younger sister, was in UCLA law, and working hard on becoming the top student. Allison sighed. She really should've known better than to ask.

Her mother cleared her throat. "And what about you, dear? We were hoping that at least you could have joined us for this holiday."

Allison felt a little spurt of anger, and quickly quenched it. "I'm working on this promotion. If we land this account, I'll be account supervisor. Before I'm thirty." Which would be in March. Not that she was thinking about that too hard.

"Well, that'll be nice," her mother said a little diffidently. "Still, you might've taken just a few days to be with your parents. I mean, the company could probably spare you."

"It's not a merger with a European conglomerate," she said, her voice even, "and it's not editing *Law Review,* but it's still important, Mom."

There was a pause on the other end of the line. "You're the one who chose advertising, Allison," her mother said, and even over the thousands of miles, Allison felt her mother's rebuke like she was in the same room. "I'm just saying, it's not quite as rigorous. If you're feeling inadequate, you've only yourself to blame."

Allison swallowed hard, but took the comment quietly.

"Oh, here's your father. They're serving dinner. I trust you'll be at the house for Christmas?" Her mother's voice was a study in forced cheerfulness. "Even your brother will be there."

What, he's not doing a deal with some African company that doesn't celebrate Christmas? "I'll be there," Allison said, keeping her own voice cheerful in response. "Love to Dad."

"All right, dear. Goodbye."

Allison hung up her phone, then threw it on the couch. She looked at her living room. There were papers everywhere. There were remnants of her Thanksgiving feast next to her laptop with the presentation slides. The television was on, the volume turned low. They were playing *It's a Wonderful Life* on cable, and it was her favorite part, when Donna Reed got caught naked in a hydrangea bush.

"This is a very interesting situation," she quoted right along with Jimmy Stewart, and she giggled a little hysterically.

The thing is, it wasn't a very interesting situation. It was a sad and vaguely alarming one.

Panic attack.

She hadn't mentioned it to her mother, for obvious reasons, but she sat on her couch, trying to will away the incipient touches of squeezy pain starting to clench at her chest. She had too much on her plate to succumb to panic attacks, of all things. Her family didn't *do* panic attacks. Just like they didn't *do* failure.

The doctor at the hospital had tried to prescribe antianxiety medicine, and a bunch of other kinds of pills, but Allison had turned them down. She had tried pills like that before, back when she was in college. Of course, then it had just been lower-level stress, and she had felt weird going to the doctor for something so stupid, but she'd gone at her roommate's insistence. Unfortunately, the medicine had made her dizzy and loopy, unable to focus.

So she'd done the only thing she could. She moved out on her own. No roommate, no pressure to go to the doctor. She still stressed out, and she lost a lot of weight that semester, but she'd managed to pull it out with a 3.85 grade-point average.

The fact that her mother had shown off her brother's dean's list 4.0 grades was not helpful, admittedly. But the point was, she'd made it through just fine.

Allison picked up her plate and headed off to the kitchen, where a pumpkin pie from the grocery store was thawing out on the counter. She methodically washed up her dishes, then looked at the pie. Then she grabbed a fork, taking the whole pie to the couch. "Happy Thanksgiving to me," she said with a firm nod…then dug in.

An hour later, with a sick but happy feeling of satiety, Allison stretched out on her couch. She managed to rough out a lot of the Kibble Tidbits presentation, but she knew that there was going to be about seven thousand more drafts, if her boss had any say in it…and, of course, he did. The account was too important for him not to get obsessively involved.

The thing was, if she kept having panic attacks, she wouldn't be able to work. At all. And that scared her more than anything.

She frowned, replaying the conversation with the doctor in her head.

"What can I do, other than drugs, to prevent these—" she'd winced, not even wanting to say the words "—panic attacks?"

The doctor was clearly not happy with her comments, and he'd frowned fiercely. "There's only one way to prevent these, really," he said, and from the tone of his voice, he didn't sound very confident. "You're going to need to relax."

"Relax. Just…relax." Allison tensed up immediately. "Uh…"

"Which I can see," he said dryly, "that you're completely incapable of doing at this point."

She bristled, even as some part of her brain said *he's got your number there, kid.* "I can…I mean, I'm sure…"

"What are your hobbies?" he asked, throwing her off.

"Hobbies?"

"Yes. You know, what do you do when you're not working?"

"I…er…" She thought about it. *Eat. Sleep. Shower. Repeat as necessary.* "Um…"

He sighed, impatient. "What was the last movie you saw? The last book you read? The last time you spent time with a friend?"

"I've been busy," Allison hedged, feeling her face redden. "So you're saying I need to get a life."

He frowned so fiercely, she thought he was going to blow a fuse. "I'm saying if you keep working this way, next time, it might not be a panic attack," the doctor warned, even though he'd kept his voice gentle. "Next time, it might really be a heart attack, Ms. Robbins. Believe me, you don't want that."

Allison sighed just remembering the exchange. Reluctantly, she leaned over, shutting down her laptop, putting her work into its neat, respective folders, and tucking the whole lot of it into her briefcase. She'd have enough time to work on it tomorrow, anyway, since a good chunk of the office would still be on vacation the day after Thanksgiving. Hopefully, it'd be nice and quiet, at least.

Then she pulled out a large piece of paper. Panic attacks, like anything else, were just a problem—a challenge. She could handle challenges. In fact, she lived on them.

First thing to do was to brainstorm. She pulled out her felt pens. On the TV, *It's a Wonderful Life* had moved on to *Funniest Holiday Moments,* so she changed the channel, not even paying attention to what was playing. Then she started scribbling away with the single-minded determination that made her one of the best advertising execs on the West Coast.

Hobbies, she wrote in fat letters.

She realized, with some distress, that she didn't have a lot of friends to hang out with. Most of the people that she had been friends with in college had drifted away, gotten married, moved. The friends she had now…well, "friends" was a loose definition. They were people from work. She barely had coffee with them, unless it was somehow related to a work project. Besides, they were people who were more than likely vying for the same job she was, now that she thought about it. Approaching any of them to join her in a hobby was probably not going to happen.

Social life, she wrote on a different corner of the large paper. Then, biting her lip, she added *Friends* to the list. Might as well work on that, too. "In my copious spare time," she said ruefully to herself.

She looked back at *hobbies,* then started listing things randomly. Skiing. Skating. Swimming. Painting. She kept adding things, getting as blue sky as possible. She always told the people she worked with to think big, and then they'd come up with how to get there. There was always a way, she was a firm believer in that. Dream it, and you could do it.

She figured this wasn't any different.

After an hour, she looked at her sprawling list. It didn't cheer her up. On the contrary, she actually felt hints of the panic creeping back.

How am I going to have time to do any of these things? I barely have time for the whole eat-sleep-shower thing!

She took a few deep breaths, and a few more forkfuls of pumpkin pie. *Just pretend it's a client project.* And slowly, logically, she forced herself to focus.

She needed something she could do locally. She crossed off skiing, camping and European travel immediately.

She needed something that incorporated exercise, if at all possible—the doctor had mentioned that exercise would also help, and she was all about multitasking. So she crossed off poker, the art-related stuff and museum visiting.

She needed something that wouldn't stress her out more than she already was. She scratched off bungee jumping, skydiving and hang gliding with a silent breath of relief.

She stared at the options she had left. She lived in Southern California. Sure, it was winter, but all things considered, that didn't mean much. She should probably choose to do something outdoors. She *was* pretty pale, as she'd mentioned to her boss. So something involving sunshine, she thought with a smile.

And maybe the water. She'd loved the beach when she was a kid, she remembered, even though she never had time to enjoy it. And now, she only lived ten minutes from the sands of Manhattan Beach. When was the last time she'd actually looked at the ocean, now that she thought about it?

So what could she do that involved the water?

"I feel like I just got hit on the hedge by a sledgehammer," a girlish voice said from the television.

Allison looked up, startled…and then abruptly started laughing.

Gidget. The classic-movie channel was playing the movie *Gidget.* Allison watched as a diminutive and driven Sandra Dee tackled the sport of surfing with the same single-minded focus that had apparently made her valedictorian, or something. Now, *there* was a fellow short blonde who knew what she wanted, and knew how to go after it.

Allison felt herself grin. She looked down at her list…and sure enough, there it was.

With a fat felt-tip pen, she circled one word in red, and leaned back, feeling better than she had in hours. She had her answer.

Surfing. She could hardly wait.

CHAPTER TWO

"HERE GOES," Allison muttered to herself.

It was Friday, and she'd snuck out of work early, taking advantage of Frank's absence to embark on her latest adventure. She wasn't quite as enthused as she'd been on her couch, after her Gidget epiphany. In fact, she felt as if every single muscle fiber in her body was tensed.

You can do this, she thought. *If Sandra Dee can hang ten, you can get your butt into a surf shop and ask for help.*

She stood up straight, and walked with purpose through the door. The faded sign said Tubes and showed a surfer—at least, she thought it had been a surfer, once upon a time—and a big, curling wave around him. The place looked run-down and somewhat disreputable. Still, it was close to her house, and in the online research she'd managed to do, people on several Web sites and bulletin boards said that Tubes was the absolute best and most knowledgeable surf store in the South Bay.

She was all about Internet research.

She walked in, looking around like a mouse sensing a cat. She hated feeling as if she didn't know what she was doing...hated feeling out of her element. Still, it was just a store, not—

"Can I help you?"

She jumped like a firecracker had gone off. The guy seemed to come out of nowhere. Well, technically, he came out of the back storeroom, obviously. Still, it was so quiet in there, and the guy moved like a ghost.

He didn't look like one, though.

She stared. He was six foot, easily, and had sandy-brown hair. Nice eyes, too, sort of blue-green-hazel, changing. *Like the ocean,* she thought absently. And he had a tan. She'd bet he was a surfer…she could make out a very nice muscled torso under the long-sleeved cotton shirt he was wearing, which sported a logo of a shark with sunglasses.

Then he smiled, and she felt her mouth go dry.

Wow. All she could think was "wow" in response to a smile like that.

"If I can help you with anything at all," he said, his tone slightly amused…and a little provocative. "Let me know."

She shook her head. *Stay focused,* she chided herself. *Don't* even *go there.*

"I need to learn how to surf," she said in a brisk, business-like tone.

He smiled a little wider, looking her up and down. He didn't seem to be doing the sexist scope-out, instead he was studying her. Truth be told, she felt insulted because he didn't really seem all that impressed.

She was wearing a Max Mara suit, she thought, and these shoes were Chinese Laundry. Exactly what was Mr. Big Kahuna smirking at?

"I see," he said slowly, although obviously, he didn't. "Don't tell me. You're a beginner."

"Obviously," she said, feeling a little waspish. Then she

noticed abruptly that she was starting to breathe a little more shallowly. She stopped herself, closed her eyes. Took three deep breaths, just like the doctor mentioned. "Sorry. I've been a little on edge lately," she apologized, grateful that her voice was more mellow. "I know absolutely nothing about surfing. I don't have any equipment. In fact, I don't know the last time I owned a bathing suit," she admitted with a small smile. "So. How can I get started?"

He blinked at her. "Um…"

"Do you have any idea how long it would take? To learn, I mean?" She whipped her Palm Pilot out of her bag. "I don't expect to be hitting pro tournaments anytime soon, but being able to stand up on the board is probably good enough, anyway. You do give lessons here, right? I seem to remember reading that on the Internet. There's a really good instructor here…but I didn't see anything advertised anywhere specifically." She looked at him, realizing that her conversation was starting to speed up, like a runaway train. She tried to slow down by focusing on the business aspect. "You know, you guys really ought to consider a Web site," she added.

"Don't I know it," he muttered, and she saw him cast a glance toward the back room. "But hey, I just work here. So how long, exactly, did you plan on spending on…er, *learning to stand on the board?*"

He was mocking her now, that So Cal drawl obvious. She crossed her arms. "I want to focus on this for the next month and a half, at least," she said, thinking of when the presentation was due. "And I'm serious about the process. I want to get started right away."

She knew that sounded ludicrous. Most people who didn't know her thought things like this were impossible. She proved them wrong every single time. For example, she'd learned Italian to near fluency in three months.

She glared at his gorgeous, yet doubtful face. She could learn how to stand on a floating fiberglass plank in a month and a frickin' half.

He started laughing, and her heart clenched. She focused on the anger, tamping down any potential anxiety. "Listen, you're not the only surf shop in town, you know," she said.

"Then by all means, go to another store," he said with elaborate graciousness. "But before you go running off, can I at least ask you *why* you need to learn to surf in a month and a half?"

She bit her lip, uncomfortable.

"I mean, is it a hazing thing?" he continued. "Bar bet? Did you claim to be a championship surfer on a résumé?"

"I don't see how it's relevant," she said stiffly.

"You've got to admit, it sounds sort of strange," he said, crossing his arms, mirroring her posture. "Let's see. You're wearing an expensive suit. Bright color, a little flashy. I'm betting something like marketing. Maybe advertising." He put his hand on his chin, a surf-bum Sherlock Holmes. "So I'm guessing you're trying to learn to surf to impress a client. Maybe you just got a new surfboard account or a new wet suit account or you're just trying to hawk soda to extreme-sports fanatics. One way or another, though, I'm guessing you're doing this for work."

She winced. She should've said bar bet when she'd had the chance.

"You're right," she said tightly. "I'm in advertising. And this is for work." In a manner of speaking, anyway. And she'd rather be dragged naked over hot coals than admit why she was really doing it.

He grinned, smug.

"So you're the Columbo of the surf world," she said. "Congratulations. So can I get surf lessons and equipment here or what?"

"A woman who gets right to the point. Ordinarily, I like that," he said, his smile sliding off his face. "Still, in this particular case, I don't think this is a good idea."

She stared at him, unable to believe what she was hearing. "Excuse me?"

"You know, you could get just as much information out of a few good surf magazines and a few books. I can recommend several. And maybe you could watch some videos…we sell a lot of great surf videos," he offered. And damn him, he wasn't making fun of her. His voice sounded like he actually wanted to help her.

"Read?" she repeated, dazed. "Watch *videos?*"

How was she supposed to get a hobby by watching *videos?*

"I really have to insist," she said, enunciating very slowly. She hated herself like this—she knew she was getting pushy, acting like her mother, or worse, her father. "I appreciate your suggestions, but what I really need is to buy some equipment and get out in the water."

Now he stood a little straighter, and his arms were still crossed. He looked stubborn. "Well, I have to insist that you're in the wrong store, then, sweetie."

"Are you kidding me with this?" She didn't mean to yell…it just sort of happened. She blamed the nascent panic attack.

He took a step closer, and she was momentarily sidetracked by the smell of his cologne…and the heat coming off of him. The guy was like a very sexy furnace.

"I'm not going to let somebody who's got absolutely no experience and no real interest in the sport get out on a surfboard and muck around in the water," he said, and his voice was sharper than his laid-back image suggested. "It's not just fun and games out there. People who aren't serious, who aren't careful, can get seriously hurt. Or *die.* So no, lady, I'm not going to just let you buy a surfboard and give you some instructions and send you out there, just so you can try to impress your boss or whoever."

"It's just *business,*" she protested. "Isn't that what you do? Sell stuff?"

"That's not," he said, his deep voice low and stern, "how *I* do business."

She was floored. "Fine," she said shakily, responding to both his refusal and his proximity. "Just…just *fine.*"

She was halfway out the door, when she turned. "What's your name?"

His eyes were low-lidded, his arms still crossed. "Sean," he said, his voice smooth as a lime margarita. "Sean Gilroy."

"Well, Sean Gilroy," she said, ignoring the shiver that his voice seemed to stupidly induce, "I was about to drop over a grand in this store. I figure, a surfboard, a spring suit, a winter suit, a couple of videos, a surfboard, some bathing suits…sunscreen, for pity's sake. You name it, I would've bought it. And I hate to say it, but it doesn't look like you guys could afford to lose the business. So thank you for your stunning display of moral conscience, Mr. Gilroy."

He leaned back, smiling at her, even though his bright gaze snapped with fire. "Don't mention it."

"Wasn't planning to."

She stormed out to her car, slamming the door shut behind

her. She was gratified to find that she wasn't shaking, that she was breathing deeply. She was also starting to have a headache. Still, that was infinitely preferable to a panic attack.

Of course, she realized, she also had no hobby.

So they were the best surf shop in the South Bay? Fine, she consoled herself, surfing wasn't the only hobby out there. She sure as hell wasn't going to grovel and convince some surfer-dude to help her. The panic attacks themselves were humiliating enough. She wasn't going to debase herself further and compound the problem.

She would've loved surfing, she thought, starting up her Jaguar. But she'd find something else. Basket weaving. Tap dancing. Anything.

She would get her hobby. And Mr. Gorgeous Sean Gilroy would see just how fine she did without him.

AT SIX O'CLOCK, Sean was closing up the surf shop and looking forward to hitting the waves, when Oz walked into the store, after taking a two-hour "coffee run." He'd been out of the store more and more lately—and when he was there, he seemed unhappy. Sean wondered what was going on there. Maybe the restlessness that he himself felt was just something that was going around. One of Oz's old girlfriends fancied herself a bit of an astrologer—maybe there was something in retrograde or something, that was affecting everyone. Or maybe, like the song said, there was a bad moon rising.

It would certainly explain a lot, anyway.

Oz looked grumpy. "What was all the ruckus about earlier, just before I left?" he asked without preamble.

There had only been a couple of customers in between Oz's leaving and now. "Which…oh." He grinned as the only memorable moment of the day flooded him. "You mean *her.*"

The word her was rich with emphasis. Sean could still picture her, as though she'd just left a second ago.

"Yeah, her," Oz said with less enthusiasm. "The little girl."

"With the big voice," Sean said, chuckling. With her silvery-blond hair and her petite frame, she looked like some kind of manic pixie…a fairy gone to war. She was cute, too. He would've said adorable, except for the Godzilla-sized attitude. She was beautiful, though, he had to give her that. "She wanted to learn how to surf in a month and a half. Can you believe it?"

"So?" Oz frowned at him. "What's the problem?"

Sean shifted uncomfortably. "I don't even know how well she can swim," Sean said.

"You could've asked."

Yeah, he could've, Sean thought, but Oz's persistence threw him a little. Oz unhappy was one thing. This was different. Normally, Oz was as laid-back as Sean himself—that's how Sean had learned it. Oz hadn't even freaked out when Sean's mother, and his then girlfriend, had bailed out, leaving the man with two young teens on his doorstep. So, seeing Oz getting worried was a little unnerving.

"I wouldn't want to be responsible," Sean said quietly. "You know we've never been just a store that pushes stuff on people. There are some basic safety issues here. She was so gung ho…she could've hurt somebody. She could get hurt, herself."

"Still," Oz said. Sean didn't like the way Oz seemed to brush his concerns aside. "You could've sold her some stuff, then directed her to the Y or something."

Sean's eyes widened. "I suppose I could have," Sean said, feeling a bit like a car salesman. "I guess it didn't occur to me."

What's worse, it didn't occur to Sean that it would occur to Oz.

Oz had the grace to redden, at least, though it was hard to notice—his skin was the leathery brown of someone who had been hard-core tanning without sunscreen for well over thirty years. "The shop hasn't been doing so well lately, Sean," Oz said slowly. "We could've used the money, is all I'm saying."

Sean sighed. So here it was. The heart of the problem.

"It was different, when you started working here," Oz continued. "Hell, even when you were sixteen, I knew I could just leave the shop in your hands and go surfing whenever, no problem. We made money no matter what we did. Now…all these posh stores cropping up all over the place. The bait shop got replaced by some high-toned shoe store, and don't even get me started on the Starbucks."

Sean smiled. "Yeah, I know. Still, Tubes is an institution. It's winter, so it's slow," he said, trying to cheer the older man up. "You know, I've been thinking about stuff we could do. To maybe turn things around."

Sean cleared his throat, thinking how best to approach the subject. It was one he'd sort of hedged around for the past…oh, ten years. But Oz really hadn't cared before—as long as the was making enough money to cover rent and pay for his surfboards, he was content.

Maybe he'd listen now.

"I don't know," Oz said, hesitant. But at least he hadn't tuned out.

Sean felt a little of his restlessness ebb as he started to talk about his plan. "For one thing, we might want to spruce the place up, you know? I mean, you own the building, right? We could repaint, maybe. And maybe get a new sign." He grinned, picturing the changes in his mind. "And then, promotion. Charlotte has a number of graphic jobs lined up, still she could work on the logo, and we could get a Web site... Ryan would be happy to help with that. It could really make a difference."

For a second, Oz perked up a little, but just as quickly, he slumped into a chair. "It sounds like a lot of work," he protested.

"You wouldn't have to worry about it," Sean said quickly. "Remember? You felt that way about the books that time we were audited."

"Don't even remind me," Oz said with a shudder.

"I'll handle it, is my point. Just leave it up to me."

For a second, just a second, he thought Oz was going to agree with him. But his heart sank a little as Oz shook his head.

"The thing is, you're going to be busy, Sean," Oz said, his voice sad.

"Busy?" Sean laughed. "Are you kidding? It's the dead season. And it's not like I've got a raging social life." He stopped laughing as he realized how true that statement was.

"Well, the thing is...I'm glad you brought up the part about the building, Sean."

Now Sean felt the slightest tickle of apprehension brush along his spine. "What about the building?"

"The thing is…"And Oz hemmed for a second, looking at the floor. "I've been thinking of renovating the apartment upstairs. You know it was just sort of jerry-rigged, never was a proper place."

"It works fine for me," Sean said, shrugging. It was sort of bare bones, but he'd made some improvements himself…and the view of the ocean was well worth it.

"I was thinking of building it out, making it a little nicer."

Sean stared at him, still not putting it together.

"Jeez, do I have to spell it out?" Oz said, looking anguished. "Kid, I need you to move out."

Sean blinked. Of all the ways for this conversation to go, this wasn't what he was expecting at all. "Is it a matter of…I mean, I guess I could pay you more, if that's what you need," he said, mentally doing some calculations. Of course, he wasn't paying much because Oz wasn't paying *him* that much, but it sounded as if Oz was in trouble. He could make some changes, if necessary. For the good of the shop, if nothing else…and he did still feel like he owed Oz.

Oz sighed. "It's not that. I'm just…I need to reevaluate a lot of things right now." To his credit, Oz did sound apologetic. "I just think that it's time to make some changes. Some improvements."

"So why don't you…"

He was about to ask *make the improvements to the shop first,* but realized that it was the wrong time. Oz was squirming like he was sitting on a bed of nails. Now was not the time to pressure the older man. "Okay," Sean said instead. "How long do I have to find a new place?"

It took Oz a long moment to respond. "Thirty days," he said in a low voice.

Sean frowned. "That's it?" After sixteen years living there?

"My lawyer says that's the best plan," Oz replied, shocking Sean even more. There was a lawyer involved? Oz stood up, looking agitated. "I'm sorry, Sean," he added. He sounded like he really was.

Sean shook his head, still reeling with disbelief as Oz disappeared into his haven in the back room. Sean went about the routine of shutting the store with all the precision and automation of a robot, even as he heard Oz puttering around in the office.

Sean knew what he needed: to get out to the waves. Ever since he was a kid, he knew it was the one place on earth where, no matter what, he could feel better.

Suddenly, a dark thought hit him. He stalked to the back office, knocking on the door frame and watching Oz's startled expression. "Does this mean," he asked somberly, "that you're selling the shop, too?"

Oz cleared his throat, shuffling a bunch of catalogs that were strewn across the beat-up desk. "I haven't made any decisions, Sean," he said.

"How about your lawyer, then?" Sean said.

Oz frowned. "Listen, this is hard on me, too. I love this surf shop, and I know how much it means to you."

Sean doubted that. He crossed his arms.

Oz sighed. "If the store were doing more business, maybe it'd be different. I don't know how to turn that around. If we made more money, I wouldn't have to make the decision," he said, and his voice was pleading. "It's a tough economy, Sean."

Sean saw the earnest expression on Oz's face, and let out a deep breath. "Sorry," Sean said. "I know it's tough."

"You have no idea. Owning a business isn't as much fun as it used to be…and I'm not a young man anymore," he said, and his voice was filled with apology. "I'm just lucky I've had you working for me all these years."

Sean nodded, feeling embarrassed by the compliment. "I've locked up," he said. "I'm going out."

"Good night, Sean."

Sean waved, and headed upstairs, to get his gear. He didn't know what else to say. He felt overwhelmed. He'd talk to the rest of the Hoodlums, he thought as he took off his clothes and pulled on his wet suit. They'd help out, but he didn't want to rely on his rich friends any more than he already did. Gabe would give him a job in a shot. So would any of the rest of them, if they could.

The thing was, he loved the surf shop. He loved living over it. There could be a really nice two-bedroom apartment above it, and they could make all kinds of—

He stopped himself. No. He wasn't going to think about it. *The waves. Just focus on the waves.*

But instead of the usual calming waves, he found himself thinking of something else entirely. The petite blonde. The pixzilla. She certainly wasn't about to let anybody stop her, he thought, with the first grin he'd had since Oz dropped the bomb on him. He bet that if she was handed news like this, she'd probably rush out and have eighteen different solutions before dinnertime.

If a woman that was five-foot-nothing could storm out like a Valkyrie, hell-bent on getting exactly what she wanted and nothing less, then a grown, six-foot guy could probably find another apartment in thirty days. In the meantime, he was going to surf.

He was still smiling as he got his surfboard, feeling better. If he didn't watch it, he'd get completely torqued...and stress was a killer. That was the one thing about the pixie he didn't envy.

"ALL RIGHT. Today, we're going to make a small pot."

Allison ignored the slimy feel of wet clay beneath her hands and sneaked surreptitious glances at the other students. She looked just like them—each of them in jeans and a smock, each of them sitting at the electric potter's wheel at the community college.

The thing is, she wasn't like them. She was more determined, for one thing. For another thing, this was the fourth "hobby" she'd tried in a week, and she was starting to get a little desperate. Watercolor had been mind-numbing and disappointing. Everyone else had managed to make at least somewhat recognizable flowers, while her paper had somehow turned into a muddy-brown Rorschach test. Then she'd tried belly dancing, which was dismal. She considered herself limber, but the teacher (the suspiciously named "Zoyana, mistress of the dance" even though she asked that all checks be made out to "Millie Blumberg") had told Allison that she was way too wooden to really enjoy the dancing and that she needed to learn to relax before she'd ever learn to belly dance. She'd gotten a refund right then and there, something that "Zoyana" seemed more than happy to offer. She needed a hobby that created relaxation. She didn't need the stress of learning to relax, just so she could do something else, for God's sake!

She didn't even want to think about the cooking class. Although she had to say that flambé seemed a little advanced for anybody, and for a beginner, the instructor might have rethought starting with crème brûlée. Handing out blowtorches was probably not the best way to start off.

So here she was, with squishy clay and an increasing sense of foreboding.

At weird points, she'd think of Sean Gilroy. She doubted she'd ever forget his name now. She was torn between laughing at the spectacle she'd made of herself, and getting angry all over again at the way he'd judged her. And, if she were honest with herself, the way he'd pegged her. Of course, maybe a lot of advertising people…well, no. She couldn't honestly think that a ton of advertising people wandered into the dingy shop.

Maybe…

"Miss Robbins? Are you paying attention?"

"What?" She looked up to find Mr. Francis, the instructor, frowning at her and her immobile lump of clay. She belatedly realized she'd been so lost in her own thoughts that she'd missed her cue. Everyone else was already forming small bowls as their wheels spun and whirred in a cacophony.

"Just start easy," Mr. Francis said, smiling a little, although she sensed he was a little impatient with her. She wondered just how long she and her lump of clay had been sitting there. "Wet your hands and just slowly work the clay. Okay?"

She nodded, horribly embarrassed that she was so far behind. She dunked her hands in the small plastic bowl of water and went at the clay with a vengeance.

"Slowly!" Mr. Francis cautioned, then started to walk away.

"Slowly," she repeated, easing her foot off the pottery wheel's "accelerator." The clay barely spun. She pushed at it. It looked…like a smushed piece of clay, she thought critically.

She had always hated art projects, she remembered for no good reason. She'd stopped taking classes as soon as she could. At least art teachers never failed you, but she had ruined her high-school A average with art class.

What in the world was I thinking?

She shouldn't be in an art class, or a dance class.

She closed her eyes. Her happiest memories were from the beach, back when she was very young. Before her father had become a CEO, then a venture capitalist…before her mother had become a successful nonfiction author and was just a sociology professor with summers off. They'd all gone to the beach, her brother, her sister and her parents.

She didn't notice that she was pressing down on the pedal, didn't register the clay slowly inching its way out from the center of the wheel. Didn't see any of it.

Sean Gilroy might be a pain in the neck, but he didn't look unhappy, she thought. In fact, she had yet to see a stressed-out-looking surfer. Maybe there was something there that she shouldn't give up on so easily.

"Miss Robbins!"

Her head snapped up with an audible click. "Yes?" she said out of reflex, tensing. Her foot floored the pedal.

The clay finally got critical momentum, and it flew across the room, a wet, heavy projectile. Mr. Francis barely squeaked before it smacked him hard in the center of the chest, knocking him over.

"Oh, crap!" Allison rushed over to him, as did several other students. "I'm so sorry. I'm so *very* sorry. Are you all right? Are you…"

He looked at her. "Slowly," he grunted. "I said *slowly.*"

She nodded, glum. "I'll…er…"

"Have you considered," he said, propping himself up on one elbow, "trying painting?"

She nodded, even more miserably. "I took watercolor with Ms. Peterson."

"And…?"

Allison sighed. "She suggested pottery."

He rolled his eyes, wincing and touching his chest. "You know," he said, getting up, "I think there's a few open spaces in the origami class."

That was it. The final straw. The last humiliation. How much worse could it get than this?

She took a deep breath. "I think this is my last art class," she said, and packed her things.

She'd just have to swallow some pride, and go back to Tubes. And convince Mr. Sean Gilroy that she had what it took to be a surfer. She convinced people for a living. How hard could it be, right?

CHAPTER THREE

SEAN SAT at the counter at Tubes, at four o'clock on a Saturday. He couldn't believe it was this slow, especially when Christmas shopping ought to be in full swing. Still, there was at least one good thing to come out of business being so wretched. It gave him plenty of time to go through the classifieds. He now had twenty-four days or so to find a new place to live. *When life gives you lemons,* he thought ironically, trying not to wince as he saw the prices of places to live. Sixteen hundred bucks for a one-bedroom that wasn't even close to the beach? He knew he had been lucky to have the sweet setup with Oz, just steps from both the beach and his job. At this rate, he was going to have to get a second job just to cover rent. And it had better be at a restaurant, because he wasn't going to have enough money left over to eat.

After an hour of combing through three local papers and the *L.A. Times,* he was glad to hear the jingle of the bell on the door. A customer. Finally. Just what he needed to get his mind off the depressing state of rentals in the Redondo/Manhattan Beach area. He also tried not to focus on the depressing state of sales at Tubes. *One battle at a time.*

He stood up, headed toward the front of the store. "Hi, how can I help—"

He stopped abruptly when he got a look at who had just walked in. Wearing an emerald-colored suit, with her hair in a loose ponytail and her highest high heels on, she looked adorable. Like a lawyer for leprechauns, or something.

Pixzilla returns, he thought, smothering a chuckle. She frowned, as if she could read his mind.

"Well, this is a surprise," he drawled instead, putting his hands in the pockets of his jeans and rocking back on his heels.

"Isn't it, though," he thought he heard her mutter. "Hello again, Mr. Gilroy."

"Hi back atcha, Miss…" He paused. "Sorry. I never did get your name before." He put his tongue in his cheek, waited for a beat. "I believe you might've been too busy telling me off to get around to proper introductions."

She took in a deep breath. He didn't think brown eyes could snap the way hers did, but she was proving him wrong, and looking awfully cute in the process.

"Robbins. My name is Allison Robbins," she said, holding out a hand. He was surprised and amused enough to take it. Her hand was soft, and tiny compared to his own. His large, callused hand engulfed hers. Still, she had a grip that meant business—something that didn't surprise him at all. "I'd like to start off with an apology," she said, her voice low and contrite. "There really wasn't any good reason for my awful display last time I was here. I…well. Let's just say I was having a bad day." He watched as her eyes clouded, and she laughed, a tiny, self-deprecating laugh that wasn't mirrored in her eyes. "Possibly a bad week."

Bad week. He looked at her. She had an angel's face, with a tiny rosebud mouth, huge eyes, the highest cheekbones he'd ever seen. Still, he noticed the tiny lines of strain etched lightly in that porcelain face.

Bad week, nothing. Honey, I'll bet you're having a bad year.

"Apology accepted," he said easily, and meant it. He saw her looking at him warily, then noticed the tiny, almost imperceptible shift in her attitude as she realized he was serious.

"Good," she said, the relief ringing through her voice. "Now, about those lessons—"

"I have to repeat," he interrupted. "I'm not going to just load you up and send you out there."

She looked startled, then shrugged. "I didn't expect you to change just because I apologized."

"No," Sean said, studying the stiffness of her posture. "But it'd be a lot easier if I did, huh? Because now you're going to have to work on me."

Her eyes widened, and to his surprise, she let out a bell-like laugh. "Well, yes," she said, and in that moment, she looked completely unguarded. He got the feeling she didn't laugh a whole lot, and inexplicably, he felt like changing that. "I'll level with you," she added. "I still want surf lessons."

"I can guarantee you're not going to be able to learn how to surf in six weeks," he said bluntly. "Or is it only five now?"

"No, I guess you wouldn't be able to teach me," she said, pricking at his pride a little, even though from her tone, baiting him obviously wasn't her intent. "But it's not completely hopeless, right? I mean, I could learn *something* in six weeks, couldn't I?"

He nodded thoughtfully, wondering what weird angle she was working now. "The basics, yeah, sure."

"All right, then. Now, we're getting somewhere." He noticed that her smile looked satisfied, almost smug, and that she'd shifted her focus from him to the merchandise around them. "And there's no reason why I shouldn't be able to go out on the water just a little, right? I mean, just to practice the basics, being very careful?"

He sighed impatiently. She was going to jump ahead anyway, that much was certain. He sensed a—well, *recklessness* probably wasn't the right word. This little woman obviously planned things to a T…and she'd had his number before she even stepped foot in the shop. No, reckless, she wasn't. Driven was more like it. Or possibly unstoppable.

She was starting to look through the wet suits, and he stood next to her, close enough to ensure she was paying attention. Close enough that she had to crane her head up to look into his eyes. He hoped his height would intimidate her, even if he doubted the results. "Okay I can't stop you if you're determined to go," he admitted in a low voice, staring into her eyes as if he could hypnotize her into submission. "Still, considering how new you are, I have to strongly urge you not to attempt even the basics by yourself. I wasn't kidding before. People really do get hurt. And I wouldn't want anything to happen to you."

She stared at him, swallowing gently. She looked beautiful, and just a little apprehensive. He'd finally gotten through to her.

Of course, standing this close to her, staring this intensely, had caused a few changes in his own body. She was pretty, and he'd been single for too long not to react to her. He took a cautious step back. "It's smarter for you to go with a buddy," he said gruffly, around the huskiness in his throat, "until you're more confident about what you're doing."

"A buddy?" she repeated, frowning. "Like, a surf friend?"

"Or a teacher," he said. "Just somebody to make sure you're okay."

She smiled, although he couldn't figure out why…until she said, "And you give lessons."

He shrugged. "Now and then. Usually to kids, or guys."

"But you don't teach women?"

"No, I've taught women," he said. "But they usually are more comfortable with a woman instructor…"

"No," she said in her firm voice. "I want you."

He felt the words like a fist in his gut, but despite the sexual tension that knotted him, he couldn't help but smile.

She blushed, her fair skin coloring like a raspberry. "I mean, I want you to be my teacher," she muttered, looking at the toes of her shoes.

He smiled. "Well, I guess I could teach you," he said. "There are a few—"

"How about every day?"

He blinked at her. "Every day?"

"I want to get up to speed as soon as possible. It'd be best if I were practicing daily," she said.

"Do you do everything this way?" he asked.

The question seemed to startle her. "What way?"

"Full steam ahead. Damn the torpedoes." He grinned at her. "No half measures."

Her eyes glowed, and she sent back a confident smirk of her own. "You have no idea."

Oh, lady, I'm beginning to. He wondered if she was that way about other things. Nonwork-related things. He looked over her trim, petite body. Physical things, say.

Immediately, his mind supplied a mental image that almost had him blushing.

Ryan's right. You do need a girl.

He shook his head. The last thing he needed was to get involved with a woman like this. She was a poster child for type-A people. They couldn't get involved with people like him—he was the opposite of type A. He was type Z, surf-Zen, so laid-back he could be mistaken for comatose under the right circumstances. People like her usually wanted to kill people like him. Something about his relaxation seemed to activate more stress in them somehow. He still wasn't quite sure how that worked.

"So, Mr. Gilroy…do we have a deal?"

"Call me Sean," he said out of reflex. Mr. Gilroy sounded alien.

"All right. And you can call me Allison. After all, we're going to be seeing a lot of each other." She pulled out—yes, he'd guessed it—a PDA. "What times work for you? I'm in the middle of this really hellish project at work, but I could manage early mornings, or later in the evenings. I know the days are short, and I might be able to sneak out at a lunch-time or something, once in a while…"

"Wait a minute. Just wait a minute," Sean protested. Suddenly, he remembered the classifieds…and his other problems to deal with. Neat, how just talking to her had managed to derail his train of thought completely. "I don't think I can start teaching you right away."

He saw it again—a mixture of annoyance and anxiety.

"Why not?" She rolled her eyes. "This isn't, like, a waiting period or anything, right? I mean, it's not like I'm buying a gun."

"You're sort of weird, you know that?" He shook his head. "Strangely, no, this isn't about you. This is about me. I have to find a new place to live in the next month. That's probably going to take up all my time."

"You can't teach me anything for a *month?*" she said, aghast. "I can't wait that long!"

He couldn't understand that statement at all—then he remembered. Client related. He frowned. "Okay. If you want me to start earlier, you can just find me a place to live, then."

"All right," she said, flooring him. "What are you looking for? What are your parameters?"

"Um…" he hedged, caught off guard. "Something I can afford."

"What can you afford?"

"I work here," he pointed out. "What do you think?"

She looked around and bit her lip. "Just give me a number."

He did, seeing her blanch a little. Well, he didn't make much. Still, he felt embarrassed, and a little defensive. She was obviously rich. Not that it made a difference.

"That's the only guideline?" she finally asked, jotting down the monthly rent target in her PDA.

"I don't want a huge commute," he said, thinking he might as well go full-out. He was having no luck. Besides, did he really want her involved in his life this much? "I still want to live close to the beach, too."

"Just curious," she said. "Where are you living now?"

"Over the store," he said, gesturing to the ceiling. He then felt guilty. He was handing her an impossible task. "Listen, you don't have to do this. I know how hard—"

"The sooner you get yourself settled," she pointed out, "the sooner you can teach me. So helping you helps me."

He just wished he didn't feel so uncomfortable about that statement. "If you say so."

"So, I'll find you a place to live, you'll teach me how to surf and it'll all work out," she said, putting her PDA away. "I'll have a qualified list of places for you to check out in a few days. Is it all right if I stop by?"

"Sure. Why not?" The woman moved at the speed of light. Still, he doubted that she was going to find anything. He'd been looking all week, and he'd struck out. So why shouldn't he let her run herself ragged? Hell, she might even turn up something. And teaching surf lessons was no hardship—it was something he loved. So why shouldn't he go ahead? "Good luck," he said with a grin.

"You don't need luck if you work hard enough," she said cheerfully, winking at him. "All right. It's a deal. Sean."

She held out her hand again, and he shook it…and held it. And for a second, as their gazes locked and he smiled at her, he felt it again, that sliding sense of attraction that sliced through him like a samurai sword.

"Deal," he murmured, and let her hand go. "I'll, er, talk to you later."

Her breathing had gone shallow, he noticed, and her eyes were round. "'Bye," she said hastily, then turned and left the store.

He could still feel his body burning, and he turned back to the counter.

Why shouldn't he get involved with this woman?

Because she was going to be trouble. He could just tell.

"HOW ARE THOSE SLIDES coming?" Frank yelled from the hallway leading to Allison's office.

She didn't even look up from her computer. "They'd be done a lot faster if you'd stop popping your head in and asking me about them every twenty minutes," she muttered.

"What was that?" he asked from her door frame.

She looked up, a smile plastered on her face. "Going fine! I should have a mock-up by five o'clock. I'll make sure you get a copy before I go home."

He frowned. "You're going home early?"

She sighed. Only in advertising was six o'clock considered early, especially since she'd come in at 7:00 a.m. "I'm doing work at home," she said.

He nodded, although he still looked a little suspicious. "You're my hero," he said. "Just get the mock-ups on my desk before you leave."

He walked out, and she glanced at her watch. He'd be back, no matter what he said, at least once before she was done.

When she was sure he had walked all the way down the hall, she toggled her screen from the presentation she was working on to the Internet, calling up the apartment-search Web site she'd been frantically working with. She still needed to help Sean find a place to live. It was harder than she had anticipated, which frosted her a little. No wonder he'd been eager to let her. He thought this would slow her down.

Not likely. She set her jaw. Once she decided to do something, she did it.

"Did any of those listings I pulled help?"

She jumped, then spun to see Gary, who had wandered behind her like a shadow. "Have you reconsidered the idea of wearing a bell?" she said, trying to calm her system.

Gary ignored her comment, frowning at the screen instead. "You realize, of course, that in that price range, I figure you're only going to find studio apartments. In demilitarized zones. And next to the beach is a pipe dream...you know that, right?"

She sighed. She did know that. She was treating this like a client project. But right now, like it or not, Sean Gilroy was one of the most important people in her life. She'd already had two mini-attacks in the past three days, and she hadn't been back to the surf shop since her last conversation with him. She didn't have a lot of time to learn this whole relaxation crap, she thought crabbily, and this little apartment-hunt diversion wasn't helping.

Having said that...she didn't want him living in a demilitarized zone, either, she realized. "Gary, what else is on my schedule? I want to check a couple of these out, if I can."

"No time," he said. "Look."

She groaned. A few keystrokes, and her color-coded daily schedule popped up. "Oy. Are there really that many hours in a day?" She groaned, putting her head on the desk. "And do I really need to sleep?"

"Well, I suppose it might be fun to watch you hallucinate," Gary said dryly. "Oh. You can cross off one block, though...your parents canceled their monthly dinner."

She felt a little pang, ignored it. "No surprise there. At least I'll see them at Christmas." She paused. "That's still on, right?"

"Your mom's secretary seemed to think so." Gary sounded like he understood, though, and cleared his throat. "Oh, she did point out that there's some friend of the family that you might want to see instead, though."

"No can do. The presentation, and this, er, other project, have to take precedence," Allison said decisively. Then, curious, she asked, "Which friend?"

"Somebody named...let's see. Mrs. Tilson? Does that sound right?"

"Oh," she said, quailing. "Aunt Claire."

"She's your aunt?"

"My godmother," Allison said, picturing the stern woman in her mind. Aunt Claire's husband, Herbert, had died a year and a half ago, and consequently, she'd stopped going to the board functions she had once worked on with Allison's mother. Aunt Claire always remembered Allison's birthday, Allison noted, and had showed up to her graduation. Still, she ought to understand that Allison was busy.

Allison gnawed her lower lip thoughtfully. She did have a little block of time, with her parents' dinner canceled, she thought with a tinge of guilt. And Aunt Claire did live pretty close to her. Just a few blocks away from her, and the beach...

Suddenly, like a bolt of lightning, a brainstorm struck.

"Gary," she said, calling up her phone book on her computer, "you are a genius."

"Yes, I know," he said with his usual understated humor. "Although what I did this time eludes me."

"Just pull those numbers for the dog-food products for me, would you? I've got a phone call to make." She felt positively gleeful. She waited until Gary shut the door to her office, and she dialed Aunt Claire's number.

"Yes?" Aunt Claire sounded as brisk and unbending as ever...but also just a touch tentative, which made Allison feel sad that she hadn't spent more time checking on her. Her guilt ratcheted up a notch.

"It's Allison, Aunt Claire," she said, keeping her own voice cheerful.

"Allison," she said, and the surprise in her voice only made Allison feel worse. "I thought you'd be working."

"I am, but I thought I'd call," Allison said. "I'm sorry I haven't been able to see you."

"I'm not some invalid that needs checking up on," Aunt Claire said, every syllable so crisp it crackled.

"Well, it would still be nice to visit," Allison responded with a smile. "I've just been, well, pretty busy…"

"You've been busy your whole life, dear. Runs in your family," Aunt Claire answered. "But if you have time to drop by for tea this weekend, well, that might be nice."

Allison glanced at the papers strewn across her desk in mountainous piles. "I'll, er, certainly try."

"Wonderful." A pause. "So. Why don't you tell me why you really called, Allison?"

Allison cleared her throat, feeling like a heel. "Well…there was something." She took a deep breath. "You wouldn't still happen to have that one-bedroom apartment, would you? Over the garage?"

"Actually, yes," Aunt Claire said, sounding surprised. "Although nobody's used it since I hired that cleaning service instead of having a maid live in. It's rather small though. I thought you still had that nice town house."

"I do," Allison said. "The thing is…well, I have a favor to ask you. I have this friend who needs to find a place to live as soon as possible."

"Really?" Now Aunt Claire sounded more than surprised. She sounded flabbergasted. "I hadn't envisioned becoming a landlady, Allison. Would this be temporary?"

"Uh…well, I suppose it could be." She hadn't really thought that far. Sean would need some kind of stability, but maybe moving to Aunt Claire's would at least buy him some time. It would definitely buy her six weeks of uninterrupted surf lessons, which would hopefully take the edge off of her panic attacks. So the arrangement might not be optimum for him *or* Aunt Claire…but it would work for the short term, she justified.

She'd worry about the long term after the Kibble Tidbits presentation.

"And who is this person, Allison?"

Allison thought about Sean, and immediately blushed. How to explain without going into the whole saga? "He's, well…he's a teacher."

"What does he teach?"

"Well, ah…" Allison winced, then bit the bullet. "He surfs. He's my surf instructor."

"Your surf instructor," Aunt Claire repeated slowly. With her shocked intonation, she might as well have said *your gigolo.*

"I know. I don't believe it, either." Not that he was her gigolo, she thought.

A quick mental flash of his smile and the way he filled out his shirt and jeans came to mind, unbidden.

Of course, if he were, she bet that she'd definitely have a vigorous form of stress relief…

"I see." Another long pause. Then, in a soft voice, "Is he attractive, then?"

"Pardon?"

"You know," Aunt Claire said. "Cute."

"Auntie Claire!"

"For goodness' sakes, Allison, I'm not asking if I'm going to have eye candy living over my garage," she scoffed. "I'm just wondering if this surf instructor of yours is attractive, that's all."

Eye candy. Her seventy-plus-year-old godmother had just referred to Sean as potential eye candy. This conversation was taking on a freak-out factor that Allison really hadn't anticipated.

"Is he…hmm." Allison briefly considered lying, but Aunt Claire would be seeing him soon enough, if all went well. "He's not ugly," she downplayed.

"Very cute, then."

Was it her imagination, or did Aunt Claire sound approving? Maybe Gary was onto something. Maybe her recent lack of sleep was encouraging hallucinations.

"All right, Allison. Why don't you bring the young man by, so I can meet him. Then I'll make up my mind."

Allison suppressed a groan, thinking of her jam-packed schedule. When would she have time to bring Sean by? "Would it be okay if I just sent him over?"

"I'm not ordering a pizza, dear," Aunt Claire reproved. "This is your favor, remember?"

Welcome to the rock and the hard place, Allison thought, and sighed. "Okay, Aunt Claire. I'll bring him by tonight. Around six-thirty or so."

"That'll be fine. Goodbye, dear."

Allison hung up, growling to herself. She'd had no idea that this relaxation business would be so damn stressful. She didn't know how people managed it at all.

SEAN WAS WAITING in front of Tubes at six-forty. Oz had gone home for the day at four o'clock, so at least he wasn't witness to this. Sean still couldn't quite believe it when Allison told him she'd stop by to show him where his new apartment might be. She'd also told him to dress up, because he'd need to talk to the owner. She hadn't been explicit, but he got the feeling that his performance was going to determine whether or not he got the place.

He was therefore waiting, patiently, as dressed up as he managed to get, in an ironed gray oxford shirt and khakis. He still wore his suede skate sneakers, however. A guy had to draw the line somewhere.

He saw Allison's silver-blue Jag humming down the street before she pulled up to the curb with a flourish. Everything the woman did had an element of flourish, he noticed. He leaned over to the window, glancing in. She was also wearing a muted blue suit, one that seemed to make her large brown eyes even darker.

"Do you mind if I drive?" she asked, and her voice sounded quick, almost manic. "I'm sorry that I'm running late, and this'll be easier than having you follow me."

He shot a quick look at his old pickup truck. Yeah, it would be faster than him following this honey of a Jag. He opened the door, climbing in. Then he did a double take. "Did you know that your clothes match your car?"

"What?" She glanced down, then laughed a little nervously. "I didn't even notice."

He didn't know what possessed him to mention it. Maybe because she, like the car, was so unbelievably luxe looking.

And way out of your price range, buddy boy, so don't get any ideas.

He shook his head. "So. Where are you taking me?"

"A very old friend of the family has a mother-in-law unit

a few blocks from here," Allison said in that quick-breathless-rush voice that he was starting to guess meant she was kind of nervous. "Just a few minutes added to your commute, really, and I think you could stay out of each other's way easily enough, and I don't know if it's going to be temporary or what, I mean, it'll be something to discuss with her, and…oh. She may seem a little straitlaced, maybe a bit brusque at first, but you'd have to get to know her. Not that you'll need to necessarily, as her tenant. I mean, you just need to overlook anything that she says that might seem a little…stern. During the interview. Not that it's really like an interview…"

He watched as her pale face turned flush. She was staring at the road like she was driving the Indy 500.

He sighed, then reached over, covering her right hand with his left one.

She flinched. "Whoa! Hey, what—"

"Just relax," he said, keeping the amusement out of his voice, and trying to project a sense of calm. "You're going to strip your mental gears if you keep revving up that way."

To his surprise, her eyes flashed and she yanked her hand away.

"Don't ever, *ever* tell me to relax," she growled.

He tilted his head, staring at her. "Why not?"

She took a deep breath, and rolled down her window. Her blond hair was up in its usual ponytail, but the wind whipped tendrils out from confinement. "Because," she said with a huff, "if people like me could relax, we'd just *do* it. I mean, it's not like we're just sitting there freaking out because relaxation hadn't *occurred* to us." She glared at him. "Really, what are you thinking when you tell someone that? Do you expect us to just sit back and say, God, what a brilliant idea! Why didn't I think of that before? I should just *relax!*"

He couldn't help it. He laughed, earning him an even frostier glare. "Duly noted. Don't tell you to relax."

She pulled up to a huge old Victorian house, similar to Gabe and Charlotte's, except bigger. With a fenced-in yard yet. Which meant that this was big money.

He got out of the car, feeling a little apprehensive. Allison, in her roundabout and adrenaline-laced manner, had been trying to warn him about the lady. Someone old and crotchety, no doubt. And from the looks of this house, a society type.

She was all of that, and then some, when she opened the door. She was a tiny, birdlike woman, shorter than even Allison's five-foot frame. Still, she had a steely gaze and looked up at him like a white-haired drill sergeant. "You'd be the…surf instructor, then," she announced.

Allison was looking up at the sky like she was praying, and Sean felt his discomfort level inch up a touch. "Yes," he said. "And you'd be Allison's old friend."

"Her godmother," the little woman corrected, offering her hand. He shook it gently—for all her tough demeanor, the woman looked as fragile as sugar glass. He and Allison followed her to one of those stuffy parlors, the type with hard furniture that had clawed cherrywood feet. Ugh. Still, the view out the window, the rolling wave of the Pacific, was very, very promising.

"So, Mr. Surf Instructor. Allison said I was her *old friend.*"

"Please," he said, hiding a grin. "Call me Sean."

"Your full name?" She sat in a high-back chair and barked the question out like a grand inquisitor.

"Gilroy. Sean Gilroy." *And I'll take a Corona, shaken, not stirred.*

He felt the faint bubbles of nerves in his system, and leaned back against the concrete-stuffed chintz couch. Gabe had often commented that Sean was the quietest of the Hoodlums…unless he was nervous.

"Then," Gabe always said, "you're funnier than hell, Sean."

Don't be nervous, you putz, Sean counseled himself. Somehow, he doubted this woman would share Gabe's sense of humor.

He glanced over at Allison, who was mangling the strap of her purse. He didn't even think she realized it. He winked at her, and she frowned at him.

"Relax," he mouthed to her. To his satisfaction, she did the eye-flash thing at him, a third-degree glare. He just grinned, feeling more chuckles forming.

Ooh, this was not going to be pretty if it wasn't wound up quickly.

"I'm sorry. I didn't catch your name." He turned back to the older woman, trying desperately to get back to business.

"Mrs. Tilson," she offered. "So, Mr. Gilroy. You expect me to just let you rent out a part of my home, do you?"

His eyebrows rose, and he sneaked a peek at Allison.

"Aunt Claire, this is really more of a favor to me than to Sean…" Allison interrupted.

"Yes, and I've been wondering about that," Mrs. Tilson said, keeping her attention on him. "Did you know that in the entire time I've known Allison, she's never once asked me for a favor? You must be an extraordinary sort of person, Mr. Gilroy."

Sean bit his lip as his mind provided a few inappropriate

multiple-choice answers to the rhetorical question the pissed-off old woman had peppered him with.

Yeah, well, Allison's never met a guy who could go all night like a lumberjack before was one of his favorites. He forced himself not to speak the thought aloud.

"Just lucky, I guess," he said instead, with a slow grin.

Mrs. Tilson straightened her back to the point where he thought he heard it crack. Of course, with these frickin' hard chairs, he guessed that happened often.

Don't say it.

"Let me tell you something, Mr. Gilroy," Mrs. Tilson said sternly. "You may be very good looking, and all of that. But I'm old. And I'm not talking doddering, amusing, purple-wearing old. I mean that I'm old-fashioned. Strict. And at seventy-eight, I must warn you that I feel absolutely no compunction anymore about being polite with someone I know nothing about. My family says that I have become ruthlessly honest."

He nodded. "I'll drink to that." In fact, he'd love to.

"The fact of the matter is, if I let you rent the garage apartment, then I'll be keeping an eye on you. Allison is my favorite goddaughter, and as competent as she believes she is, I'm not letting anyone take advantage of her. Is that quite clear?"

He knew in that moment that the little switch that usually prevented him from saying whatever was on his mind temporarily shorted out. "Well, I think I'd like to take this opportunity to say that there's absolutely nothing going on between myself and your goddaughter but surf lessons. Not that she's not a hottie, I mean an absolute babe. Especially if she could just *relax* for a minute, you know?"

Allison's eyes went round, and her face went scarlet.

"But the bottom line is, it's strictly business. And I've got to warn you…I'm not some brainless sex slave that Allison's trying to squirrel away in your mother-in-law unit."

Mrs. Tilson, if at all possible, sat up straighter. Then she made a weird sound.

Oh, God. I think I've killed her.

"Auntie Claire…" Allison said, leaning forward.

Suddenly, the old woman let out a wheezy laugh. Sean felt his heart start beating again.

"As I've said, I'm seventy-eight and no longer care what people think," Mrs. Tilson said around a series of dry chuckles. "What, exactly, is your excuse?"

"I'm told I have a cute ass," he said. "Apparently, it's a get-out-of-jail-free card."

Allison choked.

"Well, Mr. Gilroy, I'll rent you the apartment, for the price Allison asked," she said, and Sean felt a flood of relief. He didn't even realize just how tense he'd become. "When will you move in?"

He forced himself to focus, feeling a little dazed. "I've been packing for the past few weeks…I could be in by this weekend, if you're okay with that."

"That sounds reasonable. Let me get you the keys," Mrs. Tilson said, and got up slowly, walking with purpose out of the room.

"I. Cannot. Believe. This." Allison stared at him. "You have a cute ass?"

"Right back atcha," he said, then grimaced. "Did I mention that I joke when I'm nervous?"

"A fact you could've mentioned before we got here!" she hissed.

The larger picture suddenly clarified in his mind. "I've got a place to live," he marveled. "A perfect place. I owe you big time, Allison."

She blinked, as if that fact had only just occurred to her, as well. "Don't mention it," she said, her tone of voice nonplussed. Then she cleared her throat, turning businesslike again. "Besides, it was for a good cause."

He raised an eyebrow. She'd lost him. It was a common occurrence. "Now you can teach me how to surf," she said, and crossed her arms, her expression smug. "Every day."

He didn't roll his eyes, although he wanted to. "Sure."

"How's tomorrow?" she said eagerly.

He sighed. "You're like the Terminator, you know that?" He thought about it. "I'd like to pack up the rest of my things. And I know you've got to work. How about Friday, after I finish moving my stuff? We'll need to get you outfitted first, anyway." He saw her look of protest, and frowned. "You're not going straight out on the water anyway, Allison, so don't even start."

"Okay," she conceded. "But after Friday, every day, right?"

He nodded. Then, even though he was courting disaster, stood up and held out his hand.

She stood up, too, looking at his outstretched palm with what seemed like hesitancy, which wasn't like her. Then she shook his hand.

There it was again…that awareness. He stared at her, watching her eyes go low-lidded.

She stepped a little closer.

So did he.

That, of course, was when Mrs. Tilson came back with the keys. "Here you are, Mr. Gilroy…" she said.

He and Allison released their grip, jumping apart like an exploding grenade. "Um, thanks," he said, feeling his heart race.

Her eyes narrowed as she dropped the keys into his hand. "Just for the record," she said, "I'll be watching you."

He swallowed hard, then nodded.

Considering how he reacted whenever he and Allison touched, that might not be a bad idea.

But speaking of bad ideas, he thought as he pocketed the keys…being in close proximity with Allison every single day might be one of the worst ideas on record.

CHAPTER FOUR

"FOR A GUY who doesn't believe in being bogged down by material possessions," Gabe said, huffing underneath a dresser, "you sure have a lot of crap."

"Shut up and lift," Sean said from the other end of the heavy piece of furniture. "I want to get this stuff moved in by this weekend, and this is most of it. And besides, I've lived over the surf shop for sixteen years."

He and his sister, Janie, had moved in when he was fifteen years old and Janie was twelve—he grimaced a little, remembering just how tight a fit that had been, in the very bare one-bedroom.

"Sixteen years," he repeated, feeling a pang of melancholy mixed with frustration. He probably should've moved when Janie went off to college. She lived in a cute house of her own now, with her husband and two young kids. But he hadn't moved. Granted, it was a lot easier with just him rattling around in the unfinished apartment, and he loved being steps away from the surf. He would miss that.

Things changed, he supposed with a pang. It was high time he changed with them.

The two of them maneuvered the hardwood dresser into his new apartment. Sean took another look around. It wasn't huge, but his old apartment had only been bigger because it was missing a few key walls and opened up into the overhead storage. This was much more posh. He took a deep breath. It smelled like fresh paint. Mrs. Tilson, for all her fierceness, obviously wanted to make a good impression. Sean chuckled at the thought.

"I wouldn't laugh yet," Gabe warned, sounding a little winded. "You've got, like, twenty-five boxes of stuff still in the truck."

"Twenty-four," Ryan corrected, bringing one in with a huff. He was sweating profusely. "And exactly when did you get this whole fascination with books? *Heavy* books?" He dropped the box down on the floor with a thud and looked at Mike.

Sean wiped his own forehead with the back of his hand. "I read," he said, with a shrug.

Ryan surveyed the place, nodding slightly at the view out the window. "Wow. This is pretty great, actually. How did you find out about it, again?"

"Friend of mine," Sean replied, hedging. He popped back out the door, heading for the rental truck.

Ryan and Gabe followed him as Mike handed him a box. "We're your friends," Ryan pointed out with the slight laugh in his voice that signaled mischief. "Who, exactly?"

"A new acquaintance," Sean said. He hoisted the box on his shoulder, turned, and saw his trio of friends staring at him, their arms crossed. "What?"

"Guy or girl?" Ryan asked immediately.

"What do you think?" Sean sighed. "If you must know, a new surf student of mine hooked me up with this place. Mrs. Tilson, my landlady, is a godmother or something."

"Didn't know you were still giving surf lessons," Gabe

said, his tone reflective as they all carried more boxes up the stairs to the in-law unit. "How long has that been going on?"

"Haven't even started yet. Getting me a place was part of the condition of teaching, actually," Sean said.

"Man, did you come out ahead on that deal," Ryan said with a low whistle.

Sean thought of Allison…of the heat he'd felt just by holding her hand. "Not really," he said with feeling.

"What, are you kidding? What's the big deal? You're, like, the best surf coach in the South Bay," Mike said, sounding puzzled.

Sean sighed. "Yeah, but this student wants to learn how to surf in six weeks, now five." That had them all laughing, and Sean grimaced. "I know. Pretty nuts. But at least I got an apartment out of it."

Another trip to the truck, and Sean hoped that was the end of the discussion, but Gabe obviously wasn't finished. "How's it going at Tubes, by the way?"

Sean didn't answer immediately, focusing on huffing and puffing his queen-size mattress up the stairs. When he got to the room, Gabe was looking at him, concerned. "Not so well," Sean admitted…and was surprised when Gabe nodded. "You knew? Who told you?"

"I keep tabs on the neighborhood," Gabe answered. "A couple of business owners are circling around, wanting to buy the building. If nothing else, a few stores would love to move in."

Sean growled. He could just imagine some upscale clothing store or high-end gardening-supply store taking up the spot. Imagining was disturbing enough. "That bad, huh?"

Gabe shrugged. "Do you know what Oz's plan is?"

"As far as I know, he doesn't have one," Sean said dourly.

"I'll bet that Oz is under a lot of pressure. The local chamber of commerce has been complaining that Tubes is run-down…ruining the look of the street. And as far as the business side…" Gabe let his sentence run off meaningfully.

Sean leaned against the wall behind him. Hadn't he told Oz that they ought to repaint? Only one of a million suggestions that he'd made that Oz had ignored. Well, he'd make his suggestions even louder now. It was sink or swim, and the thought of the surf shop sinking was frankly unthinkable.

"Oz said that if sales turn around, he'll do more," Sean said, his voice grim. "So I was going to see what I could do about maybe increasing promotion…or pushing more stuff for Christmas. Doing whatever I can."

"Doing whatever you can with what?" Ryan called over his shoulder, carrying another box.

"With the surf shop," Sean said.

"You and that surf shop," Ryan said, shaking his head. "Man. You moving out is like the end of a legacy."

Sean tried not to think of the finality of that statement.

After several trips, they finally had the bulk of Sean's stuff in the in-law unit. There were boxes everywhere—Ryan was right, he had a ton of books. Fortunately, he now had some built-in bookshelves, a nice touch. It was going to take weeks to unload the boxes. That is, if he decided to unpack. With Tubes up in the air, he didn't know how long this arrangement was going to last. Especially once he was done teaching Allison.

He really had to thank her, he thought. Although from the gleam in her eyes when last he saw her, he was pretty certain she was going to make sure that he repaid her little favor in full…and then some.

And, let's face it…I've never looked forward to repaying a favor so much in my life.

"Well, you look pretty happy about moving," Ryan noted with suspicion.

Sean quickly wiped the grin off his face and glanced at his watch. Six o'clock. He'd promised Allison that he'd meet her at the surf shop and get her outfitted.

"Thanks, guys," he said, and meant it. The three men had been his best friends since high school. He knew how rare it was that they hadn't lost contact when they all went off to college and he'd gone to a junior college. "I really appreciate this."

"Pay us back by grabbing a beer with us," Mike said, taking a deep breath, "and we'll be even."

"Can't," Sean said regretfully. "That new surf student of mine needs to get some things. I was going to open up the store and take care of that tonight."

Mike shrugged. "So grab a beer with us tomorrow."

"I'll be working…then I'm teaching," he said. "Every night, actually." He looked at Gabe. "This is probably going to be a lot of money. Gotta do what I can."

"Don't tell me," Ryan said. "You're teaching some rich guy to surf the Pipeline in a few weeks, and he's paying you outrageously to be a drill sergeant every single day?"

Sean coughed. "Not exactly. But I've gotta get going…"

Gabe stopped him. "How much are you charging?"

Sean was afraid of this. "The usual."

"You're teaching for *free?*" Gabe looked aghast.

"You're what?" Ryan yelped.

Mike frowned, puzzled. "But I thought you said the guy was rich."

"Actually, Ryan said that," Sean said impatiently, stripping off his sweat-soaked shirt and rummaging around for a clean one. He really ought to take a shower. "Listen, I was supposed to be at Tubes fifteen minutes ago, and I hate to rush you…"

"Tubes is in trouble, you're in temporary housing…and you're going to spend the next five weeks giving daily surf lessons to some rich guy every day for free?" Gabe said, his voice raising.

"Every day?" Mike said, surprised.

"Tubes is in trouble?" Ryan picked up immediately.

"I knew I should've hired movers," Sean grumbled. "To those of you joining our program late—yes, Tubes is in trouble. Oz might have to sell. I'm doing what I can to fix that. Whether or not I can has nothing to do with the surf lessons I'm giving, but I promised I'd do that, so that's what I'm doing. And, yes, they're for free. And, yes, I'm teaching them every day." He grabbed a clean shirt impatiently, and turned to glare at them. "We all caught up now?"

"Sean, you've got a lot on your plate right now," Gabe said.

"Yeah, give us one good reason why any man in his right mind would spend all that time and effort for no money at all," Ryan said, crossing his arms.

"Sean?"

Sean looked over at the doorway. Allison stood there, her eyes wide as she surveyed the walls of cardboard boxes and the four sweaty men arguing. "I'm sorry, I didn't mean to interrupt."

Ryan smiled broadly as he checked Allison out. "No. Please. Interrupt as often as you want."

Sean quickly stepped forward, tugging his shirt on. "Allison. I'm sorry I'm late…."

"I only had the store number. I didn't have your cell." She looked apologetic. "I'm afraid I have to reschedule. I have to go back in to work."

"This late?" he said, appalled.

She sighed. "Emergency meeting. So can we do the gear shopping tomorrow? And get started right away?"

"What time is good for you?"

She bit her full lower lip, looking as unstoppably cute as usual. "How's six-thirty?"

"The store will be closed by then," he said, "But I'll open it up just for you, don't worry."

She smiled, and the expression sent a wave of warmth through him. "Thanks," she breathed. "See you then," she said. Then she waved to the other guys, turned and walked quickly away.

Sean watched her leave, admiring her gait…then realized that he had three onlookers who were about to unleash a load of grief on him. Bracing himself, he turned back.

"Guess I can have that beer after all," he said…then realized they were all grinning from ear to ear. "Oh, hell."

"You dog," Ryan said. "What happened to the monastic life?"

"It's not like that," Sean said. "She's just a student, that's all."

"That's your mystery client? I thought she was supposed to be a guy!" Mike said.

"For the record, I didn't call her rich, and I didn't call her a guy," Sean protested. "Ryan just made some assumptions."

"And man, I'm glad I'm wrong," Ryan said, walking to the door frame. "She is HOT." He turned back to Sean, his expression speculative. "You know, I've got some free time. With Tubes being in trouble and all, I'm sure you've got a lot on your plate…so why don't you let me teach her?"

"Got it covered," Sean said with an overtone of menace he didn't even realize was going to be there.

Ryan's grin widened. "Monastic, my ass," he said knowingly.

"Let's get that beer," Sean said tightly.

Ryan and Mike were still joking as they walked down the stairs, but Gabe hung back, his expression still serious. "Listen, I'm glad that your love life is getting back on track, and all…"

"It's not…*argh*," Sean said. "Why won't anybody believe that there really isn't anything between us?"

Gabe's expression stayed stern. "If there isn't anything between you and that girl, then I gotta say—it's even more reason for you to cancel these lessons, Sean."

Sean was taken aback. "Why?"

"Tubes is going to go under fast if things don't change. You're going to have to come up with a game plan. What are you going to do if you have to leave the shop?"

Sean took a deep breath. "I don't know."

"Well, you're going to need to think of something, and pretty soon, too," Gabe said. "I know you promised, and you feel like you owe this girl. And I know how much your word means to you. But we can find her another surf instructor. I can help you with that," Gabe said. "Besides, in five weeks? She sounds like some spoiled rich girl with more money than common sense. It's not like she's learning because she loves it."

Sean felt a wave of protest…and just as quickly quelled it. He didn't know why exactly she was learning, besides the fact that it was for work… Gabe was right.

"I'll worry about it when I get there," Sean said.

Gabe's eyes were sympathetic, and he clapped a hand on Sean's shoulder. "Hate to tell you, bro…but you *are* there."

Sean swallowed hard. "Let me get that beer," he said, his voice a little uneven.

He needed to think about it. He loved Tubes, and would do whatever he could to save it. And if he couldn't save it, then he'd need a job in a hurry. Every single thing that Gabe said made sense.

So why does the thought of someone else teaching Allison feel so damn wrong?

ON SATURDAY, Allison had still put in a long day at the office. She'd gone over the presentation three times with Frank…and had wound up scrapping the entire thing, much to the disappointment of the creative team, the media team and herself. Frank was going after this thing like a man possessed, and he was making everyone else crazy in the process. Four times, she'd had to excuse herself and go outside, trying to take deep breaths without drawing attention to herself.

She wished she could actually get into the water today.

Instead, she was here at the surf shop, after hours, knowing that at least she was getting one step closer to relaxation.

The only problem was, if there was one thing she hated almost more than the panic attacks, it was feeling stupid. And here in the dressing room, it seemed almost impossible *not* to feel stupid. Although "ugly" was running a close second.

"You okay in there?"

At the sound of Sean's voice, her heart raced…and not in the good way that she was starting to get used to around Sean. "Just a second," she called out.

She surveyed the wet suit. It was a winter suit, with long sleeves and full leg covering, and she was having a hell of a time getting the thing on.

She pulled the wet suit over her legs as best she could, wincing as the rubber gripped and pinched her thighs. Okay, maybe she wasn't working out as much as she should, but did the guy sneak her a child's size or something? She couldn't seem to get it around her rump. She finally got it up to her butt.

"Allison? You sure you don't need some help?"

And have him see her like this? Was he high?

"Nope! I'll be out in a minute!" she sang out in a false cheerful voice…then she sat on the floor and *wriggled.*

After a few moments of wiggling, groaning and struggling, she finally got half of the suit over her butt…and promptly kicked the door open, lying there on the floor, with her legs up. She caught a glimpse of her own horrified expression in the mirror, before looking up and seeing Sean's shocked look.

"Um…need help?"

"No," she muttered, then closed her eyes against the humiliation. "I mean, yes."

He was trying not to smile, she had to give him that. "Are you all right?" he asked with exaggerated care.

"I'm fine," she said. "Although I suddenly have a profound new respect for people who put on condoms."

She blushed immediately. What the hell had gotten into

her? She sat up immediately, whacking her head on the small bench.

"Whoa! Whoa," Sean said, all amusement erased from his face.

"You know," she said, keeping her eyes closed, "this is a hell of a lot to do to frickin' learn how to relax."

To her immense horror and embarrassment, she started crying. Tears welled up, and before she could stop them, they were running down her cheeks. She brushed them away as quickly as she could.

He sighed, and to her shock, he actually got into the small dressing room with her.

"Hey!" she protested, scooting back…or at least trying to. The neoprene of her wet suit caught the floor, effectively sticking her there. "What do you think you're—"

He put his fingers on her lips, startling her into silence.

"You and I need to have a little talk."

His tone was serious. He didn't look threatening or lecherous. If anything, he sounded tired, or maybe concerned. His soul-searching eyes seemed to look right into her.

"I'm a little underdressed for a serious conversation," she said inanely, crossing her arms over her bikini top. Not that he was ogling. She just, well, she had serious conversations in her business suits. That was the whole point to wearing the things. To be taken seriously.

She got the feeling this was going to be more than just surf instructions, and she wasn't quite sure how she felt about that.

"Humor me," he said. "Why do you need to learn how to relax?"

She hadn't meant to say that out loud, she really hadn't. Now she sat up carefully, scooting to the other side of the dressing room, which was still close enough to feel his presence, mountainous and close. She surveyed him carefully. "It's complicated."

He didn't say anything. He just stared, waited.

She took a deep breath—or at least, as deep a breath as she could. She could feel the frayed edges of panic, forced herself to stay at least a little calm. "Listen, it's nothing. I've got a big presentation coming up. The biggest presentation of my career, I think. If I land it, I'll be account supervisor by the time I'm thirty, which is what I've wanted since I was in college."

"You knew what you wanted that early?"

She looked up at him, distracted by the interruption. "Of course. Why? Is that odd?"

"No. Never mind," he said, shaking his head, even though she could tell that he obviously thought that it was. She felt a little sinking feeling in the pit of her stomach. Well, of course, planning-type people probably seemed like freaks to dedicated, superrelaxed surfer types like Sean.

"Please go on," he said, and he looked like he was really interested…like he had absolutely nothing better in the world to do than hear what was bothering her.

"It's nothing," she muttered, staring at the floor, flustered. "I just…wanted to loosen up a little. Bring my A-game. That's—"

He leaned over, cupping her chin and forcing her to look up at him. His touch was incredibly gentle, the feel of the slight calluses on his fingertips a marked contrast to her own skin. She felt her breathing go shallow.

"I shouldn't have interrupted, and I don't want you to think I was judging," he said. "I've been worried about you since you walked through this door. And I know that there's something you're not telling me. I really do want to know what's going on." And he stroked her cheek, an almost unconscious gesture, before removing his touch from her completely. "I don't think I can help you unless you're honest with me."

Maybe it was because his voice was so comforting. Or maybe it was because nobody that she could recall had asked her really and truly what was wrong. For whatever reason, she found herself telling him everything. About the meeting, about the panic attack, about the emergency-room visit. His eyes had gone reassuringly wide at that point.

"So the doctor advised that I had to go on meds, and I said I wouldn't," she told him, fearing the tears again and unconsciously wiping them with the back of her hand. Her makeup was probably a mess, but after this point, she'd already gotten as close to emotionally naked as she'd ever gotten, especially with a relative stranger in a dressing-room cubby, for God's sake. A little ruined eyeliner between confidants hardly seemed worth stressing over.

"So they told you that you had to learn to relax without meds, huh?"

"He suggested a hobby," Allison said. "So, I've been busting my ass trying to find a hobby."

"Wow," he said, and this time she wasn't insulted. "I can see now why, well, why everything."

She waited for what he was going to say next. She prayed that it wasn't going to be some previously unmentioned surf rule that crazy people couldn't be trusted out in open water. She'd be forced to kill him. A jury of her type-A peers would definitely understand. Although her peers would figure out a way to get out of jury duty.

Sean stood up, and smiled at her. He put out a hand, helping to her feet. He didn't let go, just looked into her eyes until she felt her stomach go sugary. She smiled.

Then he grabbed her ass.

"Excuse me!" She started to shove him, and to her amazement, he blushed.

"Sorry. That was a bit abrupt," he said, and pointed instead to her wet suit. "I should've warned you. Getting a wet suit on the first time, especially dry, is probably one of the hardest things you'll ever do. But trust me, you'll get used to it." He smiled at her, almost shyly. "And I'd suggest that you put some soap on, maybe, to help get it on before we go out in the water. Here, suck your breath in a little."

Like she'd taken a breath since he started talking! She sucked in a tiny bit more and held it, and he reached down. She barely felt the back of his hand before the suit went where it was supposed to, covering her butt with a small *swwokkk* noise.

"Now put your arms in, and I'll zip you up."

She did, and turned so he could pull the zipper up. "Snug, isn't it?"

"That's the point. It's winter, and you'll be cold even with the suit on." He nudged her back, and smiled more easily. "But you'll find that out soon enough."

"Really?" She felt happiness pulse through her like sunshine. "And...after everything I've said, you're still okay with teaching me?"

"Are you kidding me?" He chucked her under the chin. "You need a hobby."

"Thank you!" She threw her arms around his neck, hugging him tight. "Thank you thank you thank you..."

He hugged her back, chuckling. She could feel it through her chest. Which brought up the fact that she was in his arms, in a tiny dressing room. With nothing but a few thin layers of neoprene and spandex between them.

She backed away hard enough to hit the opposing wall. “Ouch. Oops. Sorry. It’s been an emotional day…”

“No reasons needed,” he said. “I’ll give you some privacy, and I’ll get your stuff together—your board, all that.”

She nodded, still smiling.

He winked before he shut the door. “Oh, and I have to tell you…it’s going to take a little while for you to take that suit off. Consider it a learning experience.”

She opened the door, stuck her tongue out at him, and shut it again.

He was still going to teach her—despite her outbreak of emotion, despite her crying, despite everything. She couldn’t explain it, but she felt better than she had in years.

So taking off the suit was going to be a little challenging. Learning surfing was going to be a little challenging.

In her life, just a little challenging was a nice change.

SEAN HEADED BACK to his new apartment. It was only about eight or so. He’d helped Allison get outfitted, and promised that he’d start teaching her tomorrow night—indoors. In her house, of all places, which she’d been surprised by. Then he’d gone out for a quick surf in the winter moonlight. It was bitterly cold, a real shock to the system, but after spending time with Allison, it was a welcome jolt.

He got the feeling he was going to be going for a lot of night surfs if Allison was going to be his student.

Allison. He closed his eyes for a second, picturing her

sprawled out on the floor of the dressing room at Tubes, trying with desperate fury to tug on that wet suit. He laughed at the image. She never did anything by half measures…and he bet that she wouldn't ask for help in any ordinary circumstances, even if she were on fire and he had an extinguisher.

But she'd asked tonight.

The picture of her wet-suit shenanigans was eclipsed by the thought of her face, staring up at him, her velvety brown eyes wet with tears, and her normally tense face softened in a pleading expression, asking for his understanding.

He shook his head as he walked up Mrs. Tilson's driveway toward his new apartment. Despite Gabe's good advice, there was no way he was going to abandon Allison now that he knew why she needed him.

As he got closer to his apartment, he noticed two things. One, that he hadn't turned the outside light on, and the stairs to his apartment over the garage were pretty dark. Two, that there, in the dark, were things on the stairs.

"Sean! 'Bout time you came home, man!"

Not just things, he realized. He was surrounded by Hoodlums.

Sean closed his eyes again, this time in a plea for patience. "What, is the gang all here?" he asked as he began to make out faces in the dim light. Gabe and his wife, Charlotte, Gabe's sister, Bella, and her husband, Brad, and the rest of his surf crew—Ryan, Mike and millionaire-turned-surf-bum Jack Landor. The Hoodlums was a pretty goofy name for grown men, but for whatever reason, it suited them. Especially when they pulled stunts like this. "To what do I owe this invasion?"

Gabe cleared his throat. "Let's say I activated the phone tree."

Sean made his way past everyone and unlocked his door, trying to contain his irritation. "Wish you hadn't done that," he murmured to Gabe.

"You're family," Bella said with a tone of enthusiasm that Sean frankly hated. "Besides, brainstorming is right up my alley."

No, "butting in" is right up your alley, Sean mentally corrected, then felt instantly guilty. They really did mean well, even buttinsky Bella. "I appreciate it, but I just don't think this is full phone-tree-emergency worthy, that's all."

"You had to move, you might lose your job, and your whole life's about to change…and that's not worth a shout-out to your friends?" Jack asked, his tone implacable as usual. He was so laid-back, he made Sean look like Allison, Sean thought. It would probably take a class-five tornado to fluster the man.

Sean sighed. "Well, when you put it that way…"

He didn't even try to stop them as they all filed into his apartment, which wasn't tiny but certainly wasn't quite big enough to accommodate all of them…at least, not with boxes and stuff in the way. He heard Charlotte let out a low whistle.

"As long as we're here, we might as well have an unpacking party," she said, rolling up her sleeves. "And talk as we work."

Sean sighed. Within moments, it seemed, there was a flurry of activity. Boxes were torn open, books were placed on shelves haphazardly. And everyone, it seemed, began talking at once.

"So, first off, we have to figure out what you want to do," Gabe said, grunting as he lifted a box of pots and pulled it into the tiny kitchen.

"No," Bella countered. "What we need to do first is figure out what he's going to do short term, if he's got to look for a new job."

"The thing is, Tubes doesn't have to go under," Sean replied. "I've been doing a lot of thinking about it, and the problem is, Oz has just been cruising on autopilot for years. We haven't made any improvements, haven't done anything resembling marketing for years. We've had the same customers spread the word forever. Our rep is amazing." He grinned. "Allison found out about us through somebody's else's Web site. We've definitely got credibility."

The sudden quiet at the mention of Allison's name made him realize, abruptly, he'd opened a completely different topic of discussion—one he didn't want to touch. "So if Tubes just had its own Web site," he continued hastily, "and maybe did some publicity…and if we repainted the place, spruced it up…"

"Allison, huh?" Charlotte was grinning from ear to ear.

Here we go. Sean took a deep breath. "She's somebody I'm giving surf lessons to. You know, we could really expand our surf lessons, too, get some extra income that way as well as helping out new surfers. And we might need to—"

"What's Allison like?" This from Bella, who was absolutely insane for matchmaking.

Before Sean could head her off at the pass, Ryan interjected, "She's a babe. Very high class, though." He shrugged when they all switched their attention to him. "Gabe, Mike and I met her on Friday. She stopped by."

"Really?" Bella's voice was rich with speculation. "Stopped by your house, huh?"

"It's not like that," Sean said sharply. "She got me this

apartment, I'm teaching her to surf. That's it. The woman who owns this place is her godmother. Or great-aunt. Or something."

"So why don't you ask your landlady about Allison, then?" Bella persisted.

"Because she scares the hell out of me," Sean stated.

"Bull," Mike said, laughing. "Nothing scares you, man."

"You haven't met her," Sean replied. "You don't even want to know what it was like to interview for this place. And yes, I mean *interview.*" He shook his head. "Thought I was going to need to give a blood sample, I swear to God."

"What sort of lease did you sign, Sean?" Charlotte suddenly asked, frowning. "Because when you get a new job, who knows where you'll be. You might move to another city or something."

"Another city?" Sean felt a ball of ice form in the pit of his stomach. He'd moved plenty before his mother had settled him and his sister in Redondo Beach. "I've lived in the South Bay almost all my life. Why would I want to move?"

"Because you've lived in the South Bay almost all your life?" Jack suggested gently, with an easy smile. "You never know. You might want to move to Hawaii, or Sydney. Or someplace else with really choice waves."

"And really choice babes," Mike put in, causing Ryan to laugh.

Sean sat down on the futon couch that was finally free of boxes. "I've got plenty of choice waves here."

"The babe in your life right now is pretty choice, too," Ryan pointed out. "Although if you don't want her…"

Sean's attention snapped to Ryan. "What?"

"Hey, I'm just saying, if you're not signaling this wave, I'd love to have a ride."

Sean was on his feet before he knew what he was doing, his blood boiling.

Ryan grinned. "I love doing that. If you're going to keep saying she's just a student, you're so full of crap, pal."

The rest of the group broke into loud laughter. Sean immediately felt sheepish—and set up. He'd need to think about this.

There was a knock on the door.

"What, did you guys photocopy flyers for this party, or what?" Disgruntled, embarrassed that Ryan had trapped him into thinking about Allison that way, he quickly opened the door.

Mrs. Tilson stood there, wearing a very prim charcoal suit and a string of pearls. She looked like she was visiting a lawyer, not calling on a tenant.

"I don't know if I made it clear when I allowed you to move in here," she said, and her voice could have cut glass, "but I'm making it clear now. I will not allow you to have wild parties in this unit. You will keep the noise down to an acceptable level at all times. Especially after dark. Am I understood?"

Sean looked over at his friends, who had fallen quiet and were now looking at each other with expressions of chagrin.

"I'm very sorry, Mrs. Tilson," Sean said, pretty much meaning it...although he hadn't felt quite this foolish in one night since he was fifteen or so. "This wasn't a party, it was just my friends helping me to unpack."

"Well, if your friends keep up this ruckus," she warned, "they're just going to have to help you pack up again."

He nodded, feeling anger and humiliation burn.

"And I don't care how cute your 'ass' is," she said. "I mean it. Good night, Mr. Gilroy."

Now humiliation made way for a burning blush. "Night, Mrs. Tilson."

He closed the door behind her, and then paused for a moment, not wanting to turn around and face the rest of the Hoodlums. When he finally did, it was as he expected—they were all staring at him.

Charlotte was the first one to laugh. Pretty soon, every single one of them was laughing hysterically…and trying equally hard trying not to make a sound. They were all turning purple with the exertion. Bella had actually stuffed her head in a pillow.

Jack, for the first time Sean could remember, looked shocked. "That woman looked eighty if she were a day."

"Seventy-eight, actually," Sean said.

"And…she thinks you have a cute ass?" Jack asked, bewildered.

"It's a long story," Sean said, "which unfortunately, I can't share with you right this second. Thanks for helping me unpack, gang, but it looks like this party's over."

Gabe wiped at the tears of laughter in the corners of his eyes. "Well, we're not giving up on this, pal. You do need to find a new job…and maybe a new place to live. And when you do," he added, grinning, "we are going to have one hell of a party. Who knows? Maybe your next landlady will be some hot woman who actually lets the cuteness of your ass sway her judgment."

Sean smiled uncomfortably as they all exited, chuckling.

The problem was, he didn't want to change jobs…he

didn't want to leave Manhattan Beach. He thought of Allison. *Especially not now.*

But the bottom line was, everybody else seemed to know something that he didn't: that he ought to give up hope and move on when it came to Tubes.

CHAPTER FIVE

"TRY IT AGAIN."

Allison gritted her teeth. She was lying on the carpet in her living room, with an outline of a "surfboard" made out of string lying in front of her. She felt a little ridiculous, but compared to the great pottery debacle, this was a walk in the park. She focused, crawling forward a little, and jumped up.

"Not quite," Sean corrected. "You're going a little too fast, and you're still looking down. Remember? Don't look down. You'll get rolled. You want to look out, in front of you." His voice was smooth, encouraging. "Try it one more time."

She was getting a little tired, she realized. She'd had another full day of work, and Sean had graciously agreed to come by at eight o'clock on a Tuesday night. They'd now been at it for the better part of an hour and a half. He'd had her work on her balance, stretching, the whole nine yards. It was like having a personal trainer.

She sneaked a glance at him, sitting on her couch, wearing jeans and a T-shirt, staring at her intently.

A very sexy personal trainer.

She got back down on the carpet, even though her muscles protested the action. She started to jump, and botched it. "Damn it!"

He got off the couch, walking behind her and tapping her on the shoulder when she started to lie down again. "Okay, maybe that's enough for one night."

"No, I want to get this," she said stubbornly.

"You're not going to learn surfing in one night," he replied in that gentle voice of his. "I've probably pushed you too hard already. You're going to be feeling this tomorrow, for sure."

She didn't want to admit she was already feeling it tonight. She had made progress, at least. "Just teach me one more thing," she wheedled, like a kid begging for just fifteen more minutes of television before going to bed.

He sighed, smirking. "You're like some force of nature. You know that?"

She didn't know if that was meant to be a compliment or not, so she just made a noncommittal "hmm."

He laughed, his tone resigned. "Okay, when you're standing on the board…wait a second. Which is your dominant hand?"

"I'm right-handed."

"Okay. So your right foot is probably your dominant foot." He then stood behind her, close, and she felt a little tightness in her chest. Not the squeezing sensation of panic, thankfully, but her heart rate accelerated a little and her stomach jittered. "You're going to be leading with your dominant arm," he continued, his breath tickling the back of her neck. She shivered. "Keep your arm out in front of you. That's going to be your steering, basically."

"Like this?" She stood in the pose that every surfer she'd ever seen in a movie seemed to strike.

"Um…close enough. Bend your knees a little more," he said, and she felt his hand press on the back of her thighs. Her breath caught.

Stay focused, she counseled herself, and obediently crouched a little more.

"Okay," he said…and, if possible, seemed to get a little closer, brushing against her there for a second.

What, was the guy an oven? She could feel the heat of him through her own T-shirt and sweatpants. He now put his hands on her hips, leaning her forward ever so slightly.

"Now," he said, his voice low and smooth, "what we're looking for is the sweet spot."

You get any closer, and I can almost guarantee you're going to find it.

She gasped at the naughty and eager humor her mind seemed determined to provide. "We're doing what?" she said, shooting him a startled look over her shoulder.

"Stay low," he said, his fingertips turning her chin back toward her right arm. She could hear the amusement in his voice. "The sweet spot. That's a surf term for…well, your center of gravity, more or less. It's where you're standing on your board and you're perfectly balanced."

"Oh," she murmured, embarrassed. "Got it."

She tried to pretend she was out on a wave, not on the thick plush of her carpet. She jumped on the string outline, then crouched.

"Not too low."

She corrected her posture, and felt like the Rock of Gibraltar. "This it?" she said, finally allowing a little confidence to seep into her voice.

"Let's find out," he said.

Before she knew what was happening, he'd given her a small, gentle shove. And she wound up on her knees by the coffee table.

"Crap!" She turned over, lying on her back in the middle of the living room and letting out a frustrated huff of breath. "Just...*crap!*"

"I've never heard it put quite that way," Sean said, sitting on the floor next to her companionably. "But yeah, I understand how you feel."

She gazed at him, all sloe-eyed and slumberous looking. Probably his only acquaintance with stress was reading about it in a magazine or something. "I sincerely doubt it."

"Believe me, it's really tough to find the sweet spot when you're starting out."

"I haven't found a guy yet who has," she muttered, closing her eyes tiredly. Then opened again when he laughed, groaning and turning onto her stomach, burying her face in her hands. "What is it about you? I swear, I'm usually very well behaved. And I certainly never make comments like these."

He rubbed her back. "I'll take that as a compliment." His voice was an amused rumble.

She rolled onto her side, and immediately groaned.

All humor disappeared from his voice. "Muscles hurting?"

She tried to shrug, and the effort was brutal. "A bit," she admitted in a strangled voice.

"I knew I was pushing it, but you never said anything," he said, surprising her.

"It was my fault. I was asking for it. Heck, I was begging for it," she joked, then bit her lip.

He didn't even crack a smile, making her feel even worse. "Lie down on the sofa," he said.

She blinked at him. He'd been, well, she wouldn't say he

was all that bossy, especially as a coach. But now he sounded imperative. "It's getting late," she said, still puzzled.

He sighed. "I'm going to work on those muscles a bit. Do you have anything for sore muscles?"

"Like what? Vodka?"

He shook his head, finally chuckling a little. "Like sports cream."

"Nope."

"You're going to want to change that by tomorrow," he said, and to her distress, he tugged her until she groaned and complied, lying on her soft, overstuffed couch. "You're going to be in a world of hurt. Come on, then."

She stretched out, loving the feel of the soft cushions beneath her. "Say…this wasn't such a bad idea after all," she said, relaxing ever so slightly and feeling drowsiness hit her in a wave. "You can just lock up when you're done."

"I'll do that." She could hear the smile in his voice, and was just about to smile in response when he put his hands on her back and rubbed.

"Yeeeeowch!" She winced away from his hands, turning enough to stare at him in horror. "What the *hell?*"

He looked unrepentant. In fact, he was staring at her in disbelief. "Good grief. Is that what your muscles are like all the time?" He sounded horrified. "I've felt concrete that had more give than the knots between your shoulder blades! We should've stopped over an hour ago!"

She shrugged. Rather, she tried to shrug, but the aforementioned knots prevented her from really doing more than a little wiggle. "It's always like this…it wasn't anything you did." She turned over, sat up. "I also don't think this is going to help, so maybe we should call it a night."

He sighed. "Do you at least have a heating pad or something?"

"Somewhere," she said, feeling torn between feeling disgruntled at his persistence, and being touched at his concern. "I'll be fine," she said, getting up and starting to usher him toward the door. "Really."

He stopped at the door. "If nothing else, get into a hot shower, okay?"

She nodded. "Yes, Coach."

He stroked her cheek. She could really get used to that. "You need to learn to take care of yourself."

"Not if you stick around, apparently," she said. Then, before she could stop herself, she added, "So, think you'll keep teaching me?"

He smiled, a lopsided smile that warmed her more than a heating pad ever could, making her muscles ease out in a puddle. He leaned forward, his face perilously close to hers.

"I always keep my word," he said.

She sighed, leaning forward, millimeters from his face.

And then, to her everlasting humiliation, he pulled back.

"So…I'll see you tomorrow?" she said, hating the feeling of rejection…and hating more that she seemed to be asking for even more.

"No."

She felt the sting of that like a welt. She didn't look at him, not wanting to see the rejection.

"But not because I don't want to see you," he said, and she finally looked up. "You're going to be too tired, Allison. You worked too hard tonight. From now on, when you start to feel tired or sore, you have to tell me, or I can't work with you every day. Got it?"

"Got it," she repeated, feeling relieved.

"Take tomorrow off. I mean that," he said, and she felt as if she'd agree to anything he said. "I'll see you on Thursday. Six o'clock," he said, and walked out the door.

She forced herself not to watch him walk away out her window, trying hard not to focus on the fact that she was becoming dangerously attracted to her surf instructor…or the fact that her entire body was protesting that it would be two days before she'd get to see him again.

What is wrong with you, Allison? she upbraided herself mentally. *You've got way too much to do to get sidetracked by your surf instructor.* Especially when odds were good he didn't feel anything remotely similar about her at all. They were from completely different worlds.

No, better for her to do what she always did…bury herself in work. Stay focused on the things she could control. And leave her heart completely out of it. She'd work all Wednesday, and not think about surfing, or Sean Gilroy, at all.

SEAN GLANCED AT HIS WATCH. It was Thursday night, five forty-seven…two minutes later than the last time he'd looked at his watch, actually. The shop was going to close at six. Even though he was going to suggest holiday hours for the store, for those people who might be interested in Christmas shopping for a board or something, he was glad he hadn't suggested it yet.

Allison was going to meet him at six o'clock, or rather, as quickly after six o'clock as he could get to her town house. And while he was pretty sure she'd still be a little sore from Tuesday's session, he really wanted to pick up where they'd left off.

Especially where they'd left off just before he went home.

He could still smell her perfume, still feel the soft smoothness of her skin beneath his fingertips. She was burned on his brain like he'd stared at the damn sun.

Oh, yeah. He'd never looked forward to closing up the shop as much as he did tonight.

His cell phone rang, and he jumped a little, startled out of his prurient daydream. He glanced at the incoming number… Gabe. "Hey there," he said.

"Hey," Gabe answered easily. "You know, I've been thinking about your problem."

Sean tried hard not to groan. "I was hoping you guys would've put that behind you," he said.

"Between my wife and my sister? Are you kidding?" Gabe sounded way too cheerful to really be unhappy about the idea. "Anyway, I figure nobody knows more about the trends of surf gear than you do…and you're a surfer."

"Duh." Sean glanced at his watch. Five forty-eight. Okay, he had a problem.

"Well, Lone Shark does business with these guys…they wanted to license some stuff, actually. Anyway, it's not important now. But we're looking for a regional sales rep."

"Sales?" Sean winced. "Um, not that I'm not grateful, but I'd suck at sales."

"Are you kidding me?" Gabe's voice sounded incredulous. "You work at a surf shop. You're already in sales, bro."

"Yeah, but if I were better at it, I wouldn't be in this jam, would I?" It was sort of depressing just thinking about it, actually.

"That's not entirely your fault. Yeah, sure, you could've hustled more, but I know for a fact you've had great ideas for how the store could sell more, and Oz just hasn't been that interested."

"Stop it, I'll blush." Sean's voice was deliberately jovial, but he was starting to get uncomfortable with the whole line of conversation.

"Anyway, I think you'd be a natural fit in this job," Gabe said, moving ahead like a bulldozer. "You know the products, you know the market. And it's not like you'd be schmoozing people or being sleazy. You'd just talk, and then people would buy stuff."

"Just that easy," Sean said, shaking his head even though he knew Gabe couldn't see it. "Man. Shoulda talked to you years ago."

"If I thought you'd listen, I would've brought this up years ago," Gabe countered, missing the joke entirely. "Besides, you had other stuff on your mind. Taking care of Janie, stuff like that. And I know you feel loyal to Oz."

There was that. Sean sighed, then glanced at his watch. Five-fifty. At least a few minutes had gone by.

The door opened. "Gotta go. Customer's here," Sean said.

"Want to brainstorm a little after work? We could kick around your résumé," Gabe said.

"Can't. Teaching tonight."

There was a pause. "I'm definitely calling you tomorrow."

"Can't wait," Sean said, grinning, and hung up on him. "Hi, welcome to Tubes. Can I help you?" *And could you please go away in the next five minutes?*

The customer looked like most of the residents of Manhattan Beach proper...moneyed and vaguely harried. "Hi. I'm trying to buy a surfboard for my girlfriend's kid."

A surfboard. Sean groaned internally. "Well, do you know what sort of board he wants?"

The man looked at Sean with just this side of a sneer. "Do I look like a surf guy?"

It wasn't in Sean's nature to be rude—he generally felt it wasn't worth the effort—but he was already trying to close as it was. "I get plenty of guys like you who surf." *And, yes, they're jerks, too,* he thought but didn't verbalize.

"Well, I'm not a surfer. But the kid is, or wants to be, and he said something about wanting a...potato chip? Is that something like a board?"

Sean grinned. "The kid must be good, then. How old?"

"I don't know. Young teens, I think," the guy said, scowling. "I've only been dating her for a couple of months, and I've only met him a few times."

"Kind of an expensive gift for somebody you've only met a few times," Sean mused. He glanced at his watch. Five fifty-three. "I could point you to a few boards, but it'd really be more helpful if you could bring him in. Or maybe give him a smaller gift and a gift certificate?" That'd be quick, easy to ring up. He'd have the guy out of here and close up before the watch hand hit six.

The guy thought about it, and Sean felt time stretch out painfully. "No, I want the kid to be impressed. Really blown away. I'm having Christmas at their house, and I want to make sure he remembers what he got when he goes over to his dad's house."

Because nothing says love like big, expensive presents. Sean gritted his teeth. This guy was a piece of work, but that wasn't his problem.

"Let's start with a board, and then maybe work something else. What else could I get with that?"

"Wet suit, boots…all kinds of stuff," Sean said, "but it could take a while."

"I'm off work," the guy said easily. "And it doesn't look like you're busy, so why don't you help me pick this stuff out."

Sean didn't even have to look at his watch to know how close it was. "Actually…we close at six o'clock," he said. "But I'd be happy to walk you through it tomorrow." *Or I could just pick a bunch of stuff out at random, because you wouldn't know the difference, anyway.* That might actually be easier, all things considered. But it wasn't Sean's way.

The guy instantly looked upset…or rather, the scowling had just been irritation, and now he was truly moving on to angry. Sean hated guys like this, but ordinarily, they still didn't get to him this way. "Listen, unlike you, I generally work late. And it looks like you could use the business. I'm sure a board isn't cheap," he said. "A commission on the board, and whatever else you con me into buying, could go a long way toward buying Christmas presents, you know? So why the hell don't you stay open a little later?"

And as much as he disliked the guy, he'd made a valid point…Oz could use the money, and the whole purpose here to getting more sales was to convince Oz to keep the store open. Still, he didn't have Allison's home number, so he couldn't tell her he'd be late. He hated the thought of disappointing her. He knew how much she needed his help.

"It's not that hard a decision," the guy added derisively. "So. Show me the boards."

Something in Sean snapped. "Unfortunately, I have an appointment I have to go to," he said tightly. "I honor my commitments."

"Well. Goody for you." The guy's mouth drew into a harsh line. "I'd hate for you to somehow make a profit by doing something that made you break your word. Are you kidding me?"

"Like I said, I'd be happy to help you tomorrow," Sean said tightly. "I could even throw in a discount, I could keep the store open late, I could come in early. But I promised I'd do something tonight, and I'm not going to break that."

"Fine." The guy opened the door, turning to deliver his parting shot. "I'll just go to a surf shop that's open later, and give them my business!"

"Have a nice day," Sean drawled, just before the door slammed shut. "You Lexus-driving jerkoff."

He was still fuming about the incident a little as he locked up the store for the evening. It was 6:05…he hoped that Allison wasn't waiting too long for him.

He drove fast, or at least as fast as his poor decrepit pickup truck could manage, and then he pulled up to Allison's town house. There was a light on in the front bedroom, he noticed, and immediately felt guilty. And, admittedly, a little turned on.

Would you calm down? This is a lesson, not a date!

Still, his nerves were jangling just a little as he walked up the steps and rang the doorbell.

There was no answer.

Frowning, he waited a minute, and then tried it again. Finally, he went up her driveway, peering into the garage.

There wasn't a car parked there. She must've left her light on, or had a timer. She wasn't there yet.

He laughed to himself. Here he was, rushing, and she hadn't even made it home yet!

He settled on her front porch, hoping he didn't look too disreputable. It would suck to have her come home as he was being carted away by the cops for looking like a burglar. In this neighborhood, there probably was a law against loitering while looking menacing. He zipped up his coat and tried to look as nonthreatening as possible.

By six-fifteen, he was moving past annoyed and into irritation. He could've sold a few surfboards to that arrogant doofus by now, he couldn't help thinking. Probably convinced the guy that the kid, and the girlfriend who was the kid's mom, would really be impressed if he threw in a spring and a winter wet suit, and of course a surfboard rack so he could cart the board on the roof of that Lexus of his without ruining the paint job. But of course, Allison wasn't here. He tried to think that maybe things had happened. Maybe she got caught in traffic—he didn't even know where she worked, and anywhere in the L.A area, that was a possibility.

He was giving her another five minutes. Then he was going to call her office, make sure she was there, and not stuck in traffic or in an accident.

And if she wasn't stuck anywhere or in any kind of trouble… He grimaced. He'd find out just how much of a schmuck he was being about a pretty girl.

ALLISON STARED at her computer screen, realizing that the screen was getting blurry. She'd been there since six-thirty that morning, she thought, rubbing her eyes with the heels of her palms, and it was now—she took a quick peek at her wristwatch—six-thirty in the evening. It wasn't surprising that she was getting tired, she supposed. Still, the fact that the screen was blurry was something else. That meant only one thing: at some point in the past hour, she'd stopped blinking, or at least slowed down in the pursuit. They actually had a term for it in business school: she was going fish-eyed.

There was a knock on her office door. "You know that I hate you," she said, anticipating her boss.

"Actually, you don't," her assistant countered wryly. "Never bad-mouth people who come bearing gifts."

She took a deep breath, and the scent of really strong, paint-stripping coffee flooded her lungs. "Please tell me that's—"

"A Hammerhead, aka the Allison Special," Gary said, putting a tall disposable cup in front of her. "Leaded coffee with four shots of espresso."

"Aaaaah," she muttered after taking a deep sip. "This ought to keep me going for another hour or so."

"Are we going to be here that long?"

She looked up. Gary was stoic and, as a general rule, he didn't protest if she asked him to stay late. Probably because he, like herself, had no life, she thought with a little stab of guilt. "I just need one more revision," she said, hesitant. "Is that going to be a problem?"

He sighed, and she realized immediately that it would be. "It's just…if you need me here, you know I'll stay." He shifted his weight uncomfortably from one foot to the other. "I owe you that much, and then some."

"You don't owe me anything," she protested. "Are you kidding? You're the best executive assistant in the world."

"Who just happens to have a criminal record that you've so kindly looked past," he reminded her.

"You were practically a minor," she said loyally. "And you're really, really good at what you do."

"All I'm saying is, I'd feel better about this if..." He paused, and she swore that he might've been blushing.

It was times like this that she remembered that he was only twenty-one years old. She sighed. It wasn't helping her get her presentation revised, but she guessed that would just have to wait.

"Spit it out," she said, taking another long pull off the coffee and feeling her heart rate accelerate.

"It's fine," he said.

"No, it's not, or you wouldn't have said anything." Men. Why were they so brutally blunt about some things, and so downright shy about other things?

"No, that's not what I meant," he said. "The presentation's fine, Allison. I don't mind doing the work, but I think you're just spinning your wheels. You're too stressed out."

She blinked. Then her eyes narrowed. "This isn't because of the whole emergency-room thing, is it?" she asked suspiciously, in a low voice.

"Well, that certainly backs up my opinion, yes," he said, his freckled face scrunching into a stern frown. "Why are you working so hard on this one?"

She sighed. "The in-house presentation is happening in just a few days. I've got to nail it. You know my game plan."

"Yeah, I just don't know why you're letting this one get to you. It's more than just the account supervisor thing," he said. "So what is it?"

She sighed. "Once I get the account supervisor's job, it won't be as much of an issue," she said. "And...I just feel like...I'm losing focus lately. I'm letting things slide."

He barked out a surprised laugh. "Slide? Are you kidding me?"

She felt herself blush for no good reason. She was gratified that he hadn't noticed it…but she had. She wasn't able to focus the way she used to.

The way she did before she started taking surfing lessons. Or, more to the point, before she'd met Sean Gilroy.

She couldn't quite explain it. She'd found herself daydreaming at odd times, like in meetings. And in the shower. And when she was supposed to be working, or driving to work. Pretty much anytime she was awake, she was fair game to a Gilroy fantasy.

It was reaching ludicrous proportions. Thankfully, she had her work to keep her from being a complete and utter gibbering idiot.

"I just know that you said you were going to have to relax," Gary said, his voice high and cracked with concern. "So I figured, as your assistant, I ought to…you know. Say something."

She sighed. "I'm taking care of myself."

He pointed to the clock on the wall: six-forty. "Really."

She shook her head. "I'll leave as soon as I get the kinks ironed out. Besides, I'm already learning to chill out a little. I even have a hobby."

She thought of Sean again…then suddenly, a little chime went off in her head.

Sean.

Hobby.

Six-forty.

"Oh, crap," she panicked. "I'm late. I have to…oh, crap."

"Ladies' room is down the hall and to the right," Gary joked.

"Just shut the door, 'kay?" she said, and was already

dialing Sean's cell-phone number before the door had closed all the way. She'd need him to understand. Of course he'd understand. He had a resting pulse of twelve, why would something like this cause a problem?

She realized the pounding of her heart was only partially attributable to the mass quantities of caffeine she'd been consuming.

The phone only rang once before Sean answered it. "You're stuck in traffic," he said without a greeting.

She winced. "Actually…" She considered lying, just for a moment, but knew that she really sucked at lying and the stress of it would only exacerbate the situation. "Well…no."

There was a pause on his end of the line. "You're not hurt, are you? In a hospital? You didn't have another panic attack or anything, did you?"

She winced again. He sounded so sweet, so nervous. "No. Nothing like that," she said, feeling like an absolute toad.

Another pause. Then, in a tone of utter disbelief, he said, "Please, please tell me you're not…"

"I just got a little caught up," she pleaded. "Work ran a tiny bit late. I'm so sorry. I'll be right over."

"I've been waiting for over half an hour," he said, his voice flat.

"I lost track of time," she said, her voice pleading a little. "I'll be there as soon as I can."

"Don't bother."

She felt her stomach knot. When was the last time she ate? When Gary had pushed lunch onto her desk sometime that afternoon. "I said I'm sorry and, Sean, I really, really mean it."

"I mean it, too," he said, and she realized she'd never

heard him angry before, not like that. She didn't know he was capable of feeling anything quite that strong. "Don't bother. Stay at work. I don't care."

If possible, she felt worse. Then, to her surprise, anger leaped to the fore, a defense mechanism that usually only crept out when she was truly backed into a corner. "Listen, I don't know what else to say," she said, trying to keep her voice reasonable. "It was only one time. I can promise that it won't happen again."

"Once was enough. Besides being stuck on your steps for the past thirty minutes, I rushed a customer out of the shop to make sure that I made it here on time. And I told him, in no uncertain terms, that it was because when I make a commitment—when I give my *word*—I keep it."

"Why is this such a big deal?" she snapped, letting the rein slip on her temper. "I've already said I'm sorry. I'll buy you dinner, I'll…I don't know, I'll make it up to you. But I'm only forty minutes late, I've apologized, and it's not like my lessons are time sensitive. It's not even in the ocean yet, remember? It's on my living-room carpet! What, were you afraid the tide was going to go from high plush to low shag?"

"That's hilarious," he said, his tone suggesting that he found it anything but. "You're the one this is supposed to be important for. Not me. I've got other things to do, and I'm hanging up now."

"So that's it? I flake on one lesson, and you're just cutting me off? Thanks for the apartment, have a nice life?"

She could hear him take a deep breath. "The only reason I agreed to take you on wasn't for the damn apartment," he said in a voice so low she had to struggle to hear him over the crackle of the cell phone. "I agreed to teach you because you said you needed help. Because you had to learn to relax. Because…oh, hell. Because of that night, in the dressing room."

Now she was definitely blushing. "So help me," she whispered.

"If you're serious, you have to want it," he said. Then, after a beat of silence, he added, "And I know that, now that you're back at work, and the attacks haven't been creeping up…you're just going to call me when you need me, or when you're not really caught up in work. And frankly, I'm sorry, Ally, but that really doesn't work for me."

"But…" she protested, frustrated.

"'Bye, Ally," he said, and then she heard the annoying buzz of a dial tone.

She stared at the phone. He'd hung up on her. Just like that. He'd hung up on her.

She felt a little shell-shocked. Then, the anger that she'd been suppressing and smoothing out suddenly bubbled up like lava.

Mr. Surfer is saying that I'm a flake? He's giving me grief because I'm not being committed *enough?* Was he serious with this?

She felt a cold sort of calm engulf her, accompanied by a low buzzing in her ears. With that, she stood up, opening the door to her office.

Gary looked unnaturally busy, moving papers from one side of his desk to the other. It was obvious that he'd been desperately trying to overhear what she'd said, and was now just as desperate to look as if he'd been doing no such thing. "Bad phone call?" he said with elaborate casualness.

"About the presentation," she said in that same low tone of voice, confident that at least she could fake being calm.

"Sure. You want me to order dinner? Stay late? No problem. No problem at all."

"It's staying as it is," she said decisively. "I'm just leaving it alone."

It was funny—although people wouldn't realize he was surprised, she could tell from the way his eyes widened behind his wire-rimmed glasses that he was clearly startled. "Uh, okay."

"Just make copies of the handouts when you get in tomorrow, okay?" Still that calm. It was as if the fury burning through her was so hot, she couldn't feel it.

"Sure." He looked at her. He was used to seeing her, too, so he wasn't fooled. "You going to be okay?"

"Definitely," she said. "See you tomorrow."

She walked down the hallway. She wasn't okay, not right that moment. But she was about to get into her car, and head over to Sean's.

One way or another, she was going to feel okay, though. Especially once she'd talked to Sean Gilroy, and given him a piece of her mind.

CHAPTER SIX

SEAN SAT ON HIS FUTON sofa, in his new apartment, nursing a Corona and staring out the window. There was a sliver of moon, just a slender crescent, and it was too dark to see the ocean. Still, he could hear it, and more importantly, he knew it was out there. Just imagining it was the only thing keeping him calm at the moment. He was too pissed off to actually go out into it. The surf was too strong, for one thing, and in his current state of mind… He shook his head. How many times had he told the kids he taught not to hit the waves when they were upset? If he were one of his students, he wouldn't let himself go out there. So there it was.

He was, he realized with some surprise, stressed.

He turned on his small stereo, listening to some neo–folk music he'd picked up from a coffee-shop band he'd listened to. He saved the CD for special occasions, when he needed a little soothing. After a full day of baby-sitting for his sister Janie's two young ones, he usually played a couple of tracks. After helping Oz move to his new house, he'd listened to the whole thing.

He got the feeling tonight, he'd listen to it a couple of times. While drinking beer. Possibly let the thing run all night.

He'd never met anyone who was able to get under his skin as quickly, and as thoroughly, as Ms. Allison Robbins.

So how many times are you going to be a schmuck?

The thing was, he never really had been. He'd never really gone out of his way to get in a woman's good graces. He hadn't needed to, honestly. He'd had plenty of girlfriends. All casual, all relatively brief, as his sister liked to point out. She'd even gone so far as to say that he was lazy. And it wasn't as if he'd never been shot down. He'd asked out plenty of women who had said no. He'd just thanked them and moved on. No sweat, no blood, no foul.

This was different. This sort of stuff—bending over backward, putting everything else in his life on hold for a girl who really couldn't care less—there was a reason for not doing it.

You may be overreacting just a bit, Gilroy...

She'd only been forty minutes late. But it was a sign, he argued with himself, downing the rest of his beer. The thing was, he knew, in his heart, that this was different. He'd booted a guy out of the store. He'd rushed to her house like some teenage boy. Just to teach her. Hell, just to *see* her.

He couldn't seem to get enough of her, and while it wasn't a problem now, he wasn't so dumb that he didn't recognize just how much of a problem she'd be down the line.

No, better to just cut the cord as soon as possible. Sure, he felt badly, and sort of indebted because of the apartment. But he'd probably be moving soon, wouldn't he? And hadn't Gabe warned him not to give lessons? He was just being smart. A preemptive strike. That's all. And once she got over her snit, she'd probably just get sucked back into whatever the hell was on her computer. She'd go on the meds. She'd do whatever.

Whatever she winds up doing, the bottom line is, it's not your problem.

There was a knock on the door. He closed his eyes. There were a few options of who could be knocking on his door at seven-thirty on a weeknight. His landlady, who came up his stairs just to complain that he was pondering too loud. His friends, who were off to be their usual helpful selves. Or…

He opened the door. Allison, still in work clothes and a determined expression, stood on his step.

"We need to talk," she said, and pushed around him, walking into the living room.

Or it could be a woman who has more determination than good sense, his mind supplied. Fantastic. Well, she might be determined, but he was downright pigheaded stubborn. And he was just too fresh from his whole "feeling stupid" experience to know that there was no way in hell he was going to keep teaching her.

"Allison, you're wasting your time. I think—"

"I handled the whole thing badly today," she said. "But I know that, before I leave tonight, you'll see why it wasn't actually all that bad, and we'll be able to move forward with absolutely no problem."

Don't let yourself be charmed by this one. Stand tough. She might think it was all cut-and-dried, but he wasn't going to play that way. He crossed his arms. "You did handle the whole thing badly," he agreed. "And I don't just mean being late, which did suck, incidentally."

He saw her eyes flash, and he knew that she was just as ticked off as he was. "I've already apologized," she said between gritted teeth. "And I'm not going to walk over hot coals because I've got too much on my plate."

It was an interesting phenomenon. She looked like Tinker Bell, but with that voice, she sounded like Dirty Harry. *Now, that's my girl.*

He shook his head. She wasn't his girl, he reminded himself. "I'm not trying to add more to your plate, Ally," he said, keeping his own voice calm.

"You know my life is busy," she said. "You knew that was the whole reason I'm doing any of this!"

"I know that," he said, feeling a few twinges of guilt creeping in. Of course he knew that she was stressed out, and busy, and that she had a ton going on. So why had he made such a federal case out of all of this?

Because you don't want to be with someone who puts you last in line.

He cleared his throat. "The thing is, you came to me. You asked me for help. And like you say, you're the one who needs this to get over your stress at work. So when you cancel because of work…"

"I didn't cancel!"

"Okay. When you flake out because of work," he corrected, and her eyes flashed again, "then it shows me that you're not really serious. And people who aren't serious about the lessons are the ones who get hurt. And, frankly, I've got a lot on my plate, too, Allison." He paused a beat. "You're not the only one with a life, you know."

He watched as she absorbed that. Then she took a deep, quavering breath, and nodded. "I can respect that," she said, her voice now subdued. "And I am really, really sorry." She looked at the floor, the first time he'd seen her look quite this reticent. "What can I do to make this better?" she asked in a small voice.

He hated seeing her like this. He felt as if he'd kicked a puppy or something. He sighed deeply, then nudged her chin up with a finger, getting more disturbed as he noticed that her eyes had filled with tears.

Good going, Gilroy! Take a girl who's already on the edge, and then push at her because your ego hurts. He thought he was a schmuck because he'd gone a little crazy over a girl this beautiful. But he wasn't helping her because of her face. He was helping her because she was Allison…a really strange, really neat combination of strength and fragility. The fact that she was beautiful was just icing.

"I'm sorry," he said, his voice a little bit gravelly with emotion. Then, on impulse, he put his arms around her. She fit neatly against him, and he tucked her head under his chin. After a second, she put her arms around his waist, hugging him back. "I just take this really seriously, you know?" More seriously than she'd realize. And at this point, he wasn't just talking about the lessons—he was talking about her.

"I take everything seriously," she responded. "I just screwed up."

The words stabbed at him, and he nudged her away to look at her face. "You didn't screw up," he said. Then he laughed. "Well, you made a mistake, and you forgot a lesson. But I screwed up when I said that you didn't want it as much as I do." He paused, thinking about the words. "You do want it, right? The lessons, I mean?"

"Definitely," she breathed, and her eyes were bright.

"Then I'll apologize for jumping all over you and threatening to cancel lessons and we'll make a deal—you'll show up when we agree to lessons, or you'll let me know in advance if something comes up. Deal?"

She smiled, and it was like a punch in the gut. *Damn, she's beautiful.* "Deal."

He felt the overwhelming desire to kiss her, and took a crucial step back.

"So," he said gruffly. "I guess we could continue your lesson tonight, if you're not too tired."

She smiled brightly, then her face fell. "Uh, I don't have any of my clothes with me." She bit the corner of her lip, hesitant. "Because we were going to meet at my house, where I'd have the chance to change."

He suddenly got the inappropriate idea of her practicing, naked, in his living room. Took another step back.

It's not her problem, bro, it's yours. He had a complete, full-blown, ridiculous crush on his pint-size student.

He cleared his throat again.

Her eyes narrowed. "You're not coming down with a cold or anything, are you?"

"No, no," he reassured her. "Uh…well. I could loan you some sweats," he said, thinking that a good, thick layer of fleece might be just the thing to keep him from continuing in this vein. "And we could just practice here."

"Okay," she said amiably.

He went into the bedroom, digging out a T-shirt and a pair of his sweats. Then he let her close the door, and sat in the living room. He finished off the beer in a few quick swallows, hoping that the numbing effect of the alcohol would cool the racing of his blood.

He'd never overreacted quite this strongly to a girl before, either, he noted with some distress. And he was going to be in close contact with the woman, daily if she had her way. And as cute and vulnerable as she was, he got the feeling the last thing she needed was her surf instructor putting the moves on her. She was stressed out as it was. If she wasn't interested, he knew her well enough to know that she'd feel terrible about rejecting him. And she was comfortable with him as a teacher—she hadn't picked another one. He had a responsibility here. There was a reason there were teacher-student ethics, he reminded himself. Just because it had never come up before in his life didn't make it any less valid.

She's the student. You're the teacher. Now chill, damn it.

He was pretty sure he had a grip on his emotions when she stepped out of the bedroom. Then, after a moment of stunned silence, he burst into laughter.

She was swamped in his clothes. The T-shirt was more like a dress on her petite frame. And the sweats…she'd pushed the ankle elastic up to her knees, and the material still draped down to her feet. She tapped one of her bare feet impatiently.

"I guess this is just suitable punishment for not having my act together and meeting you at my house," she said with mock severity, even though her eyes gauged his reaction.

"You look adorable," he said, and then, damn it, cleared his throat one more time. "At least you won't get your work clothes all screwed up. Okay, let's start with warm-ups."

He forced himself to get down to business, walking her through the warm-ups and stretches. Still, he couldn't help but notice the way the thin material of the T-shirt molded itself to her when she stretched in certain ways.

It was around then that he realized she wasn't wearing a bra. He almost broke his neck, snapping his gaze away from her. *What the hell?*

"Uh, okay." He grabbed string and made the board outline

on the carpet, after he'd moved the coffee table out of the way. "Practice your pop-ups."

"Okay," she said, and stretched out on the carpet, on her stomach.

He glanced again, furtively. Nope. No bra strap. Probably thought it would've been too uncomfortable.

Oh, for pity's sake. Stop thinking about her breasts, you idiot!

After an hour, he was sweating like he was the one doing all the work. "That's enough for one night," he said, a tiny bit out of breath, to his embarrassment.

She pushed her sweat-soaked bangs away from her face. "Are you sure?"

"You don't want to be any more sore than you already are," he said, refusing to look at her. There was sweat on her chest, causing the T-shirt to cling, just enough to get his mouth watering. *You are such an idiot.* "So, are we on for tomorrow?"

"Definitely. I won't forget this time," she said. "Thanks, Sean. For everything."

You wouldn't be thanking me if you knew just what I was thinking for the past hour. "Don't mention it," he said, his voice a little strangled.

"All right. Let me change, and I'll get out of your hair."

"Just take the clothes with you," he said.

"Good idea. I'll wash them at my house." She stood in front of him. "I must be a mess. I always get this sweaty, just practicing in a living room."

He desperately forced himself not to look at her. "So...uh, what time tomorrow?"

"Seven okay?" she asked. "Or is that too late?"

"Not a problem at all," he said eagerly, then realized he probably sounded too eager. "Just don't cancel on me."

"Not a chance," she said. "And Sean?"

He focused on her face. "Yeah?"

"Don't give up on me," she said quietly.

He felt his blood calm, and he stroked her cheek, unable to help himself. "Not a chance," he repeated.

OKAY, ALLISON THOUGHT. This was it. A few days' worth of carpet-leaping under Sean's watchful eye, an hour's worth of wriggling into her wet suit…and she was now standing on a beach. It was late on a Saturday afternoon, with the sun starting to go lower in the sky. It'd be full dark by five o'clock, but she figured two hours in the surf would probably be plenty. Her muscles no longer ached the way they used to when they started. The important part was, she was ready for the challenge.

He'd already been in, she noticed as she walked over to him. His blond hair was damp, curling slightly at the nape of his neck. There were beads of moisture on his wet suit already. He put his board in the sand and grinned at her, studying her slowly, from her bare feet to her ponytail.

Even though it was breezy, the California concession to December, she felt a wave of warmth go through her body. She smiled back. "So? Do I look like an authentic surfer girl?"

"You sure do," he said, his eyes approving, and she felt the heat concentrate on her cheeks.

Don't blush, you idiot. She was a grown woman. This was not the sixties. And despite certain physical similarities, she certainly was not Gidget.

"Of course," Sean added, "you're still standing on the sand. It's easy to look like a surfer when you're not in the water."

She probably should've been insulted, but her brain had already locked into work mode. "That's what I'm here to tackle," she said firmly. "Bring it on."

He sighed. "First, some safety rules."

She listened carefully, if somewhat impatiently, as he outlined the rules of etiquette for surfers…what to watch for, hand gestures to show that you or another surfer was claiming a wave. Signals to show you were in trouble. She repeated them back perfectly, moving from foot to foot—it was starting to get a little chilly she couldn't help but notice.

"All right," he finally said, and she did a little dance. "You're ready. Let's get in there."

"About time," she muttered, and grabbing her board (no simple feat, considering it was about a full foot taller than she was), she headed for the surf.

Then put one foot in the water, yelped and abruptly dropped the board.

Sean burst out laughing. "Okay, you don't really look like a surfer anymore," he noted as he watched her dance away from the lapping waves.

"Cold! Cold cold *cold!*" She hopped, wondering if she was ever going to get circulation to her right foot. It was as if the water had frozen it solid…she could barely feel the sand squish between her toes. "It's frickin' freezing in there!"

"Um…it's December," he noted. "And at least you're wearing a wet suit. I should've thought to get you booties."

"I'm not that big a baby," she said, trying hard to neither pout nor wince as she put her feet back in the water. Now, at least, both her feet were equally numb.

He laughed again. He had a nice laugh, she thought, although she imagined she'd like it a lot more if he'd stop laughing at her and her absolutely amateurish displays.

"*Booties* is just what they're called. I wasn't implying anything," he clarified.

Fortunately, she already felt stupid, so his definition couldn't really add much to her feeling of humiliation. "Right," she said tightly, and then walked in calf deep. Thank God for neoprene, she thought silently. The wet suit at least allowed her to retain feeling in her legs.

She struggled to pick up the board from where she'd dropped it, and was gratified when he leaned down and picked it up for her. She also couldn't help but notice that his shoulders rippled from beneath the wet suit. The guy had guns, she thought appreciatively, wondering what he'd look like without the wet suit in the way.

Not naked, she quickly amended…and damn it, there it was, that blush again. What was it about the guy? Ordinarily, she was a perfectly cool customer. She felt sure that she had a private and unpleasant nickname among her coworkers at the agency, and while she'd never been called it to her face, she felt sure the term "ice" or "frigid" was somehow involved in the title. Now she spends a week in the company of the Big Kahuna of Manhattan Beach, and she was turning into a red-hot simpering idiot.

"Allison, knock it off," Sean said curtly.

She spun, staring at him. *What, he can read minds?*

"No, I can't read minds," he said, startling her, "but it's easy to tell that you're thinking about something else. Probably work. And if you're not going to be one hundred percent focused on this, then I'm taking you back in. You could die out here if you do it wrong, Allison. You've got to be all in or you're going to get rolled. Clear?"

Suddenly, the all-business stance that she'd started the afternoon with snapped back into place. "Crystal clear," she said, and walked with purpose out into the water, shuffling her feet the way he'd taught her so she wouldn't step on anything, like a stingray or some spiny fish that would get angry at her stepping on it.

As she got in to her neck, she abruptly realized that while she felt as if her wet suit was beyond skintight, there was a slight gap between her actual skin and the suit…and in that tiny gap, the icy water managed to sneak in. She gasped at the cold.

"You'll get used to it in a minute," Sean said, standing behind her. The sound of the waves was both loud and soothing, but he was close enough that she could hear him without his yelling.

She nodded, setting her jaw grimly. "What do I do now?"

"Okay…get your board out in front of you."

She slid the board on the waves, struggling to hold on to it as the water battered it forward.

"Okay…get on."

She remembered the sessions on her carpet. Of course, her carpet hadn't been a wet piece of fiberglass. With more determination than finesse, she managed to pull herself belly first on the board.

Abruptly, a wave snuck up behind them. "Watch it," Sean said, one second before it crested just before them. He tried to hold the board, but it slipped…and she slipped off the board, getting completely submerged. She came up, spluttering and embarrassed.

"Damn it!" she exploded as her head suddenly felt cold. "I was on and everything!"

"Get used to it," Sean said placidly. "Okay, let's try it again."

It took the better part of twenty minutes for her just to get on the board and stay there. When she finally got on, she felt tired, but grimly determined. "Now…now what?" she huffed.

He looked at her, his sky-blue eyes darkened with concern. "You okay?"

"Yeah, I'm fine," she said, brushing his comment aside. She felt like enough of a feeb, thanks. Offhand, she wondered if she was the worst student he'd ever taught. And if she was the only woman he'd ever taught.

Immediately, a wave rolled the board over, and she was plunged into the icy silence of the ocean.

"Damn it!" she roared, spitting out the saltwater she'd accidentally ingested as the waves had knocked her in.

"Whoa! Whoa. It's okay."

"No, it's *not* okay," she countered, trying to get a grip on the board. It was tethered to her ankle, a protective measure, but it wanted desperately to let the tide carry it back to shore…and her with it, consequently. She was moving from tired to exhausted in a hurry. "What sort of idiot can't even stay on the board? On her belly? This can't be that difficult!"

"Everybody learns at their own pace," Sean said. "Maybe we should go back in."

She stared at him, aghast. "Are you kidding me?"

"No, I'm really not," he said, and despite his laid-back demeanor, his eyes meant business. "You're tired, and we've been out here for half an hour."

"Let me just try to stand up. Just once."

He sighed. "You wouldn't happen to be Irish, would you?"

She blinked at him. "Okay, Mr. Non Sequitur. What brought that on?"

"Well, I'm half-Irish, and my mom always said that's the reason I'm so stubborn," he said, his eyes twinkling with amusement. "I was just wondering what your excuse was."

She grinned at him reluctantly, feeling some of the irritation at herself and the board slip away. "Well, I've got a cute ass," she said, throwing his words back at him.

"That you do," he said with enough appreciation that she was startled...and warm, despite the arctic temperature of the water. "But I don't think it really contributes to your stubbornness."

"No," she answered when she found her voice again. "But it does mean guys like you will put up with my stubbornness and let me keep going."

He sighed. "Okay. I'll push the board...we're not going to really try catching one. It's choppier than I thought it would be today."

"Okay," she said, and she clung to the board for dear life. With all her strength, she pulled herself on, and was gratified that she stayed on, feeling the movement of the ocean beneath her.

What does this feel like? It was vaguely familiar, the soft rocking, the up-and-down motion...

Immediately, she started blushing yet again.

"Focus!" Sean yelled, and just like that, she pushed her wayward thoughts aside. The board was her world.

"Okay," Sean said. "Steady...steady...now pop up, just like on the carpet."

She pictured the move she'd been practicing all week. With one fluid movement, she "popped" up, half jumping to her feet.

And then fell ass over teakettle back into the ocean.

When she surfaced, she felt like crying.

"Okay, that's enough. We're going back in," Sean said.

"One more time," she countered, but was startled into silence when she felt his arms on her waist.

"No. That's enough, Allison," he said, warming her neck with his breath. "We're going in *now*."

She couldn't breathe, and it had nothing to do with the water or being tired. She simply nodded, and followed him back to shore. She unstrapped the board from her ankle, and was grateful when he carried it back to shore, where their towels were.

"You did really well," Sean said.

She snorted. "Don't humor me. I sucked."

He stared at her quietly.

When she couldn't take it anymore, she finally stared back. "Yes?"

"If you're always this hard on yourself…" He trailed off thoughtfully, then shook his head. "No wonder."

She bristled. "No wonder what?"

"No wonder you're having anxiety attacks."

She bit her lip. He had her there. "Well, at least I'm trying."

He took a deep breath. "How are you feeling?"

"Like—" She stopped before the words that suddenly popped to mind leaped out of her mouth.

Like a failure.

"Tired," she said instead.

He studied her, and she had that disconcerting feeling

again…like he was reading her mind. "You don't do many things that you're not good at, do you?"

"I'm not good at plenty of things," she said.

"Yeah, but how often do you do those things you're not good at, is my point?"

She fell quiet. Boy, wasn't he just full of insights today?

"This isn't going to help," he said, and his voice was pensive. "I need you to loosen up."

Don't even say "stress," she warned her internal voice. Thankfully, it stayed silent.

"I'm really sorry, Sean," she finally said. "This is about as loose as I'm going to get."

He was quiet for a minute, and she braced herself for the inevitable—that he couldn't teach her, that the lessons were over. That she'd have to find some other way to learn how to relax.

"What are you doing tonight?"

Startled, she blinked at him. "Um…working."

"Can you take a few hours off?"

His eyes were hypnotic. She cleared her throat, to buy some time before she answered. "Uh…why?"

"Because I think I know a way that we can get you to learn to be okay with making mistakes. A way to loosen you up, as it were."

"Really?" She felt suspicious, sure, but some part of her also felt really, really hopeful. "How?"

"I want it to be a surprise," he said. "I'll pick you up from your house at around eight. Is that all right?"

"Uh…" It sounded suspiciously like a date. Not that he'd be dating her—this was all in the interest of teaching. Call it surf academia. "Sure. Why not?"

He smiled, and it warmed her more than the setting sun.

"SO, WHAT ARE WE DOING here again?"

Sean smiled at Allison's insistent question. "We're here to teach you how to relax, so you can surf better."

Allison looked around the inside of the bar, Sharkey's. A Hoodlum hangout. "So, I'm going to be surfing drunk from now on, am I?" she said with a hint of curiosity.

He laughed. She was wearing jeans, which he had to admit looked strange but great on her, and a cherry-red top that tended to bring out the roses in her otherwise pale cheeks. She blushed a lot, he noticed.

He noticed a lot of things about her, he noticed.

"No, you're not going to be surfing drunk," he corrected.

"So, what am I going to glean from this?" She glanced at him, suspicion ripe in her expression. "Because if you're planning on getting me drunk and then relaxing, I have to tell you that I have a fairly high tolerance to alcohol. Which is weird, considering I rarely drink."

"Are you *sure* you're not Irish?" He smiled at her. "Well, I have to admit, I was planning on making sure you had a drink or two, just to take the edge off. Hi, guys," he said as he saw Mike, Ryan, Gabe and Charlotte walk in.

"Hi there." This from Charlotte, who nudged Ryan hard to get him to stop grinning so lasciviously. Sean was grateful—he would've had to do something if Ryan continued with the leering smirk. "I'm Charlotte. You must be Allison."

"Guess I must be," Allison said, smiling shyly. "You're all friends of Sean's, huh?"

"We're the Hoodlums, yeah," Ryan said, then winked when he must've noticed Allison was staring at him blankly. "He didn't tell you about us?"

"He told us about you," Mike pointed out, and Sean could've kicked him.

"He did?" Allison tensed up, drawing tight as a piano wire, and Sean winced just looking at it. "What did he say?"

"That you were tense as all hell," Sean put in. "Mike, go get the lady a drink, will you?"

"Sure." Now Mike was grinning, not lasciviously, but mischievously. "Exactly how relaxed do we want her?"

"Not incapacitated," Sean said sternly.

"Incapacitated?" If possible, Allison tensed up more.

Sean couldn't stand it anymore. He leaned over, put an arm around her shoulders and squeezed. "Don't worry. I'll make sure you're okay. You believe that, right?"

"Uh..." She looked around at the others, and...ah, there it was. That blush. A man could get addicted to that blush.

"I just don't want to make an ass of myself," she whispered to him. He had to lean his head close to her lips to catch the words she obviously didn't want the other Hoodlums to hear.

"Ally," he finally said, "do you trust me?"

She blinked. Then she looked down, and then looked back at him.

"You know, I do trust you." She sounded surprised by it.

"Then don't worry."

She smiled.

"Although I do have to warn you—you're going to make an ass of yourself tonight."

Sproing! Return of the piano wire. He sighed. "Sit in front of me, will you?"

She stared at him. Finally, he dragged her chair in front of his, and then began to physically work her shoulders. The knots in her shoulders were like cords of wood.

"Sean!" she protested, trying to jump out of her chair like a jack-in-the-box, but his strong grip prevented her from fleeing. "I don't think this is appropriate."

"Can I sign up for the next one?" Charlotte asked. "I've been working some rough hours, myself."

Sean grinned as Gabe moved himself behind his wife, doing the same thing that Sean was doing, rubbing his wife's shoulders. Of course, he was a little more intent, and he kept punctuating his massage with whispers and nipped kisses on Charlotte's neck.

Sean glanced at Allison's neck. She had her hair up in a ponytail. The little curve where the back of her head swirled into her jawline and met the pale, thin column of her throat. She'd taste like vanilla, he bet, and honey.

Might want to curb that "tasting" talk, buddy. That's really, really not the point here.

No, it wasn't the point. The point was, he was trying to get her to relax, which, whether she wanted to or not, she was starting to do under his fingertips. He got the feeling if he kissed her neck, she might go the completely opposite direction. In fact, she might explode.

"Here we go, a drink for the lady," Mike announced, then surveyed the scene. "Jeez. I go to the bar for a minute, and this place turns into a massage parlor?"

"Don't look at me, pal," Ryan said, smirking. "I only work on women."

"What'd you get her?" Sean said, ignoring Mike's scowl.

Mike's smile returned. "A fire-and-ice shot. She'll love it."

He glanced at her. It was a pretty strong shot, but she said she could hold her liquor. Well, this was her chance to prove it. "Bottoms up," he told her.

"What is it?"

"I'm not entirely sure, but if you can handle it, then you'll be feeling a lot less tense in about, oh, fifteen minutes." If that.

She looked at it, then at Sean, then back at the drink. Then, as if she were standing at the open door of an airplane she was skydiving out of, she took a deep breath.

"To relaxation," she said, and then she downed the shot manfully. Ryan and Mike applauded, and Charlotte laughed. To his amazement, she didn't even cough. Her eyes did widen, though, and she swallowed hard.

"Okay. Now you're ready."

"Ready? To do what?"

Sean smiled, bracing himself. "To pick a song, of course."

She stared at him blankly. "A…song?"

"For karaoke."

She didn't seem to put it together for a long minute, but he knew the second that she did. She had a look of horrified shock. "Oh, no. Oh, *hell* no."

"It's okay. The whole point of this exercise is for you to get used to failing."

"You don't understand. I'm terrible. I mean, really terrible. William Hung terrible. Legendary."

"Perfect," Sean said. "Ally, nobody's going to see you again."

"Except us," Ryan added, smiling. "But don't worry, we won't tell."

"I refuse to do this," Allison said, standing up. "I insist on going home *right now.* If I had known—"

"You wouldn't have even shown up." And this had seemed like such a good idea at the time. "Allison, we'll be up there with you. But the whole point is, I want you to actively pursue something that you're terrible at. If you keep knocking yourself out and trying to be perfect at surfing, right out of the box, you're going to get shellacked. You've got to learn not only to be okay screwing up—you've got to look for it."

"Oh, no," she muttered. "Oh, God."

Charlotte leaned over. "We'll go up there and sing with you for the first one. Won't we, guys?"

Sean nodded. "I'll be with you," he assured her. "The whole time. Don't you worry."

Allison was not paying attention to him, but she'd stopped protesting. Now he could just see she was wishing for the earth to swallow her up. Of course, there was precious little chance of that, but he didn't want to dissuade her.

They dragged her up, en masse. It was a Saturday night, but there weren't really any serious singers at Sharkey's on karaoke night, not until later, like midnight. It took a full hour for Allison to get relaxed enough to pick a song—and she picked "Walkin' After Midnight," a nice easy Patsy Cline with very little range, which he appreciated.

"Never would've taken you for a country fan," he noted.

"I'm a woman of many facets," she said. "One of which is escape artist. You're really going to make me go through with this?"

"Mikey, get her another drink."

Half an hour and two shots later, the group of them went up for a loud and rowdy rendition of "Love Shack." He didn't think Allison did more than mouth the words. By this point, most of the patrons of Sharkey's had also had a few drinks, and were feeling more friendly and less judgmental. The Hoodlums' efforts were met with thunderous applause.

He took Allison's hand as the rest of them started to walk off. "Nope. This is it. Your solo."

She turned whiter, if possible. "But I sang!"

"Not really," he said. "Listen. I want you to not only sing, I want you to be absolutely the worst possible."

She looked close to tears. "Sean…please. Please don't make me do this."

"I'm going to be right here," he said. He looked at the deejay, who cued up the music.

"I'll do it if you do a song," she said, her tone desperate.

"All right," he said easily. He would've agreed to anything.

She stood up there, and the words started scrolling across the screen. Her first notes were low, almost inaudible.

"Can't hear you!" a heckler in the back yelled, and Allison actually took a step back.

After sending the guy a glare that would've torched an iceberg, Sean stood in front of Allison, just to the side of the screen, and held her hand. "Screw them," he said, capturing her gaze and holding it. "Just focus on me, and sing your heart out."

She sang a little louder, with a tremor in her voice.

"Sweetie, just sing."

She smiled…and sang.

It wasn't Ella Fitzgerald, but by the end of the song, she was heard by the back of the room…and even a blind man would hear the sweet smile in her voice.

When she sang the last note, the crowd burst into a roar that rivaled a stadium concert. Allison blushed, then went pale, then went teary. Then she bolted, with Sean hot on her heels.

She went out the back, startling the guy smoking out there. She went back, out toward the street. She was crying.

"I'm sorry," Sean said, feeling like a complete jerk. "I'm so sorry. I'm an idiot. I just thought…I thought it might help…"

"I sang," she said, even as her tears glistened in the moonlight. "Did you hear me?"

He couldn't help it. He reached out, stroking the tear off that petal-soft cheek of hers. "Sweetie, everybody could hear you."

"I've never done that." There was a tone of marvel in her voice. "I didn't even know I could do that."

"You weren't that bad," he said. "If you decide that you want to ditch that whole surfing thing, you might pick up some blues…"

He wasn't expecting it. She tugged him toward the curb, pushing him onto the street. "Uh, Allison?"

She was staring at the high curb, then at him. Then, without warning, she put her arms around his neck and kissed him.

He didn't quite know what was going on at first. But as soon as that heated, mobile mouth of hers hit his, most of his logical brain functions shut off like a light anyway, and he was lost to a world of pure emotion. He let his hands move to her hips, pulling her closer to him, and he leaned down to give her better access. She took advantage of it, kissing him deeply.

For a tiny girl, he had to admit two things: she could hold her liquor, and the woman sure could kiss.

He didn't know how long it went on, but it was both longer than he'd expected, and not nearly long enough. She was the one who pulled away, staring at him as if she couldn't quite believe what had happened, either.

"Allison," he said, but she put up a hand and stopped him.

"I don't normally do that," she said. "But I usually don't drink. And I never sing. So I guess…I guess we can call this a night of firsts."

"As long as we're not calling it a night of lasts," he said quietly.

She cogitated on that for a second. "What song are you going to sing?"

He almost stripped gears mentally, trying to keep up with her change in topic. "Uh… hadn't thought about it." His mind came up with a few inappropriate ones—"Why Don't We Get Drunk and Screw?" topping the list—and for some strange reason, the only other ones that were coming to mind were the drippiest, sappiest love songs he'd ever heard.

He felt as if he'd been clamshelled by a twenty-footer in the Hawaiian Pipeline.

He wanted to sing a love song to Allison. In front of all his friends.

He cleared his throat. "How about 'No Woman, No Cry'?" he suggested.

"Okay," she said, smiling…and then she took his hand.

Oh, yeah. He was in trouble.

CHAPTER SEVEN

"OKAY, THIS IS HOW this is going to run," Frank said, with all the relish of a commentator at the Colosseum, about to announce the release of the lions. "Three of you have new creative concepts that we're going to test run for the Kibble Tidbits account. Each of you will have fifteen minutes to present your ideas, and then five minutes to defend the ideas. The one that wins my approval and the general approval of the team will be the one we go with in the new business presentation, to the client, on December thirty-first." He paused for dramatic effect. "He or she will be the point person for that presentation. And, as if the stakes weren't big enough—he or she will be in very strong consideration to run the account, should we get the business."

"What happens to the people who don't get chosen?" Jerry, a new guy on the account team, whispered in a nervously joking manner.

"They battle to the death in the lunchroom," someone else muttered back. There was a titter of laughter that was quickly quelled by Frank's glare.

Allison forced herself not to quail. Strangely enough, she actually wasn't as nervous as she would be ordinarily. For the first time, she was completely, utterly preoccupied with something other than what was probably the second most important presentation of her career—one that would make the most important presentation of her career possible.

You had to go and kiss Sean Gilroy.

She closed her eyes. She had needed to get Sean to take her home, and in her drunken haze, she'd realized that she was probably going to feel some embarrassment when she sobered up. That, she discovered, was possibly the biggest understatement of her entire life. The next morning, she had awoken feeling like death and, when she remembered her behavior from the previous night, wishing that she had gone ahead and died. She'd called Sean, and in a croaking voice had canceled the lesson they'd had scheduled for Sunday. No way was she facing frigid waves and a wet-suit–clad Sean. He'd laughed, and volunteered to help her pick up her car from the karaoke bar. She'd taken a cab. Now she was scheduled to have a lesson with him that night, in his living room. She'd managed to avoid him for twenty-four hours.

She was looking forward to that with even more dread than today's presentation could even remotely engender.

"So, the three people who are making the presentations are—Kate, Peter and of course Allison."

"Of course," Jerry muttered, not caring that Allison could hear him.

Maybe she should cancel tonight's lesson, too, she thought as she watched her co-worker Kate stand up and start to give her presentation. She felt like a coward just considering it. And it wasn't his fault that she had glommed on to him like a drowning swimmer and then kissed the daylights out of him. And he hadn't made a move, hadn't taken advantage of her. Worse, he'd acted as if everything was normal and made no mention of her passionate indiscretion when he'd called her that morning, checking in on her. So she could make two conclusions: one, that the kiss, while enthusiastic, hadn't really been anything to write home about… and certainly hadn't been enough to stir her mellow surf instructor into a frenzy of passion; two, it had been tepid enough that Sean obviously would have no problem teaching her. He probably just found the whole thing funny.

And if that wasn't enough to frost her cookies, then nothing was.

"Allison! What did you think?"

Allison stared at Frank, who was looking at her expectantly. "About what?"

His left eyebrow went up. "Oh, I don't know. How about Kate's presentation? Which you've just been listening to for the past fifteen minutes?"

The silent *you idiot* was heavily implied.

She winced. "It seemed okay to me."

"Really?" He grimaced. "Okay. Anybody *else* have any insightful comments?"

Peter, the guy who was going to be up next, cleared his throat. "It wasn't bad, Kate," he said in a tone that suggested the complete opposite. "Still, I'm sure you meant to mention a few things but were just short for time. Like…"

And with that intro, he proceeded to take the next five minutes to completely tee off on Kate's presentation. His comments were phrased politely, but were completely bloodless. By the time he was finished, Kate was flushed bright red, even though she did nothing more than nod.

"Okay, Pete. Your turn. Show her how it's done," Frank said, his voice proud and encouraging.

Allison tried to pay more attention this time, even though he felt bad about what had happened to Kate. She'd seen nough of these in-house competitions, and had participated ı enough of them, to know that it wasn't personal. Still, if you ,eren't tough, it was enough to leave you pretty beat up, ıentally.

Pete started making his presentation, and insidiously, ıoughts of Sean kept creeping back. She didn't want to be coward, and didn't think she was being one. Now that she ıought of it, she might not even really need the lessons nymore. She barely had what her doctor would consider "a obby" and yet she hadn't experienced a full-blown anxiety ttack since that one day. Maybe it was just an aberration. ure, she still had flutters. And she could deal with them, as ɔng as she kept an eye on it.

Maybe I don't need to go back to Sean's at all. Maybe I on't need surf lessons anymore. Maybe…

The mix of feelings that that single thought kicked up was oth strong and startling.

"Allison? Still with us?"

Allison blinked. "You got it, boss."

"In case you were wondering," Frank said, his sarcasm ıick, "I want to know what you think of Peter's presenta-on. Come on. Let 'er rip."

She sighed. "It was fine."

"'Okay?' 'Fine'?" Frank sounded baffled. "What the hell ind of constructive criticism is that?"

She should've known better. She took a deep breath. "I'm ɛserving judgment."

"I'm not," Kate said, her tone borderline vicious. She was till smarting from Peter's polite autopsy of her presentation, and she proceeded to go nuclear on his idea, tearing it apar with glee.

"There's absolutely no way the client would go for some thing like this," she concluded.

"You're just upset because I pointed out all the holes i your presentation!" Peter yelled, the vein in his foreheac pulsing dangerously.

"I might've missed a few points, but at least I thought m idea through," Kate countered, standing up. "My five-year old could come up with a better design concept than yours!

"Whoa, whoa, easy," Frank said, laughing. "Allison? Yo sure you don't want to jump into this one?"

The entire room turned to look at her. She cleared he throat.

"Since I'm up next," she said slowly, "and the one wh wins this is going to be getting promoted, basically…do yo really think it's appropriate for us to tear into each other whe we've obviously got so much to lose?"

As soon as the words were out of her mouth, she clampe her lips shut, but it was obviously too late. Kate and Pete also went silent, staring at her. Frank, and Flashpoint Adver tising, for that matter, always encouraged this kind of ope blood sport. Only the fittest survived. She *knew* that.

"Well, I'd hate for you to do something *inappropriate,* Frank said, and she knew she'd screwed up.

She felt the room grow warm, and she felt her stomac clench, since she knew it had nothing to do with the thermo stat. The confrontation had made her nervous. She'd basi cally insulted her boss and his managerial style. Now it wa her turn to step into the arena.

She got up in front of the room, knowing that she'd star

sweating and hyperventilating in a moment if she didn't do something, fast.

Focus on surfing.

She took a deep breath. Cool water. No, make that frickin' *cold* water, she thought with a grin. The waves pounding against the sand, pounding against her hard enough to cause an ice-cream headache. The silence as she was rolled underneath the swirling blue-green surf.

Her breathing evened, and she smiled.

"Anytime you're ready," Frank said, his tone dour.

Immediately, she felt a sting of panic.

You're going to make an ass of yourself, I hate to say.

She felt as if she'd been goosed, as Sean's words of encouragement popped into her head. That was completely different, she thought, stunned. That was in front of a bunch of people she didn't know. That was singing in public, for no money, no prestige, no purpose whatsoever.

Of course, she hadn't thought of it that way at the time. She'd panicked. Hyperventilated. Sweated.

And then he'd been there, standing in front of her. Holding her hand. She focused on that sensation of his hand in hers.

"Allison?" Now Frank's note of impatience was mixed with a questioning concern.

She focused with all her might on Sean standing next to her. Believing in her.

"Well, here's my concept..." As if in a haze, like she was singing at Sharkey's, she pictured her presentation as if it were scrolling across the screen of the karaoke machine. She could almost smell Sean's cologne. It was more calming to her than the sound of the ocean ever could be.

She wasn't robotic, even as she realized that she wasn't

at her best. She wrapped up her presentation, then looked at Frank and stuck her chin up.

All right, boss of mine. Let me have it.

"All right," he said, stalking around the conference room, his voice intent. "Who wants to go first?"

To her surprise, nobody volunteered.

"You've got to be kidding me," Frank muttered. "Pete. Come on, I know you've got something to say."

Peter looked at Allison, and to her surprise, he actually looked…guilty? Puzzled? "Well, I've got a few questions…."

They were valid, but they were also a lot gentler than his initial assault on Kate. Allison fielded them easily, still focusing on either her surfboard or Sean.

Frank shook his head with an expression of disgust. "Kate? How about you?"

Kate looked as if she'd set her jaw, and flipped through some notes. "Well, I don't want to be *inappropriate,*" she said, almost mimicking Frank's earlier sarcasm, but with a hint of hesitation.

Allison sighed. "I didn't mean that you were being inappropriate before," she said, feeling inexplicably tired. "I meant that it probably wasn't the greatest idea for us to critique each other, considering."

"So what she's saying is, it wasn't your fault, it was mine," Frank said. "Isn't that right, Allison?"

She looked at Frank, who was grinning smugly, having neatly twisted her words. And at this point, she was too tired to care.

"Yup. That's pretty much what I was saying."

He blinked. Kate gaped.

"Uh…you might want to rethink ending it with a graph,"

Kate finally stammered out." But otherwise, it was a good presentation."

"Thanks," Allison said, then looked at Frank.

Slowly, to her surprise, a smile crossed Frank's face. "Damn, Ally. You must have ice water in your veins. I don't know a single other executive that would have the balls to call me out on my managerial style in a team meeting."

She shrugged. It was rather like dealing with a bear—if she tried to apologize or turn tail, he'd probably rip her to shreds.

"That's the kind of gutsiness we're going to need to land the account," he pronounced, and she forced herself not to let out an explosive breath of relief. "You're point person on this presentation."

"Thanks," she said, working on a Mona Lisa smile even as she felt like bolting for the nearest exit.

"Of course, it's going to need polishing," he stated. "You're going to need to put in a hell of a lot of overtime to whip this thing into shape. You're going to be eating, breathing and dreaming this thing."

The rest of the team were looking at each other, obviously unsurprised by the turn of events.

"I thought Kate and Peter had some really good concepts," Allison heard herself say, and the grumbling stopped immediately, as if somebody had hit the Mute button.

Hello. What did I just say?

The rest of the team was staring at her, as if they, too, couldn't believe that she'd said it. These meetings were winner take all. It was as if she was trying to snatch defeat from the jaws of victory. And what was up with that, exactly?

Frank bobbled, nonplussed. "Uh...well, yes. I think that goes without saying."

And usually does, Allison realized for the first time. "If we're all agreed on my concept," she said, "I'd love to have Kate and Peter's assistance. Really make it a team effort."

Kate sat up a little straighter. Peter didn't even try to disguise his look of bafflement.

"Uh…okay," Frank said. "We'll talk about it later. You guys will want to get to work."

The rest of the team filed out, and Allison headed for her office, feeling clammy and weak-kneed. She felt like a fraud. She'd gotten what she wanted, but the thought of eating, breathing and dreaming about the project was enough to make her want to pass out. So she'd decided to throw a bone to her opponents, and had consequently made it sound as if she didn't have what it took to take charge. Not exactly the kind of image that she wanted to project for a promotion.

She'd panicked. Gotten nervous. Been on the very edge of an anxiety attack. And the only thing that had saved her sanity hadn't been surfing.

It had been Sean.

AT SEVEN O'CLOCK on Monday night, Sean had already closed Tubes down and had been waiting in his living room for the past forty-five minutes. He had grabbed some dinner with Oz, some take-out food, but he'd barely touched it. When he did get home, he made sure that the living room was perfectly clean, he'd pushed the coffee table out of the way. Then he'd taken a shower and changed his clothes.

If any of the guys had seen him, they would have ribbed him mercilessly, but then again, they hadn't experienced what he'd experienced on Saturday. That kiss had practically paralyzed him.

No way does a woman kiss a man like that if she's not interested in him. That wasn't a random-occurrence kiss. That was a full-bore, all-systems-go, I'm-so-into-you kiss. He'd had several of those, although none that rivaled the intensity of Saturday's "kisstravaganza."

It figured, he thought with a grin. Anything that Allison wound up doing would be done with intensity.

At the time, he'd been too floored to really pursue it...and she'd frankly been too embarrassed. He knew that from when he called her the next day. She was also a little too inebriated on Saturday for him to do much more than enjoy what she was offering, and wait for a better time to act on what he now knew.

The time to act was tonight. He was going to ask Allison Robbins out on a date.

He was a little nervous, but not nearly as nervous as he could have been. It was a relief, not just to know that she was interested, but to realize that it wasn't one-sided. He'd felt foolish long enough, and more foolish over Allison than he had over any woman in years. So tonight, he was going to take the next step. He'd ask her to dinner. Someplace special, maybe. And he'd keep teaching her, naturally.

Considering all the elements up in the air in his life, what with Tubes shutting down, it probably wasn't the best timing. Still, he didn't have any control over that. He did have control over this—and he was going to ask her out. She'd done everything but wear a T-shirt saying that she wanted him, and he knew he sure as hell wanted her.

There was a knock on his door, and he jumped off the sofa like a jackrabbit. He forced himself to calm down before opening the door.

Allison was there, smiling shyly. "Hi, Sean."

Before he could say anything, he heard another voice. "Mr. Gilroy. Nice to see you."

He felt his libido go from a nice medium-rev to stone-cold zero. "Um…hi, Mrs. Tilson," he said. "Is there anything wrong? I haven't been too loud or anything?"

"No, no. Nothing like that. I hope you don't mind," she said, although her voice indicated she didn't particularly care if he minded or not. "Allison asked if I'd like to join her, and see how the lessons were progressing."

He looked at Allison, who for whatever reason seemed to be avoiding his gaze. "Did she, now?"

"I just thought it'd be nice," Allison said in that high, fast-paced, breathy voice she used when she was really nervous. He remembered her slipping into it before he'd interviewed with Mrs. Tilson the first time around. "I mean, I hardly get a chance to see Aunt Claire, and I'm over here quite a bit now, so no reason not to kill two birds with one stone, and besides, she's always been a bit curious…and I think it's a good way for you two to get to know each other besides…"

He walked up to her, and he swore he could see her hold her breath. "Relax," he whispered.

She didn't react, didn't even glare at him, just stared at the floor.

Uh-oh. He'd deliberately tried for a hot button, to try to jar her out of whatever weird frenzy of nerves she was currently cycling in. For her to just pass on the opportunity must mean that she was well and truly freaked out. And the fact that she'd brought Mrs. Tilson over couldn't be promising.

He frowned. So much for his "kisstravaganza" theory, he

thought with a mental sigh of frustration. Still, a woman couldn't fake a kiss like that. She might be nervous, might be embarrassed. And she probably didn't know how he felt.

"So, how does this lesson progress? And indoors? I thought you'd need to be in the water," Mrs. Tilson said, her voice crisp but curious.

He glanced at Mrs. Tilson, who was staring at the two of them intently. Of course, he was going to have a hell of a time showing Allison how he felt, with Mrs. Tilson right there, watching him like a hawk.

He glanced at Allison. "Why don't we start with stretches and warm-ups. Mrs. Tilson, if you'd like to have a seat on my futon, make yourself comfortable."

Mrs. Tilson took a glance at his admittedly old futon. "I get the feeling I can do one or the other but not both," she said, but the little hint of humor in her voice suggested she was teasing. It was a hard call, though. She chose to sit at his small kitchen table instead. The straight-backed chair probably seemed more like her own furniture, he supposed.

He tried to ignore the fact that he had an audience, and moved Allison to her pop-ups. She still wasn't looking at him. He could practically feel the embarrassment coming off of her like a cloud. "Okay. We're going to focus specifically on balance." He grinned. "Let's see if we can't find your sweet spot today."

"I beg your pardon." This, from Mrs. Tilson.

He sighed. "It's just an expression," he said.

She sat up straighter. "For what?"

"Center of gravity," he said with a hint of irritation, although he noticed a small smirk hovering on Allison's lips. "Find that funny, huh?"

She finally, *finally* looked up at him. Their gazes locked, and he smiled at her…a full, warm smile.

Her eyes widened, and then she stared back at the floor.

He sighed. Okay, they were getting nowhere at this rate.

It went on like that for half an hour, until the sheer frustration of the situation had his muscles cemented in knots. Mrs. Tilson kept making helpful comments: "Why does she have to do that?" "Allison, you're not standing properly. Sean, would you go ahead and show her? He said don't look at the floor!" He thought the lady was nice enough, but if she kept back-seat coaching, he might be tempted to strangle her. Finally, sweating like he'd just jogged around the block, he gave up.

"I think that's enough for one night," he said.

Allison was sweating, too, and she let out a sigh of relief. "Yeah."

"You're ready to head back into the water," he said. "So just let me know when you'll be available for some sunlight surf time, and I'll check the tide table."

He turned to see she was staring right at him, no longer embarrassed or hiding. "Really? Back in the water?"

"You're practicing, you're doing well. Mrs. Tilson's right…you'd be better off learning in the water at this point." He shrugged. "It'll be cold, but you can handle it. I'll just make sure I get you some booties."

"Okay! That's great! No…that's fantastic!" Her smile was wide and dazzling, and for a split second, it looked as if she wanted to throw herself into his arms for a grateful hug. In fact, his body tensed in anticipation of just that, but she threw a quick, wary glance at Mrs. Tilson, and just stood there, shifting her weight from one foot to another. "Well. I guess

I'd better be getting Aunt Claire back, and then I've got a bunch of work I still have to do tonight. Thanks for the lesson, Sean."

"We'll pick up where we left off tomorrow," he said, not letting her off the hook that easily.

She bit her lip, and nodded. "I'll let you know when I can get some time to hit the waves," she said with a nervous laugh.

He nodded. Then he looked at Mrs. Tilson, who was taking in the whole interchange with a sort of sharp interest. "Hope you had fun," he said.

"Allison? Go along without me," she said, causing Sean's heart to fall a little. "Mr. Gilroy here will make sure I get back all right."

Sean sighed. He wondered if this was going to be Allison's way of telling him to back off…the family connection, like a mafia don in Chanel, warning him away from the golden goddaughter.

"Aunt Claire?" Allison looked surprised by this announcement, and Sean felt a little cheered.

"Go on, Allison. I'm not an invalid," Mrs. Tilson said impatiently.

Obviously baffled, Allison pressed a kiss on Mrs. Tilson's cheek, then looked at Sean. For a second, he almost leaned down and kissed *her* cheek. Instead, he smiled at her, winking.

She smiled, blushed and fled.

He sighed, watching her head down his stairway and walk out. Then he turned to Mrs. Tilson. "I'm sorry. You had questions?"

"Just one, primarily," she said. "What in the world are you waiting for?"

He stared at her. "Sorry?"

"You're obviously completely enamored of my goddaughter," she said, her words completely no-nonsense and businesslike. "So what are you waiting for?"

He let out a bark of laughter. "Uh...hmm. How about the fact that her seventy-eight-year-old godmother was right there with us the entire time?"

"What does that have to do with anything?"

He blinked at her. "I don't know. I would've felt a little weird putting the moves on Allison with you there, Mrs. Tilson."

She made a puckered little face at that one. "I did *not* say put the moves on her. Good grief. Are you crazy?"

"I'm starting to wonder," he responded dryly.

"I'm simply saying, you could've shown that you were interested in her. You could have asked her if she was busy the following weekend, maybe. Asked her out to dinner." She glared at him. "Kept it completely gentlemanly."

He was being told off by an irate septuagenarian, who was basically instructing him on how best to court and/or woo her goddaughter. Hell had basically frozen over.

"Listen, as much as I appreciate it, I don't really need dating advice, Mrs. T," he said patiently. He sighed. "Besides, I get the feeling she's busy this weekend."

"Allison is busy every weekend," she said with a dismissive wave of her hand. "That's her whole problem. She thinks work is the answer to everything." Her eyes were bright, intense. "I think you could be very good for her."

Sean smiled. "Thanks for the vote of confidence."

"You don't have the full vote yet. I think she needs someone a bit more...how should I say this?"

He winced. *Oh, I don't know. Rich? Cultured? Ambi-ous?*

"Proactive," she said with a nod of her head.

"Proactive?"

"You're not going to get my goddaughter to go out with ou if you just sit there and wait for her to throw herself at ou. She only does that sort of thing for business." She niffed. "Not that I can blame her. But the fact is, you're oing to have to jar her out of that way of life of hers. She's riving herself to an early grave with all that work."

"Well, we'll see what we can do." This had to be one of ie weirdest conversations on record, he thought with a rueful rin.

She got up and headed toward the door, and he moved to ccompany her to her house. Then she turned, frowning so ercely that he paused, startled.

"Although I must say," she said in dire tones, "you might vant to watch it with that *putting the moves on* business."

"Right," he said, and damn it if he wasn't blushing.

'OR MAYBE THE FIRST TIME in her life, she wished that her unt Claire owned a wet suit.

Allison gritted her teeth as she paddled on her board, eeling Sean's presence by her side. It was reassuring, of ourse—she didn't know what the heck she was doing—but t the same time, she seemed hyperaware of the feeling of is hand on her back, or stroking her side gently, just guiding er. There was absolutely, positively nothing sexually harged about any of the touches. He'd even say the least flir-atious and most sexually uninspiring instructions, such as you're looking like a dead fish, come on, Ally, paddle." So she knew the guy had nothing more on his mind than getting her amateur butt to stand up on her surfboard.

"Pop up, now, just like you practiced," Sean said. And then gave an offhand stroke of her back that she felt through the layer of neoprene like his hand was an iron.

She took a deep breath, then popped up. And for a second, just a second, she was standing, the wave moving underneath her.

"I'm standing!" She felt adrenaline rush through her system, and for a second, there was no work, no confusion about Sean…no nothing but the board, the wave and her. "I'm—"

Whoosh.

She choked on a mouthful of saltwater as she submerged, covering her face as Sean showed her so the board wouldn't whack her. She was underwater for a while, it felt like, as the wave rolled her. She finally surfaced, spluttering and shivering.

"You did it!" He walked up to her, laughter and happiness in his voice.

"I really did it," she said, slicking her hair back with one hand while she rode herd on her board with the other. "I did it!"

"This calls for a celebration," Sean said. "How about a coffee? Your lips are turning blue."

"*Coffee.*" She chanted the word like a prayer. "You read my mind. But can I…"

She paused when he frowned at her. "Just one more time? I loved the feel of that."

A strange look crossed his face…and for a second, the heat from his blue eyes made the chill of the water seem nonexistent as it scorched her down to her toes.

"Okay, one more time. But you're sunk," he said. "Once you learn to love surfing, you won't know how you survived without it." He looked away from her, and she wondered if she imagined the look that passed between them.

Minutes later she carried the board out, putting it down on the surf. "So…where are we getting coffee?"

"There's a coffee place, local, in Redondo," he said. "It's close."

She'd parked her Jag right behind his beat-up pickup truck. Abruptly, she noticed a problem. "Uh…I have to go up to…" She looked around. "Where can I change out of my wet suit?"

He looked at her, puzzled. She realized that after most of her lessons, he'd stayed in and surfed, or on karaoke night, they hadn't been parked near each other at all. "What do you normally do?" he asked.

She shrugged. "I put a bunch of towels on the seat, over a seat cover," she said. "Don't want to ruin the leather or anything." She paused. "What do you do?"

He grinned. "Um, normally people just use towels. Don't worry, you'll get the hang of it."

She laughed nervously. She glanced around. The water was cold enough to scare off all but the locals, and the tide was wrong for the true surfers. There wasn't anybody around, only the odd car driving by. She felt strangely, deliciously naughty. "Okay," she said. "Maybe you could keep a lookout for me."

"Actually, I can hold up your towel for you, if you want," he suggested.

She felt her heart start pounding against her rib cage. "Um…I don't think that'll be necessary," she sputtered. "I went to junior-high gym class, after all. After that, all girls can change clothes completely showing no more than one square inch of flesh between their neck and their knees."

"Really?" He smiled, and she felt like a gibbering idiot. "You know, I've always wondered about that." He crossed his arms.

"What, you're going to watch me?" she squeaked.

"With a claim like that? You think I'd want to miss it?"

She swallowed, hard, then grabbed her towel and her dry clothes, propping them on the trunk of her car. She became aware of his curious eyes. She wondered if it was entirely appropriate...then blushed.

What are you? A schoolmarm?

Deliberately, she wiggled out of her wet suit, something she'd been practicing at home. Left in only her two-piece bathing suit, she shivered as the cold air hit her wet skin. Any thought of being possibly sexy immediately left her head, although she had her embarrassment to keep her warm. She pulled the sweatshirt over her head, then maneuvered the top piece off à la *Flashdance.* He gave her a golf clap. "I knew girls could do that," he said. "You sure you don't want me to hold a towel over your...over the bottom part?"

She did go ahead and blush on that one. "Um...possibly..." She glanced at her jeans. Then she realized...he'd have to be very close to her to hold the towel to shield her. "NO. No. That's fine. I can manage."

"Okay," he said, crossing his arms. "Just trying to be gentlemanly."

"Thanks," she muttered, then wrapped the towel around her like a sarong. She took a deep breath, then stripped off the wet bikini bottoms, putting on dry underwear carefully.

For one brief, breath-stealing moment, the towel almost came loose. She finally tugged her jeans on, taking off the towel with a flourish. "Ta dah!"

He whistled appreciatively. "Good job."

"So, shall we go?"

"Gotta get into dry clothes myself," he rumbled.

She surveyed his wet suit. "Oh." She smiled wryly. "Need help?"

He looked at her…that heated look, part two.

"Actually, yes."

She cleared her throat. "Come on. It can't be that tough to get your towel around you. I bet you do this all the time."

"Yeah, but I don't usually have help readily available," he said. "And you offered."

She put her arms behind her back, like a small child who's been warned about a very hot oven. And Sean was, let's face it, one hot oven.

"Chicken," he whispered, and she felt it like a kiss on the small of her back. She jolted, as if goosed. "Well, fine. If I've got to do this by myself, you might want to look away."

"Oh, no," she said, determined to give as good as she got. "If you got to watch me through that embarrassment, I get to watch you."

He shrugged. "Suit yourself."

He wrapped the towel around his waist, and then methodically unzipped the wet suit, peeling it off to the waist.

Her breath caught in her throat.

She'd never seen him without his shirt before. He was cut like a diamond, all rippling muscles and tanned skin, even in the winter. He looked like the volleyball scene in *Top Gun.* He looked good enough to eat.

She swallowed, hard. Then she noticed he was readjusting the towel around what he'd just peeled off. "Just like a man," she said with a slight quaver in her voice.

He glanced up from his concentrated effort on the towel. "How's that?"

"You're making it much more difficult." It was easier to rib him. "Why didn't you just take the wet suit off, then just cover the bathing suit with the towel, instead of trying to take everything off altogether? Honestly."

He had turned away from her, showing her a truly gorgeous back. At that statement, however, he glanced over his shoulder, the bangs of his hair falling rakishly over his very amused eyes. "Honey, I'm a real surfer."

"So that means you do everything the hard way?"

"No," he said patiently, and his grin was downright wicked. "It means I don't wear a bathing suit under my wet suit, sweetie."

"You—"

She abruptly took in the fact that he was taking off his wet suit…and then it was just one thin layer of terry cloth between her and his…and…

The towel fell loose, and he caught it…but not before she got a tantalizing glimpse of a few inches of backside, and that perfect cut of muscles from his abdomen down to his…

She shut her eyes as if she were going to be turned into a pillar of salt. Her rapid breathing had nothing to do with panic, she knew, and everything to do with that man.

What happened to not thinking of him inappropriately? she chastised herself. Of course, it wasn't her fault that he was a true surfer.

"It's safe now," he said, and she opened her eyes to find

him a few inches in front of her. He was grinning, and his eyes held none of the mind-bending heat that they'd displayed just a few minutes ago.

"Just show me where we need to go," she said. "I'm dying for some coffee."

He laughed as he went back to his truck, and all she could think of was his soft, caressing statement.

Chicken.

She thought about what would've happened if he'd held her towel…or she'd held his. Arms around each other. Practically naked.

Chicken?

You're damn right I am.

CHAPTER EIGHT

SEAN HEARD OZ COME IN through the store's back door, and he braced himself for the confrontation he was about to embark on. As a rule, Oz didn't like talking about much of anything serious, especially not the business. This fact had gotten them into a whole lot of trouble a few years ago, when it turned out Oz had been miscommunicating with the accountant, and the taxes had been filed incorrectly. Oz had never really recovered from that flub, and the shop had suffered from it, Sean knew. Instead of being more open, Oz had gotten even more secretive about how the business was run—or how it was doing. Which only made Sean more concerned.

He knew his friends were telling him to give up on the business. He had basically been working as a clerk for the past, what, sixteen years. A lot of that had been loyalty to Oz, he knew, and because of that, he wasn't going to give up on the shop without discussing it. He knew how stressed out Oz was...he wasn't going to compound the situation by leaving in the lurch the man who was sort of like a father to him.

Oz walked in, in a hooded sweatshirt that said Surf Bum on it, and a pair of jeans. He had a cup of coffee in his left hand and the local Manhattan Beach paper in his right.

"Morning, Oz," Sean said.

Oz grunted in return. "I'll be in the office if anybody needs me."

It was ten o'clock in the morning, they'd just opened and it was the winter season. Sean sighed, and then walked with purpose to the door frame of the small office.

Oz was behind his desk, the paper already opened. He looked up. "What? Is there a problem?"

Sean gritted his teeth for a second, then dived in. "You tell me. Is there a problem with the shop?"

Oz stared at him for a second. "Sean, I told you at Thanksgiving, I've been going through some stuff lately…"

"How bad is it?" Sean felt badly, pinning him down like this, but there wasn't any other way.

Oz sighed, sitting up and crossing his arms. "I haven't had enough coffee for this conversation," he groused.

"So drink fast, because we're having it."

Oz looked at him, as if trying to find even a scrap of leniency, but for once Sean wasn't going to back down for the sake of Oz's comfort. Reluctantly, Oz took a few gulps of coffee, then sighed again. "At this point, the shop's barely breaking even. The economy's been bad, you know that. And the neighborhood's changed. We've got all these bougie shops all over the place… Victoria's Secret on the opposite corner, for Christ's sake, Sean. The tattoo parlor got replaced by an Urban Outfitters."

"That's a good thing," Sean argued. "The shops they've put in? Those are the shops that people who spend lots of money go into."

"Yeah, well, they're not surfers, apparently," Oz said. "And they haven't been spending money in here."

"We could change that." Sean went back to the counter, grabbed the notes he'd written out. "And before you ask…here's how. I've been thinking about it since Thanksgiving."

Oz looked at the notes, a bewildered expression crossing his face. "Holy cow. I didn't know you—" He stopped in his tracks. "Well, I should've known you were capable of this, Sean. You were always a smart kid."

"I love the surf shop," Sean said. "And I really think we can turn things around. Just doing half the stuff I've suggested would make a difference." He took a deep breath. "I'll work extra. I'll try it myself. You don't have to do a thing. If the shop doesn't make any more money, then you can go ahead and sell it. But if it does…" Sean paused. "If it does, tell me you'll keep the place open."

Oz sighed heavily, sounding like a growling bear. "Sean, I wasn't going to ask you how to save the shop."

Sean stilled. "What do you mean?"

"I mean…hell, even if we were doing gangbusters…" He rubbed his hands over his face. "I should've told you. I'm going to sell the shop regardless, Sean. I knew how freaked out you were just from my telling you to move out, and I was hoping there'd be an easier way." His weathered face looked mournful. "I'm really sorry, Sean."

Sean felt numb. He'd worked so hard…his friends had told him, hadn't they? Warned him? Seen this coming in a way he'd refused to?

Oz stood up, clapping Sean on the shoulder. "It's just getting to be too much for me, Sean. Hell, I'm getting too old. And it's too much business. Any joy I had for this place is long gone. Now I don't even have a retirement, Sean," he said, a note of pleading in his voice. "If I sell the shop, then I do get a retirement. If I didn't have that, I'd keep it open and you could work here forever."

Sean swallowed thickly. "Thanks."

"But you know? You're in your thirties, Sean. You've been working here since you were sixteen years old. It's time you tried something different. You're cut out for a lot more than this."

Sean wished, desperately wished, that people would stop saying that to him. He might deserve more than the surf shop, but it was all he'd ever wanted.

"So, when are you planning on selling it?" Sean's voice was even, almost mechanical.

Oz seemed not to notice—or more likely, pretended not to notice. "February. I figure, in January I can get it spruced up a little, try to get the most money possible out of it. It's in a really prime real-estate location…the broker said that it wouldn't be any trouble getting a buyer."

"February?" Sean said, aghast. "That soon?"

"I already said I'm sorry," Oz grumbled.

"No. No. That's okay. You have to do what you've gotta do," Sean said.

Which meant that he had to do what he had to do. Whatever that was.

"You look tired," Oz said in a low voice. "You can leave early today. It's been slow… I don't expect a Christmas rush, or anything."

Sean nodded. "I'm teaching tonight, anyway," he said, holding the vision of Allison as a lifeline.

He always felt better when she was around. Now he'd have to figure out what he was going to do…and he had a deadline.

"ALLISON? WAIT UP. I need to talk to you."

Allison was halfway down the hallway, headed toward her office, when Frank stopped her. "Um, okay," she replied, forcing herself not to look at her watch. She'd promised Sean she'd see him tonight, only this time, it wasn't going to be in the water…it was going to be at her house. There wasn't going to be any Aunt Claire to provide a buffer. It was just going to be him, her and a monstrous amount of self-control that frankly she wasn't quite sure she possessed.

"Allison? Yo! Earth to Allison!"

She blinked, and saw Frank beckoning impatiently from the doorway of his office.

"Sorry," she said quickly, hurrying over to him. "I was just…thinking of something."

Like Sean, standing there in just a towel against the backdrop of a gray winter sea…or the way his smile lit up his blue eyes…or the way his palm would brush against her…

"Generally I like to encourage thinking in my staff," Frank rumbled, the irritation in his voice clear as a bell. "But I have to say, you're thinking an awful lot lately, and I don't see it translating into a smoother new business presentation. So what are you thinking about?"

She schooled her expression to look properly contrite. At any other time, it wouldn't be an act. She would be more than contrite, she'd be appalled that her work was not up to her own high, exacting standards, much less her boss's.

He's right. What the hell are you thinking about?

She'd managed to keep things on the level and professional with Sean, kept sex out of the equation entirely. And here she was, still acting like a complete and utter idiot who couldn't focus on her job.

"You can't seem to be able to listen to a conversation from beginning to end. I ask you to make changes, and maybe half of what I ask for gets done. You're more than losing your edge, kid… I feel like you're losing 'it' entirely! You see my concerns?"

"You know, actually, I don't."

She heard the words coming out of her mouth as if some stranger had walked into the office and said them. She almost turned around to see if there was a smarmy, obviously unafraid-of-being-fired ventriloquist standing behind her.

"Excuse me?" Frank said in a shocked tone.

She took a deep breath, and tried somehow to get herself back on track. "Frank, can I be honest with you?"

"What, you're only starting now?"

She swallowed hard. "I'm going through a lot right now."

"Ah. I see," he said, and…she grimaced. Damn it if he didn't look smug. "I figured it'd be something like that."

"Something like what?" she asked curiously.

"You're having relationship trouble or something, aren't you?"

Her mouth dropped open at the sheer sexism of that statement. "How did you guess?" she said, her voice dripping sarcasm.

He didn't notice. "Well, you don't talk about your private life much, and I didn't think you were dating, but then, I never really asked. It's your business," he pronounced magnanimously, making her want to strangle him. "Still, when it starts to affect what could be one of the biggest promotions of my career, it becomes my business. So spill. What's going on and how can we fix it? I need you at one hundred percent."

"Are you kidding me with this?" she blurted out.

"No," he said, and he looked as if he was gritting his teeth. "Listen, I know my questions are invasive and awkward as all hell. But it really is affecting your work, kid. So if you can't talk to me, you're going to have to talk to somebody." He paused. "Or I'm going to have to take you off the account. It's pretty much as simple as that."

She processed that for a long minute. Then she took a deep breath. She considered telling him about the panic attacks. The surfing. The whole nine yards.

"Let's say, for just a second, that you're right," she said instead. "If it's a relationship thing...what in the world could you possibly tell me to fix it?"

Now he looked distinctly uncomfortable. "Would depend on the problem."

There was no way in hell she was telling her boss that she was obsessed with Sean Gilroy. "I can't do this."

"Well, I'm serious. You're going to have to do something," he said.

"Like what? Just get rid of him?" she spat.

"Hell no!" Frank sounded aghast, and she stared at him in surprise. "This close to the presentation? The last thing I need is you knocked out of commission, all weepy and wrecked."

"Your concern is overwhelming," she said softly, with a wry smile.

He rolled his eyes. "Sorry. I mean, any other time, I'd work on the whole sympathy thing," he said. "But this account is too important."

"So what would you advise?" she said, only half-serious.

He pondered it for a second. "I'd say do whatever you can to keep it smooth sailing. And definitely keep yourself happy. Don't tackle anything big until after the presentation."

"Tackle anything big," she said, laughing.

"You think it's a joke, but I know women like you," he said, obviously not even caring how un-PC he sounded. "You've got a huge project on your plate, and you think, hey, *now's* the perfect time to dissect my relationship. You have 'the talk.' You ask about where you're going. You make everything way more complicated than it needs to be."

"When I ought to be…doing what, exactly?"

"When you ought to just ride with it, enjoy it as much as you can and just…" He cleared his throat. "Well, if you were a guy, and if I hadn't had the lawyers already talk to me, I'd say just enjoy the sex and leave the heavy stuff for Valentine's Day like normal dysfunctional people."

She couldn't help it. She burst out laughing.

"There. Now you're looking a little less shell-shocked," he said, sounding satisfied. "So. About the revisions I asked for?"

She took a deep breath. "Still being honest…Frank, you're going a little nutso with the revisions. Just trust me, they're going to be fine."

"They're—"

"They're going to be *fine,*" she said in a firm voice.

He stared at her, then to her surprise, he backed down. "They'd better be," he conceded. "Okay, I'll leave the revisions alone. Still, I'd like you to stay late to meet with the design team on the graphics they're building around your concept. I'll meet you at your office in a few minutes, so have your ideas ready, okay?"

"Mmm-hmm." She barely even registered his last statement. Instead, she was still focused on his last little epiphany.

What if he's right? Maybe you are just making it all too complicated.

She knew that she was wildly attracted to Sean. She knew that it was distracting her beyond the point of reason. What she hadn't considered was, maybe the fact that she hadn't given in to it was what was making her so crazy.

Like a cool mist, she slowly began to calm down. To her shock, she relaxed. She walked to her office, and it must've shown on her face, because Gary followed her in.

"Wow. What happened?"

"I think I just had a breakthrough," she said, surprised at the enthusiasm in her voice.

Frank knocked on her door. "Sorry, quicker than I thought. The design guys are ready to go right now, so I thought I'd collect you."

"I have to go," she said.

He looked at her. "But you just said this was okay."

"I can't work late tonight, I forgot."

He shook his head. "Get this taken care of, Allison," he warned.

"It will be," she said. "In fact, I'm going to take care of it right now."

Frank stood there for a second, staring at her, as if she might change her mind. When she just stared back, he finally gave up, walking away and muttering.

Gary gaped at her. "You are so my heroine," he said, approval rich in his voice. "I've never seen anybody stand up to him. Ever."

"Yeah, well, he can't say he didn't ask for it," she said,

still feeling a delicious euphoria start to thread through her system.

She was going to solve her problem, she thought. Tonight's lesson was going to teach her to relax for good.

SEAN SHOWED UP at Allison's place. It had been a while since he'd been there—was it just, what, a week and a half ago since he'd been stranded on her steps for forty minutes? It seemed like longer. It seemed like he'd known her for months. Maybe years.

At the risk of sounding desperately melodramatic, it felt like he'd wanted her forever.

The thing was, he would take things as they came. He knew Allison was now trying to do the same. And he was taking Mrs. Tilson's advice, of all things. He was showing Ally that she did indeed want him. She was a type-A stress case. She probably needed all kinds of reassurances. She needed a game plan. She needed to proceed with caution. And, all things considered and his hormone-riddled body notwithstanding, he was okay with caution. He generally had a slow, easy approach to life, himself.

With that in mind, he walked up to her front door. Tonight, he was going to work with her on her arm strength...basic weight training, plenty of paddling. He was going to see what he could do about stirring up those hormones of hers, he thought, remembering their last encounter at the beach. He was going to slowly and incrementally show her exactly what she was missing. And then, maybe, he'd give her the tiniest kiss on the cheek.

Oh yeah. By Valentine's Day, at the latest, she'll be more than ready to start dating.

He grinned with confidence and knocked on her door.

She opened it, and his heart stopped.

She was wearing a gray tank top that molded to her body like spray paint and a pair of sweatpants that rode low on her pelvis. That glorious blond hair of hers was up in a high ponytail, emphasizing that perfect face.

"Well…hello there," she greeted in a purring voice. "Want to come in?"

"Um, sure. Hi." At a loss, he walked inside, watching as she shut the door behind him…and locked it. He smiled, trying to get his stride back. "So, are you ready to work out?"

She surveyed him like a cat eyeing a small flightless bird. "Boy, am I ever."

Suddenly, his whole "going slow" scenario seemed ever so slightly out of place.

"Today, we're going to work on your paddling," he said, deciding to downshift into the lesson plan. She was still interested in surfing, and teaching was something he'd done for so many years, it felt like a security blanket. "You're going to need to develop some serious upper-body strength if you want to become a true surfer."

"You've got a great upper body," she noted.

He felt himself get warm, and it wasn't from the way she was checking him out—although that helped. No, he got the feeling he was perilously close to blushing.

Who stole his girl? This was not the same one who had brought her elderly godmother over to his apartment to make sure there was a buffer zone between them. And it wasn't the sweetly shy female who had deliberately not peeked when he'd taunted her by stripping out of his wet suit. No, this was a woman on the prowl.

Not that he was necessarily complaining, he thought as his body started the sequence of *all systems go.* It was just, well, he wasn't expecting it. A guy like himself needed a little warm-up time.

She walked over to him, staring up into his eyes. "So, how did you want me?"

He felt his mouth go dry.

A very little warm-up time.

He circled her, and she just kept staring. "I was thinking of some light-weights stuff," he said. "Arm curls, some resistance stuff, that kind of thing. Do you have weights?"

She shook her head, her eyes like melted chocolate.

"Anything we can use as weights? Heavy books, paint cans…anything like that?"

"Nope." She was practically pouting.

He shifted, smiling. "Well, how are we going to have you work out, then?"

Her responding smile was downright wicked.

He swallowed, hard.

"Why don't we back-burner the weight training for the time being," she said. "I think I've got a better idea."

"Really?" He was starting to get some better ideas, himself.

Instead, she led him over to the couch and sat him down. "I think maybe it's time I addressed something important," she said, sitting next to him.

He could smell her uniquely intoxicating scent—something delicate, flowery, and still shot through with hints of something exotic and spicy. He couldn't help but lean a little closer to her, and noticed she wasn't backing away. "What was it you wanted to talk about?" He was having a hard time staying focused.

"I want you," she said.

He choked on a surprised laugh. "I'm sorry," he said immediately. "It's not that it's funny. It's just...I wasn't expecting it."

"You weren't?" For a second, the sex-vixen facade fell away, and she looked like pure Allison...puzzled, intent, problem-solving.

He wanted her even more. Smiling, he pushed a stray lock of hair away from her jawline, stroking the delicate skin on her neck. "I suspected, I hoped. I just...you didn't seem all that comfortable with it."

"I wouldn't say I'm necessarily comfortable now," she said in the cutely grumpy way he was learning to crave.

"Seemed pretty comfortable to me," he said. "When you opened the door, I thought my blood pressure was going to skyrocket."

She smiled, now with a hint of mischief. "I thought about not saying anything and just jumping you."

He got the mental image just seconds after she said it. His body, already primed, went hard in a rush.

"You don't say?" he squeaked, then cleared his throat. "Well, why didn't you?" he continued in his normal deep voice.

She laughed. "But I thought I'd be pushing my luck."

"Please. Go ahead. Push all you like."

Her eyes glinted, and before he knew what was going on, she was straddling his lap. "How does this strike you?" she murmured, then slowly, deliberately, started kissing his neck.

He groaned, leaning back as that little rosebud mouth of hers went to work. "Strikes me like a bolt of lightning," he muttered, his hands gripping her hips then smoothing their way up her back. She shivered, and he felt like his blood was boiling.

He waited until she edged a little closer, pulling back slightly to look into his eyes. Then slowly, deliberately, he kissed her, gently, the way he'd always wanted to. Neither of them were drunk, impaired or in any way compromised. She knew exactly what she was getting into, and so did he.

He brushed his lips against hers, coaxing them to part, then he nipped at her full lower lip, drinking in her gasp of pleasure. This was going to be fun. He could do this for a couple of hours or so, he thought.

That is, until her hips shifted, and it was all he could do not to give in to the hunger and take her right there.

"This is as good as I thought it would be…*oh,* yeah," she breathed when he sucked at an earlobe and she pressed her chest against his. "This is *better.*"

He couldn't think for a while after that. He pulled her tight against him, kissing her madly. He didn't know at what point they shifted, from her straddling him to the two of them stretched out on her couch. She tugged her ponytail loose, and he had his hands buried in the silkiness of her hair even as she seemed ready to devour him.

It all felt amazing, powerful. Overwhelming.

Something's hinky here.

For a quiet, internal voice, sometimes his conscience could yell. He tried very hard to ignore the implications, especially when Allison was lying on top of him, a compact ball of fire, trying her damnedest to burn him alive.

Trying her damnedest.

He sighed, and nudged her away from him for a second.

She jumped, startled. "What? What's the matter? Is something wrong?"

And there it was.

She was talking in that high, breathy, hundred-miles-an-hour voice. The one that signified she was nervous. She wanted him—he didn't doubt that—but at the same time, she was approaching this the way she approached everything else. Full tilt, as if she'd die if she didn't give a thousand percent.

He sighed. "Slow down, sweetie."

"Slow down?" She repeated the words as if she couldn't believe he was saying them. He didn't blame her. He had trouble believing it, himself. "But…don't you want to…"

He waited for her to finish her sentence, then realized she wouldn't. But then he saw her gaze dart nervously toward the hallway that led to her bedroom.

"Let me preface this with the fact that you have to believe that I want to." He kissed her again, gently, then less gently when she gave in, molding herself to him. He groaned, and tore his mouth away, breathing heavily. "You've gotta believe that one," he rasped.

"So what's the problem?" She was out of breath, too, her voice taut with frustration.

"Ally, what do you want to happen here tonight?"

She sat up. "Are we having one of those talks?"

The way she asked it made him prop himself up on his elbows, half sitting, staring at her. "Is that a problem?"

"Well…I thought guys didn't want to complicate things. I thought we didn't *need* to complicate things," she said, and her voice sounded genuinely puzzled. "I've wanted you since you agreed to teach me how to surf. I just didn't know it. And it's been making me crazy. I can't think of anything else. I can't focus on anything else." She smiled at him, a gentle, hesitant smile that was pure Allison. "So I thought, why don't I just do something about it?"

Put that way, it did make sense, he supposed. She was the ultimate problem-solver. "So…you were having trouble focusing, and you figured you'd sleep with me to get it out of your system?" he paraphrased, knowing that he was twisting her words way out of proportion. Who really thought that way? Still, he wanted her to admit it…admit that there was more going on between the two of them than just sex as stress relief.

She bit her lip. "Well, of course it's going to sound bad when you put it that way." She paused. "And I don't mean…I'm not trying to use you. I just didn't think it would be a good idea to get into the whole stress of a relationship right now."

The words hit him like a brick. "So, no matter how it sounds…that's really what you're doing here tonight? You're trading one set of lessons in for another?" He paused. "You're basically making sex with me a *hobby?*"

She frowned. "Okay, now you're just being melodramatic."

He nudged her off of his lap, shivering at the oversensitivity of his body and, at this point, of his wounded psyche. He'd felt stupid about being more interested in a woman than she was in him, back when he'd waited at her house. This? This was about a hundred times worse.

"I don't know if you realize this, but I've tried to point out over and over that I'm not just teaching you because you got me my apartment," he said, his voice sharp as a knife. "I'm teaching you because I care about you. Get that? *Care.* You're vulnerable, you're sweet and sometimes I swear to God you're the most messed-up woman I know."

"Ah, and *that's* attractive," she bit back at him, her eyes starting to well with tears. "Why are you making this so difficult?"

"Because I don't just want to have sex with you!" he exploded, anger bubbling through his words like lava. "Because I *care* about you, damn it!"

She stared at him like he'd grown another head. "I don't know… Sean, I wasn't expecting…"

"Yeah, I know you weren't expecting," he said bitterly. "I'm a little too tired to help you out today, Allison. Have a nice Christmas."

"Sean, wait," she said, but he shrugged her hand off of his shoulder and walked out the door.

CHAPTER NINE

"MERRY CHRISTMAS, honey."

Allison smiled tightly at her mother, who was holding out an elaborately wrapped gift. She was sitting in her parents' picture-perfect living room. The twelve-foot tree stood in the corner of the cathedral ceiling–covered room, right next to the Italian-marble fireplace. The place was absolutely beautiful—the decorators had gone overboard this year. It looked even better than it had two years ago, when *Architectural Digest* had done a holiday display on the house. From beyond the fireplace, she saw the ocean through the floor-to-ceiling windows.

Sean.

She took a deep breath, and unwrapped her gift.

It was a gorgeous leather briefcase, in a deep mahogany brown. It felt like butter beneath her fingertips. "Thank you," she said, luxuriating in the feel of it.

"I picked it up when I was doing that promo stop in Milan," her mother said. "I told you about that, right? It was *such* an ordeal..."

"At least you got time to shop," her father joked. "The last time I was in Germany, I didn't see outside of a conference room!"

Allison noticed that her sister and brother laughed appreciatively. Allison joined in a little late. "It's beautiful," she admitted.

Her parents then handed her siblings their gifts…and to no one's surprise, they each had some kind of leather item. Her brother, Rod, got a handsome laptop case…her sister, Beth, got a beautiful leather portfolio. There were oohs and aahs all around.

Then it was time for her parents' gifts…and Allison felt her stomach clench a little. This was always the stressful part of the program.

She couldn't remember the last time she truly enjoyed a stress-free Christmas, she realized. She also realized she was gripping the briefcase too hard, and forced herself to release it.

"This one's from Rod," her father said, shaking it.

"Don't shake too hard," Rod cautioned. "It's fragile."

Her father smiled broadly, and then handed it to her mother, who carefully removed the paper, drawing out the moment like a noir suspense movie. Allison swallowed hard.

"Oooh!" Her mother clapped her hands. "Look! Matching PDAs!"

Allison fought not to roll her eyes. Her brother's company manufactured PDAs. How hard could getting that have been?

"Those are prototypes, the absolute top of the line," Rod said proudly. "I've been working eighty hours a week to get those babies to market. We got 'em out in time for Christmas. They're loaded up with all the latest…wi-fi, Web access, the works. Now you'll always be connected to your e-mail…"

As he listed the various features of the phone, Allison felt her heart sink a little bit. It actually was a perfect gift for her parents, especially since now Rod had set up a family Web site so they could all coordinate their calendars for family dinners, and it was uploadable to the handheld organizers. It was kind of ridiculous how busy they all were.

"Now, let's open Allison's," her mother said. They always did them by age.

Allison took a deep breath. She'd purchased the presents months ago, as was her habit…she was always busy, but she knew that this was going to be important, so she always scheduled it in. She held her breath as her mother unwrapped the gift.

The term "what do you get the person who has everything?" came leaping to mind.

Her mother smiled. "Look. More Waterford for our collection. How thoughtful."

Her father nodded, giving a few obligatory noises of assent. Allison felt her heart sink a few notches lower. Talk about lack of enthusiasm.

"Now, what did Beth give us?" Her mother opened the packages. "Ooh! Watches!"

Now, how the hell did a law student afford two Cartier watches? Allison didn't mean to begrudge her sister—she'd worked hard in college, and it wasn't as if she was spending any money while she was in school, so of course she had gift money.

Organizers. Watches.

"It was the best I could do," Beth said demurely. "I really didn't have the time to shop. I can't believe how busy I've been, between my classes and editing *Law Review.*"

"Know what you mean," Rod grumbled. "I've been

tempted to set up a bed in my office, I'm spending so much time there!"

Her parents were watching the exchange between siblings with interest and pride. Allison felt herself shrivel up, stuck literally in the middle on the couch as her brother and sister played the "who works harder" game.

Allison realized abruptly that she'd always felt this way during holidays…ever since she was a little girl. Family gatherings weren't just something to enjoy. They were always a contest of some sort. And she'd never felt like she won enough of them.

She got up and walked toward the tree, taking a deep breath of the pine scent. There was potpourri on the mantel, smelling like dried oranges and ginger, all overlaid with the smoky smell of the wood fireplace, which was crackling happily. She looked outside, and, even as she noticed that everyone was watching her, she opened the balcony door and stepped outside, closing the glass behind her. It was cool out, but bright, and she drank in the scent of the ocean like alcohol. The sound of the surf was even better than the Christmas carols wafting through the house out of the Bose stereo.

Her father stepped outside. "Honey? You all right?"

She nodded, smiling. She'd always felt closer to her father. "Just tired. It's been…"

She was starting to say "busy at work," then realized that's what she always said. At every family gathering. She was just getting in on the contest.

"I've been a little stressed," she said instead, feeling a little odd at being so honest.

He nodded. "Work?" he said, and although it sounded like a question, she knew that it wasn't.

"Sort of." Like there was anything else in her life. "Actually, it's a bit more than that."

He looked surprised. "More than work?"

Now her mother stepped out, shivering. "It's freezing out here. What in the world are you doing?"

"It's California, Mom," Allison said with a smile. "It is not freezing."

"Well, for us natives it is," her mother admitted. "But you're right…I just did a signing in New York, and *that* was freezing. But come inside anyway."

"Allison is stressed," her father stated, and Allison winced.

"Work?" her mother asked.

"What, am I wearing a sign?" Allison said, laughing weakly.

"No," her father said, and the fact that it wasn't work was no doubt the reason he was bringing it up.

"It's not that big a deal," Allison said, hoping to head this off at the pass. "You were in New York? That was just before you guys went to the Bahamas, right? I don't know that you told me about that one."

"If it's not work, what is it?" Her mother wasn't dumb, and she wasn't going to be deterred by something that obvious.

Allison could see her brother and sister still arguing on the couch inside. "It's not that big a deal," Allison repeated.

"You're not involved with somebody, are you?" Her mother sounded skeptical.

Allison started…then realized she thought immediately of Sean, and smiled before she could stop herself.

"You *are* involved with someone!" Her mother's voice was jubilant. "Good heavens, why didn't you tell us? Who is he? Do we know his family?"

"Whoa, whoa. Hold your horses. I'm not involved with anyone," Allison said quickly.

"You really should have told us," her father said.

"I would if I were involved with someone," Allison retorted.

"So we don't know him?"

"Hello? Am I talking to myself here?" Allison shook her head. "I am working hard, I am not involved with anyone and that's it."

"So what's so stressful?" Her father's puzzled concern was humorous in its single-mindedness. At least she came by that honestly.

My family, to start?

"Just…life."

Her parents stared at her as if she'd suddenly started speaking in tongues. "Life?" Her father repeated carefully, waiting for her to correct her statement.

Allison nodded, then began to wince as they kept staring at her. "It's no big deal," she repeated.

Her mother patted her shoulder, looking at her as if she'd gone off the deep end. "I'm sure it will be fine," she said, as if she was trying to convince them both of that fact. "Everyone's life gets hectic."

"Especially around the holidays," her father added with a smile, apparently feeling better that they'd identified the problem and made it a lot less nebulous than the generic "life." "Holidays make everyone crazy."

"Come back inside," her mother said, "and we'll have Susie serve dinner, and it'll all seem much more in perspective."

Allison wanted desperately to believe her, but as soon as

she opened the door, she heard her brother and sister squabbling.

"My girlfriend doesn't even see me anymore," Rod complained.

"I don't even have a boyfriend," Beth countered, as if that was something to be proud of.

"It's only going to get worse... We've got another new-product launch in March."

"This is my last year...and I've got to start lining up my internships. I'm aiming to work for a ninth circuit court judge."

"We should be making a few more million this year..."

Allison swallowed, hard.

"I have to leave a little early, after dinner," she said carefully.

"Well, I'm going to have to start boning up for the bar," Beth said, oblivious to Allison's statement.

"I felt that way after taking the GMAT," Rod said, also ignoring Allison's comment.

"Ha! The GMAT can't even compare..."

"You shouldn't leave early," Allison's mother said a little nervously. "You'll feel much better after dessert."

Suddenly, it occurred to her siblings that, despite her avoidance of the subject of work, Allison was getting all of the attention. "What's wrong?" Beth said, obviously surprised.

"Nothing," her father put in. "Your sister's just stressed, is all."

"What does Beth have to be stressed out about?" Rod said, equally surprised. "She works in advertising. It's not even her company."

"Thanks, Rod," Allison murmured.

"You know what I mean," he said, at least having the grace to look embarrassed.

"I know," she said. "And I just need to leave a little early, that's all."

"Whatever in the world for?" her mother said, the nervousness really moving to the fore.

She smiled. "I thought maybe I'd go surfing."

She couldn't help it. She laughed at the mirrored looks of shock on her family's faces. The similarity in expression was priceless.

"I'm sorry, did you say surfing?" her father asked.

"Yup," she said.

"You can't go surfing!" Her mother's eyes were wide.

"Why not?"

Her mother goggled. Her father picked up the ball. "Don't be ridiculous. You're kidding. Surfing? Whatever for?"

"Well, I may just go out and look," she said. "Let's eat."

If nothing else, she thought, as her parents continued to harangue her, *I'm going to see what Sean's doing.*

SEAN SPENT CHRISTMAS the same way he'd spent almost every Christmas since his sister had kids…over at her place, playing with the babies and loading them up with tons of toys. It was heartening, since watching people open stuff like sweaters or gift certificates was kind of pointless. So he spent Christmas Eve there, helping them last-minute assemble toys, and then he spent the morning playing. Today, his niece Sarah had her first tricycle. His nephew, Paul Junior, pretty much just played with the gift wrap, but since the kid seemed to get a serious charge from it, he had a pretty good time, too. Then, they'd packed the kids (with one toy apiece) into the car, to go visit the in-laws and have Christmas dinner. Sean had dinner over at Gabe and Charlotte's house. The evening was pretty idyllic…not perfect, not by a long stretch, but pretty nice.

It would've been a lot better if the last incident with Allison hadn't been quite so ugly.

I can't believe I turned her down.

He parked his truck in Mrs. Tilson's driveway, then closed his eyes and rested his head on the steering wheel. It all seemed like a surreal nightmare. Allison, only one of the most beautiful, amazing women he'd ever met, had invited him over to her house…for sex. And he'd actually said no. Turned her down. Took the high road, went monastic, however you wanted to call it.

If it were possible to feel more stupid, he didn't want to know about it.

You'd do it again.

He sighed. And there it was—the thing that made him feel even worse.

The bottom line was, with any other girl, he would've been more than happy to be her booty call and "stress relief," as she'd so inelegantly labeled it. He wasn't a monument to higher morals. But she wasn't any other girl. She was Allison. He knew she didn't mean it, just as he knew (or hoped he knew) that it wasn't what she meant.

At least, he prayed that she didn't mean it.

He thought back to all the times he'd talked to her—her heartfelt confession in the dressing room topping the list. The way she'd opened up after karaoke. The way she basically lived her life. She was stressed out, and she made what she'd thought was an easy decision—what she'd thought he'd be open to. Something that should've been simple for the two of them.

The thing is, for the first time in a long time, he wanted something more. It was a new and unnerving experience for him.

He sighed. He had the rest of Christmas night to think about it. It was one night too late, but he got the feeling he was about to be haunted by three ghosts: the Ghost of Mistakes Past, the Ghost of Problems Present, and the Ghost of What-the-Hell-Am-I-Doing-with-My-Future.

At a time like this, there was only one thing a guy could do: get good and hammered.

He was starting to walk to the stairway up to his apartment when he glanced back at the main house. Mrs. Tilson had presumably gone off with family that morning. So why was there light up on her second-story patio?

He noticed that it wasn't just light. It was an orange glow.

It took a second for his brain to register, but when it did, it weighed in heavy.

Fire.

He immediately started running, yelling "Mrs. T? Mrs. T! Are you all right?"

He had bolted up the stairs and tripped on the top step…only to find Mrs. Tilson sitting comfortably in a teak patio recliner, wrapped in a quilt. In front of her was a terracotta fire pit, with a small fire blazing merrily.

She stared at him like he was insane.

"Um…Merry Christmas," he finished feebly, abruptly realizing that as the adrenaline started to wear off, his body hitting the deck planking hurt like a son of a bitch. "Ouch."

"That was perhaps one of the most gallant and least graceful rescues I've ever seen," Mrs. Tilson noted. "Still, thank you. And Merry Christmas."

"I didn't know that you had one of those fireplace things," he said, getting up and trying to retrieve his decorum.

"Did you have a nice day?"

"Yeah. For the most part." He paused. Now that the immediate threat of fire had gone, he felt funny—like he was intruding. Still, she didn't seem happy. "How about yourself?"

She smiled, but it never reached her eyes. "How would you kids put it?" she mused, then sighed. "It sucked, Sean. It well and truly sucked."

If it had the prim-and-proper Mrs. T swearing, it had to be a bad time. "What happened?"

"It occurred to me today that all I've been doing is waiting to die," she confided, staring at the fire. Her voice wasn't dramatic, or low. It was practically without inflection. "My children have their own lives, and they seem intent on proving that I'm not competent to handle mine. All of my friends—and there are precious few of them—are either vapid, spiteful, complaining cows…or they're dead. And frankly, I'm wondering what I'm hanging on for anymore." She paused, then looked at him. "Merry Christmas, indeed."

He sighed. "Well, I have to hand it to you. You're making me feel a whole lot better about my problems."

She quirked an eyebrow at him. "And what would those problems be?"

He sat in the deck chair next to her. "Well," he said, "my boss is selling the surf store I work in…the store I practically grew up in, which I love. The short story there is I'm losing my job. Which means I probably won't be able to afford to stay here in my apartment much longer. Which means I won't have a place to live because I won't have any money really. And to top it all off, I'm falling hard for a girl who is completely out of my league and seems to see me as a form of human Prozac for her work stresses."

Man. Just saying it out loud should have, in theory, made him feel better. Instead, it simply seemed to put the depths of his loserdom in sharper relief. "Yikes."

She nodded. "I have to admit, you're giving me a bit of a run for my money. At least you have your youth."

"I'm thirty-one."

She grinned, and for a second, she looked years younger. "I take it back. Your life sucks as badly as mine does."

He laughed, then stood up. That trip was going to leave some marks, he could tell. Just one more thing to add to his bitch list, he supposed.

"Well, I think it's time for me to indulge in another tradition," he said. "I have a gift from a friend waiting for me in my apartment."

"And opening it on Christmas night is your tradition?"

"No, I know what it is," Sean said. "I get the same thing from Mike and Ryan every year. They get me a case of Beers of the World...you know, beer from a bunch of different countries. The tradition I was mentioning was to get hammered like a railroad spike."

She let out that papery dry laughter of hers. "You traditionally get drunk every Christmas?" she asked around chuckles.

"No, I traditionally get drunk when my life completely and utterly sucks," Sean corrected, and she laughed some more. "However, the holiday is sort of conveniently coincidental this year."

"Well, I'd hate to be the cause of a break in tradition," she said. "Good night, Sean."

"Night, Mrs. T," he said.

She looked proud, sitting there in the firelight. Stoic. And so damn old, all of a sudden, in a weary way that had nothing to do with the seventy-eight years she was wearing.

She looked alone.

He thought for a long minute, paused at the top of the stairs. Then he cleared his throat.

"You know," he said speculatively, "you haven't lived until you've had Nigerian beer with a Belgian-ale chaser."

She simply looked at him for a moment, then a broad smile affixed itself on her face.

"Sounds disgusting," she said.

"I'll bring it right over," Sean said with an answering grin.

"You do that."

ALLISON FOUND HERSELF in Sean's driveway, several hours after her very unmerry Christmas at the home front. He was home, from the looks of it…she'd just parked behind his pickup truck. She couldn't see the light on in his living room, though, even though she felt pretty sure he'd still be up. It was only ten o'clock, after all.

Maybe you'll be waking him up. Maybe he's busy. Maybe you should just start your car, head back to your town house and forget you ever had the idea of bothering him. She could always send him an e-mail, she reasoned. Well, maybe not an e-mail, since she didn't have his address. Maybe a text message on his cell phone. Hell, maybe a messenger-delivered letter, come to that.

Her idea to come over here and clear the air seemed more and more stupid by the minute.

She deliberately shut off her car and pulled the keys from the ignition. No. It had been two days and way too long since the Big Screwup, as she was calling it. He cared about her, and she cared about him. She'd handled it badly. And what had possessed her to actually consider Frank's dating advice anyway? The guy was working on his fourth divorce!

You thought there was an easy way around this.

After all these years, you would've thought she'd remember there was no easy way.

Taking a deep breath, she got out of the car. The answer might not be easy, but at least it was straightforward. She was going to go up, admit she cared about Sean and ask his forgiveness. Then, and only then, would she see where they were going to go from there.

Considering she'd never seen him quite that angry before, she walked toward his apartment over the garage with a strong sense of foreboding.

As she started to head toward the steps to his apartment, she noticed something—voices, coming from Aunt Claire's second-story deck. Low laughter, and from the looks of it, someone using the clay fire pit that Aunt Claire owned but, to Allison's knowledge, never used. She could've sworn that Aunt Claire would be at her son's house for Christmas. Who was up there?

Curious, and admittedly eager for a distraction, she headed up the stairs to the deck. As she got closer, she could make out the two voices.

It was Sean, she felt quite sure. And the other voice was way too low…and way too happy. And way too female.

Allison froze on the steps.

Oh, God.

Of course. Of course Sean would have a girl with him! He was only gorgeous. And yeah, he might "care" about her, but he'd also never said that he was exclusive. Maybe he'd found some nice surfer girl, with way fewer hang-ups, someone who was actually sane most of the time, someone who cared about him right back and wasn't afraid of admitting it.

Suddenly, she was roiling in her own foolishness. Why couldn't she just act like a normal person, keep her job tucked safely away in her office and enjoy life for a change, instead of overthinking every single damn thing!

She turned around quickly, almost tripping on her high heels (which she'd kept on to look good for *him,* her brain added with masochistic glee). She was almost to the bottom step when she heard Sean's voice.

"Ally? Is that you?"

She winced. God. Just when she'd thought it couldn't get any worse.

"Is that Allison?" the woman's voice called out.

"Aunt Claire?" She quickly walked back up the steps, disbelief spurring her forward.

Sure enough, Aunt Claire was rolled up like a taquito in the antique quilt from the living room. She looked… Allison searched for a word. Mellow?

"Well. This is a surprise," Sean said slowly.

"I was just about to go to bed, dear," Aunt Claire said, enunciating carefully. "I hope you don't mind."

"I'm sorry I'm coming so late," Allison said, feeling immediately guilty.

"No problem. No problem at all," Aunt Claire said. "I've been having a fine time, talking with Sean, here. Perhaps you could sit with him and take over for me?"

Aunt Claire's voice was smooth, clear…ever so slightly musical. And that's when it hit her.

"Aunt Claire…have you been drinking?" Allison said, now officially floored.

Aunt Claire laughed as she slowly got up out of the chair with Sean's help. "I've just been taking a bit of a…world tour, I suppose you might say."

Allison watched as both Sean and her aunt laughed, finding that cryptic statement uproariously funny. "You're supposed to be at Clarence's," Allison said, referring to Aunt Claire's son.

"I was, but I insisted that they bring me home. I didn't want to spend another painful holiday at that pompous ass's house, pretending to like his wife's dry turkey and pretending that I don't notice that they hate having me there," she said. "So I had beer with Sean instead, and I must say, it's the happiest Christmas I've had in some time."

Allison didn't have any response to that, so she shut up and simply stared. "I'll leave the quilt out for you…the fire's not that strong and it's pretty chilly out," Aunt Claire told them from the sliding glass door. "You keep Sean company, dear. After all, I don't expect you to even pretend that you're here to see me…not this late at night."

Allison stammered, but Aunt Claire had already closed the door, leaving only her ghostly chuckle behind.

"Is she going to be all right?" Allison asked instead, finally turning her attention to Sean now that her inebriated godmother had gone off to bed.

"I'm sure she'll be fine. We really didn't drink all that much, and I stopped her by the time we got to the Scandinavian countries," Sean said.

He didn't sound slurred, or impaired…or even as happy as he'd sounded when he was talking to Aunt Claire, she noticed worriedly. She felt her courage immediately fail her, and she swallowed hard.

He stared at her, the light from the dying embers making his blue eyes glow almost red. "Want to have a seat?" he said politely, his voice low.

"Aunt Claire was right," she admitted as she sat down next to him. "I did come here to talk to you."

She paused as he leaned over and gently placed the quilt around her shoulders. Then he leaned back in his own chair, studying her, and waited.

He wasn't going to make this easy on her, she realized. And honestly, she couldn't blame him for that.

"I wanted to apologize. For the other night," she said, the words all coming out in a rush.

He still said nothing.

"The thing is…I really do like you. And care about you. You're maybe one of the nicest men I've ever met."

She saw how he winced at the "nice" label, and realized she wasn't helping matters. "Not just nice. I mean, it would make it easier if you were just nice. But the thing is, I can't stop thinking about you. I thought that I must be losing my mind, and with all of the other stressors in my life right now, I thought maybe you were just another symptom…something that I was focusing in on to try and get my mind off of all of my work. And you have to realize how incredibly, amazingly hot you are. I mean, I haven't thought this much about sex in…" She paused, doing some quick mental calculations. "Well, ever, actually. Now that I think about it. And the fact of the matter is, I thought that maybe if I just gave in to it instead of fighting it all the time, I'd get some of my sanity back. But there wound up being another problem. I really *like* you, is the thing. I really care about you, so for you to say that I was just, well, to make it seem like I was just using you…well, I suppose that it *was* like I was just using you… Oh crap, I don't know!" She felt tears spilling over onto her cheeks. "Why do I always cry when I'm around you, damn it?"

He just stared at her for a long minute, and she thought, *Good idea, Allison. Go tell him how you feel, and see where you can go from there, huh?* The only place that she was going was back to her car, back to her house, and back to her office, hoping that somehow she could get so engrossed in paperwork that she'd blot out the past week, and Sean Gilroy, entirely.

She was still working on that escape plan when he stood up, and she held her breath. If he just walked away…oh, she'd die. She'd just die on the spot.

Instead, he scooped her up, quilt and all, and sat down on the lounger, putting her on his lap like she weighed nothing. "Do you even breathe when you give monologues like that?" he asked, his voice mildly amused.

She sighed. "You're telling me to relax again, aren't you?"

He smiled that warm smile that never failed to soothe her…and stir her up. She let herself give in to resting her head against his shoulder.

She was both surprised and thrilled when he pressed a kiss against her temple and stroked the back of her hair.

"I have never known anyone quite so tightly wound as you, sweetie," he said with a small sigh.

"I'd be angry, if I didn't realize just how painfully true that probably is," she said, snuggling against his chest.

"And yet," he continued, "I find myself falling for you anyway."

She didn't say anything, simply savored the warm thrill the words shot through her. She wriggled, ignoring his low groan as she made sure she could look into his eyes. The pain was still there, she noticed, as well as the irritation…and a kind of defensiveness.

Slowly, deliberately, she kissed him. Not the full-frontal assault that had been her desperate attempt in her living room. The kiss was sensitive, and sweet, and thorough.

"I've never met anybody like you," she whispered against his jawline. "And believe it or not, I've never quite felt like this. I screwed up. I seem to do that a lot with you."

He laughed, some of the pain ebbing out of his expression, and he kissed her back, still keeping it light. Still keeping it tentative.

"So, since it's obviously not just sex, what's our next step? Because just speaking for myself—Sean, my life is so nuts right now. I don't want to lose you," she said gently.

And just like that, she handed the next step over to him, waiting nervously for what he would say. As a woman used to making all the plans, being the "point person" and the "go-to gal," this was more nerve-racking than, say, skydiving naked.

He stared at her, and she doubted he realized just how much she trusted him, to just hand this over, and see what he'd do.

"My life's pretty complicated, too," he admitted. Then he continued kissing her. The sensations washed over her like a roaring high tide. She drowned in the taste of him, moving so she had better access…feeling the delicious strength and heat of him.

"I don't care how complicated my life is, I'm not walking away from this," he finally said in a ragged voice.

She felt relief, acute and overpowering, hit her like a wave. "Good," she said. "I don't want to walk away, either."

"When's this big-deal presentation of yours?" he ground out, his hands stroking her back.

"In about a week," she said, arching against him.

"Which is about the same time Oz closes the shop down," he mused. "Listen, things are about to get crazy for me, too. But after then, they'll calm down. I just need to focus on a few things. And it sounds like you do, too."

She nodded.

"So for two weeks, let's just take things slowly," he said. "That way, we'll be sure we're doing things for the right reasons. I'm not going anywhere, Allison. I'll be right here, whenever you need me."

As comforting as that sounded—and it did sound comforting—she cleared her throat. "The thing is…I really want you, Sean."

With that, he kissed her, nothing gentle about it. It was explosive, and she groaned as she was crushed against him. This was more like it. This was what she wanted.

She realized it was the wrong place, the wrong time. She tore herself away. As much as she wanted him, she understood—this was bigger than she had anticipated, as well.

"So, where does that leave us?"

He sighed. "With the longest two weeks of my life."

She kissed him, then smiled. "Think I can still have my surf lessons?"

He smiled back. "No way am I stopping those now. No matter what."

CHAPTER TEN

"GABE, WE NEED TO TALK."

Sean said the words like he was announcing that somebody had died, and in a way, he felt like it. He had the day off, but Oz was just going to keep the store open for another week or two anyway. He needed to get this sorted out.

Oh, who are you kidding?

Yes, he needed to get his life in order, and, yes, the shop was closing. But he never moved quickly in his life. He had savings. Ordinarily, he'd take at least another week or two, and draw out more of his options. He still felt a dull ache at the idea of losing the surf shop. But now, things needed to move just a bit more rapidly.

Because of her.

He sighed. As long as his life was up in the air, he didn't feel as if he could get seriously involved with Allison. And when it came to Allison, his involvement was as serious as it came.

Gabe had agreed to meet him for lunch for this one. "I came over as soon as I could," Gabe said.

Sean looked at him. "I know I said it was important, but I didn't need you to dress up for it," he tried to joke, to take the edge off of the desperation he was feeling.

Gabe laughed back ruefully as he loosened the tie he was wearing, pulling it over his head and tucking it in a pocket. He still wore a navy suit with a white shirt, and he still looked like a lawyer or a banker or something. "Had a big meeting with some distributors this morning. Can't wear surf shorts to those, unfortunately, although I still lobby for it."

Sean sighed. "Guess that's what I have to look forward to, then."

And he waited.

Gabe's eyes widened as realization dawned. "You're agreeing to take a job with Lone Shark?"

Sean took a deep breath. He hated the idea of being locked inside an office all day. Hated it with a passion. On the plus side, he liked eating, drinking and living in a house.

And he really, really liked Allison. If he had a steady job, and all the stuff that a steady job could bring, he wouldn't be in such limbo. Which would mean that he'd have a much better shot at lasting with Allison, the girl who liked her answers in black and white, her dates on a calendar and her life in alphabetical order.

"Well, that's what I wanted to talk to you about," Sean said. He took a deep breath and continued. "I know that I haven't been all that interested, but I had some questions about the position."

Gabe smiled, nodding thoughtfully. "Shoot."

"What would I be doing, exactly?" Sean didn't mean for his voice to sound so suspicious—and so ungrateful. So he modified it. "I mean, I want to make sure that you're getting the right guy for the job, you know?"

"Lone Shark puts out a bunch of products. Wet suits,

clothing, stuff like that," Gabe said. "So you'd be a sales rep. You'd have a book of business. You'd send out catalogs, take orders, work your way up to more locations."

Sean smiled. "You mean, like Darren, our Lone Shark sales rep?"

"Like that exactly," Gabe said. "You could do that, easy. Hell, you know all our products because of all your time in the surf shop."

Sean fell silent for a minute. As a general rule, he really liked the products. Lone Shark was a good company, and they didn't skimp on quality. Still, all they put out was clothing. It was fun to help people figure out which sort of wet suit worked best for them, but the rest of it was all pretty boring. People bought the clothes because they wanted to look like surfers or to show they were locals.

"I don't suppose you guys are considering making any surf gear?" Sean asked hopefully.

Gabe frowned. "What, you mean like surfboards? No. Not really. It would dilute the brand too much."

Sean nodded. He knew that it would seem too dumb for a clothing company to put out boards, but it was worth asking. "Well, at least I won't be in an office much," Sean said.

"Actually, you wouldn't be in an office too much at all," Gabe said. "You'd be traveling a bit, though. I think your territory would go all the way down to San Diego."

"How many surf shops are there? Sounds like a lot of ground." That could be fun, Sean thought. He'd been to surf shops whenever he saw one, usually to see how they did business and to talk shop. Surfers hung out with other surfers.

Gabe cleared his throat. "Actually…you wouldn't be covering surf shops. Or at least, not just surf shops."

Sean looked at him blankly. "If I'm not…. Wait a sec, where would I be selling stuff to?"

"Well, malls, actually," Gabe said.

"Malls?" Sean said, horrified.

"And sporting-goods stores, stuff like that," Gabe added hastily. "Places that sell wet suits."

"You're selling wet suits in malls all of a sudden?"

Gabe sighed. "No, we're selling clothing in malls. The women's-sportswear line is selling well in those women's stores, so we're pushing to sell more aggressively there."

Oh, ugh, Sean thought. He wouldn't even be working with surf shops. He'd be hanging out with teenage girls and trying to push sleeveless hoodies at those places that sold clothes that made thirteen-year-old girls look thirty-five and headed for their second divorce.

"Listen, I know it's not optimal," Gabe said. "But it'll pay twice what you're getting paid now. Maybe three times as much."

Sean nodded soberly. "I don't mean to seem ungrateful. It's just…a change. That's all."

A big, hairy, hideous shock of a change. He shook his head.

Gabe sighed again. "Why don't you think about it for a while, before you jump in? I mean, I know you hate to rush things."

"How long do I have to think it over?" Sean asked before he could stop himself, gripping at the chance to take a breather before committing himself like a man clutching at straws.

Gabe grimaced. "Well…not much longer than a week. The guy in charge of sales is new, and I know that he's going to want that position filled soon, now that he's got the budget for it."

A week. Everything in his life seemed to be converging in one big week. "I do appreciate this," he said.

Gabe seemed to relax, shrugging easily. "Hey. You're family. And besides, I trust you. When you give your word to do something, you do it."

Sean nodded. Which was precisely why he didn't want to just agree to this, when his gut was sending all kinds of warnings. "Maybe we should talk about something else for a while," Sean said, feeling tension in the back of his neck.

Gabe leaned back, smirking. "Okay. How's Allison and the surf lessons going?"

"How about we talk about a different something else?" Sean suggested.

Gabe laughed. "I'm just asking about surf lessons, not about whether or not you're hooking up with a short blond hottie that it's obvious you're completely crazy about."

"I'll tell Charlotte you just called Allison a hottie," Sean warned. "You'll be sleeping on the couch for a week."

"One, she'd call Allison a hottie herself, because it's just a fact, not an opinion," Gabe said. "Two, Charlotte knows there isn't anybody else in my life who could ever tempt me. And three, she knows that anybody who even looks at Allison cross-eyed would probably get murdered by you, so no worries there."

Sean groaned, covering his face with his hands. "She's…complicated," he said. "God, that's an understatement. I have no idea what's going on with all of that."

"What's the problem? You're crazy about her, I'd venture a guess that she's very into you…so what's the holdup?"

"My life is in a complete shambles right now, Gabe," Sean pointed out. "It's not exactly the perfect time for me to get a girlfriend."

"News flash—if you wait for the perfect time, you'll never get a girlfriend," Gabe said sagely. "Jeez. No wonder you've been single for so long."

"Cheap shot," Sean said with a grin. "This is different, anyway. She's really busy, too, and her life is crazy. She's got this really big presentation in the next week, and her work…" He thought about it. "It makes her nuts, and it's obviously crucial to her. I don't know where I'd fit in to all of that. And I hate the idea of waiting by the phone—just waiting for her to have a second where she can squeeze me in."

Gabe laughed. "Metaphorically speaking."

Sean winced. "Unfortunately, only metaphorically speaking so far." He closed his eyes. "And I don't know that you need to share that one with Charlotte or the guys."

"Figured. You're way too wound up to have gotten laid."

"Maybe we should talk about the job again," Sean said sourly. "At least that's less stressful."

"Hey, it's not my fault your monastic streak is still holding strong," Gabe said, needling him like they were back in high school. "The guys would've bet on it, but I actually thought you would've closed the deal by now."

"I could score, believe me," Sean said sharply, then abruptly realized the rest of the café was now staring at him. He grimaced, then took a swig of his soda. "But that's not the point here. She's special, man. She's not somebody I'm just trying to hook up with."

Gabe smiled, a Buddha-like smile of contentment and wisdom.

"Which is exactly what you were trying to get me to admit," Sean said, rubbing his temples. "You might want to wipe that smarmy smirk off your face before I kick your ass."

"Whatever helps you sleep at night, grasshoppa," Gabe said smugly. "The important thing here is, you're finally getting out of your slump. You've been stuck in neutral for a decade, man. It's time you started making changes. It's time you stepped up to the plate."

"I haven't been stuck in neutral, damn it," Sean said in a low voice. "I like the surf shop. My life's been pretty good. What's wrong with that?"

"Nothing," Gabe said. "But you've been just resting comfortably. You've been atrophying. Now you've got stuff at stake and something to risk. Something worth taking risks for. So...are you going to just sit there and watch the pitch fly by or are you going to take a swing?"

Sean gritted his teeth. He hated feeling pressured. Hated the sensation of going against his instincts, of rushing, of being forced.

But do you hate the idea of losing Allison more?

He grimaced. "Set up the interview," he said. "And let's order some damn lunch."

ALLISON SAT AT HER DESK, staring out the window. Still, she wasn't looking at her view of the freeway or the trees that lined the parking lot. She wasn't really looking at anything. She just stared, a funny little smile plastered on her face.

That kiss.

She couldn't stop replaying it. It was a fixation. She knew that the big presentation was just days away...that it was going to be the biggest New Year's Eve of her life. She needed to focus.

She had her computer playing CDs because she loved music while she worked, and a love song started playing. She sighed.

"What is *with* you?" Gary said, walking in and wrinkling his nose with an expression of disgust.

"Huh? Oh. Nothing," she protested, even though she knew that was anything but true. "I'm just…thinking."

"You've been 'thinking' for the past two hours," Gary said. He didn't sound irritated, exactly, but he did sound frazzled. "We need the final revisions on the deck for the promotion, design still hasn't gotten the posters right, and you've still got your regular stuff…something went wrong with one of the Super Flashlight ads, didn't run in the newspapers we said, and I've been fielding about eighteen different calls from some of your other clients," he explained.

She sighed. "I thought nobody worked during the holidays."

"Apparently these guys do."

She looked at him. "Gary, do I thank you enough for all the work you do for me?"

He shrugged.

"I'm serious," she said.

"I know you appreciate my work, boss. And just having the job is thanks enough."

"You do an amazing job. I'd be out of my gourd if it weren't for you. In fact, I've been thinking about suggesting you get promoted to the account team, and I've let myself get too swamped to do something about it. You can't keep yourself stuck just because of your past, Gary."

He looked as if someone had hit him in the back of the head with a two-by-four. "Uh…thanks, Allison." He sounded like he had something caught in his throat, and he shifted his weight from foot to foot. "That's the phone. I'll go get it," he said, even though she had heard no ring.

She meant every word. She'd miss him because he was really someone she leaned on…but at this point, she wanted him to move forward. He deserved to do more with his life than what he was doing, even though she had to say she'd never met anyone who took care of her and supported her as much as Gary.

Except possibly Sean.

"Allison, *what* have you been doing?" her boss said without preamble, busting into her office.

Since her last thought had been of Sean, she felt pretty sure she was still wearing the same goofy grin that she'd been wearing all morning, and she quickly tried to school her expression to something a little more sober and businesslike. "What can I do you for, Frank?"

"It's, what, two o'clock on the twenty-ninth, and you're asking me what you can do me for," Frank said, his voice the operatic heights of drama. "How about the bloody presentation, for starters!"

"You know, one of these days, you're going to blow a gasket," Allison tried to joke, even as she felt her own blood pressure start to rise in typical fight-or-flight instinct. The tickles of adrenaline started. "Gary's already told me what's on my plate. I'm getting it handled. So how, exactly, is yelling at me getting you anything that you want?"

Gary had been standing in the doorway, and his eyes widened like saucers. Frank looked as if she'd turned purple and grown wings.

"Allison, I know that we've worked together for a couple

of years now, and I know that you feel pretty confident. I'm sure I contributed to that a bit—I mean, everybody knows I've favored you. But you're crossing the line."

She swallowed, hard, and felt her heart start to pound in her chest. "I'm sorry. I didn't—"

"Just shut up," Frank said, and she felt a small part of her soul shrivel up. "This is too important for you to snap on me. You say that you can get this done, well, it's time for you to put up or shut up. Meet me in my office at five o'clock. No doctor's appointments—which I know was baloney, by the way—no excuses, no nothing. Have all the final details for the presentation on my desk for review at three o'clock, we'll do a practice run-through tomorrow, then we lay out the presentation on the thirty-first. Is that clear?"

She nodded, looking down at her desk, suddenly feeling fourteen years old again. Tears started to sting her cheeks, and she wanted to just curl up in a ball under her desk.

"Fine." Frank strode out.

Gary walked in, closing the door. "Are you okay?"

She couldn't break down. Not now. She simply nodded. "Tell all my current accounts that I'll handle their stuff after the new year, to their satisfaction," she said, glad that her voice was able to stay even. "Put out whatever fires you can. Tell design I want the stuff on my desk in the next hour. I'm going to finish the slides myself."

Gary nodded. "You sure you're okay?"

"Just fine," she said numbly. "And Gary?"

He turned in the act of opening the door and leaving. "Yes?"

"Don't let anybody come in my office, okay?" She was ready to crack. She just knew it. She wasn't ready for anybody else to see her this way.

He nodded, understanding written clearly on his face. "You got it."

She worked steadily for the next hour. She got the presentation posters, the design mock-ups, the whole nine yards. Went over things until she thought her eyes would bleed. And didn't cry, even though her throat felt scratchy and she really, really wanted to. At three, she stood up, took a deep breath and prepared to face the lion's den.

"You can't go in there," she heard Gary saying in as foreboding a tone as his high voice would allow.

She paused. If she didn't know better, she would've sworn she hated this job.

She opened her door, prepared to tell off whoever was there…and the words died silent on her lips.

It was Sean, looking amazing in a pair of black slacks, a striped shirt and a tie with a sport coat. He looked like something out of *GQ*. He was even wearing real shoes, not his usual sneakers.

He looked good enough to eat, and all the feelings of this morning—the giddy, sugary feelings of happiness—quickly crowded out her feelings of misery, like the sun coming out from behind storm clouds.

"Sorry, Allison," Gary apologized, glaring at Sean. "I know you're off to your meeting…"

She was. She should be. She took one look at Sean.

"I just wanted to see you for a minute," Sean said. "I knew you'd be busy, but—"

He stopped as she grabbed him by the arm and tugged him into her office. "Tell Frank I'll be five minutes late," she said, then slammed the door shut and dived at Sean.

SEAN WASN'T QUITE SURE what stupid impulse had brought him to Allison's office. He'd dressed up, prepped to the gills for this interview that Gabe had set up, and he surely didn't want to let down his best friend. But as he'd gotten ready, every minute brought an ever-increasing sense of dread. Especially tightening his tie. It had been like taking a step up to the gallows—there had to be something wrong with a job that forced you to wear a noose to qualify.

You're doing this for Allison, he'd reminded himself. And when that wasn't enough, he'd found himself looking up Flashpoint Advertising on the Internet, and then found himself driving over there. It wasn't too far from Lone Shark, after all. And he knew that there was something about Allison that spoke to him—spoke to his soul.

And now that he was standing in her office, and she'd leaped at him, suddenly that sliding sense of reality slipping away from him came flooding back in a wash.

This. This was why he was willing to wear a tie, sing in public, do whatever it took. This woman was worth doing absolutely anything for.

She pulled away, and he felt the regret of the loss of contact like a stab wound. He held her against him. "Wow. Hi," he said.

To his surprise, she leaned against his chest, and he abruptly realized that tears were spilling out of the corners of her eyes.

"I've had the most awful day," she said. "The most awful week, without the surfing. Without you. I had no idea how much I'd miss all of it." Her voice broke, a heart-wrenching sound.

He made quiet, hushing noises, rubbing her back with

little circles. "Sweetheart, it's okay. I'll make sure it'll be okay." He had no idea how, but at this moment, with her in his arms, he'd figure out how to stop the sun from shining if he thought it would make her feel better.

"I'm sorry, I always keep doing this," she said, leaning back and rubbing the tears away with one hand. She cried pretty, he had to give her that one. "I…I don't know. It's been tough. I can't seem to focus the way I used to."

"You're working too hard," he said, stroking the last vestige of tears from her cheek, then leaning down to kiss her softly, just a whisper of a kiss. Before he could go in for something a little more serious, he saw her smile.

"You're all dressed up," she said. "You clean up awfully nice, Mr. Gilroy."

Which brought him back to the whole reason he was there…which effectively doused his ardor with a bucket of ice water. "Yeah, I've got an interview," he said. "I just thought I'd see you beforehand…sort of as an inspiration."

She blinked at him, and he swore she looked disgruntled. "I'm your inspiration for getting a job? Because of what I do?"

"No," he said, chuckling a little ruefully. "Because of what happens when my life settles down."

She still looked puzzled, then understanding dawned on her face and her brown eyes turned heated.

"But you're still more important," he said. "Hell, I could reschedule or cancel the thing, if you want me here."

"No, I know how important this is," she said, and he felt a little let down—realizing just how hard he was reaching for another excuse not to go to the interview. "But can we go surfing tonight?"

After the interview, he felt sure he'd need to. And the thought of Allison in the water, and surfing, was like being wrapped up in a comforting blanket. "Definitely."

"Thanks," she said, her voice low and husky. "You always make me feel better, you know that?"

He sighed, cuddling her against him, and the warmth in his chest had nothing to do with the fact that she was pressed against him. Or rather, everything to do with it, but not in any way he would've imagined.

"I guess you've got to go," she said finally, the regret in her voice mirroring his own.

"Yeah," he said, but before he could completely pull away, she got up on tiptoe and kissed him, harder than she had when he'd walked in initially.

He groaned and leaned into her, feeling the soft silkiness of her lips beneath his. His fingertips dug into her waist, pulling her tighter to him. Her lips parted, and he deepened the kiss, gratified to hear her soft moan of approval.

"Allison, Frank says you've got to…" Gary said, first knocking directly on the door. Then, just as abruptly, his voice stopped as he took in the scene, and he retreated, shutting the door quickly.

Allison and Sean broke apart, staring at each other. "You've got to go," she said, her breathing uneven and ragged.

"Right." It took Sean a minute to get his brain back on track and remember why he had to go anywhere but here, with this woman who made him silly. "Yeah."

"And I've got to go."

"'Course."

"But I will definitely see you later," she said, and her voice rang with promise.

He couldn't help it. He leaned down, kissing her one last time, like a man leaving for war or something. "Count on it," he whispered, then forced himself to walk out the door.

CHAPTER ELEVEN

ALLISON'S BLOOD was still buzzing from the kiss as she made her way to Frank's office, her arms overloaded with posters. Kissing Sean in her office was a dumb idea, no doubt. Still, she had to admit, it had taken her anxiety down a few notches.

She liked the way he winked at her, she thought. She liked the way he smiled. He reminded her of being on the ocean, not surprisingly. As immense and chaotic as it was, there wasn't anything complicated about actually being on the ocean. When she was out on the waves, feeling the water beat against her and the wind stroke her face, she felt free, like some kind of sprite or spirit or wild animal. Not like somebody trying to claw her way out of her own life.

She almost tripped as the last bit of that thought cleared up for her. Good grief. Was that what she was really feeling?

So why the hell am I staying here?

She thought of her parents. Of the way they listened so raptly to Rod's stories, and to Beth's law tales. It just seemed like such a long time since she'd felt special. It might seem pathetic, it might seem dumb, but just *once,* just once, she wanted to be the one that got that praise. The one they thought had really "made it."

How could she live like that? How could anyone live like that? Were those her only options…get promoted or die?

There has to be another way.

She never would've thought of it if she hadn't started surfing lessons, and now that she had, she might be crazy but there had to be more to life than this single-minded pursuit of pursuing. She had to get off this nutso thing.

As Sean would say, she was "hamster wheeling."

Frank was staring at her as she put everything down on his desk, so he must've caught the grin that spread at the thought of Sean. "You're smiling. You must've nailed it. Tell me you nailed it."

"Nailed what?"

He rolled his eyes. "The presentation. Got all the changes." He sat at his desk, leaned back, looked at her expectantly. "Come on. Wow me."

She suddenly felt like…well, like a stripper, she thought, abjectly horrified.

"Frank, how long have I worked for you?"

"Two years." He fidgeted, his irritation clear. "I take it I'm not about to be wowed."

"How often have I been able to wow you?" she asked instead. "Seriously. That you remember."

He frowned. "Up until the past few weeks, kid, you've always, always, *always* wowed me with your work."

"Yeah, but how often have you told me that?" she said. "Before whatever presentation we've had to do was done? Or even after, for that matter?"

He paused, thoughtful. "Is that what this is all about? You think I don't appreciate you?" He rubbed his left temple with his fingertips. "Come on, Allison, you know what this business is like. If I haven't complimented your work, then I'm sorry. I know, I'm hard on people I work with. But after the work's done, you know that I tell everyone how stellar your work was. I don't take credit that's not mine. I don't mess anybody over."

"I know that," she said…and she did know that. Frank might be monomaniacal, but he wasn't unfair.

"So, could you please tell me if what you've been going through lately is a mental aberration?" Frank said, crossing his arms. "Or is it all stemming from this 'you don't bring me flowers anymore' crap? Because if it is, frankly, you're in the wrong line of work. If you want strokes every time you do what we pay you to do, you're better off someplace else."

She winced. "Nicely put," she said softly. "Let's just chalk it up to mental aberration, then."

He stared at her, as if he was testing her response. Then he sighed heavily. "Sit down. Let's talk about it."

She sat down, if only to get over the shock. Talk about it? With Frank? Since when had he gone all paternal?

"Come on, spill. Are we talking gambling debts? Family problems? Boyfriend issues?" He leaned back, with the same sort of look of expectation he'd sported when asking for the presentation. She got the feeling he wanted her to "wow" him with the extent of her inner turmoil, and almost giggled nervously. "Doctor's in."

"What if I just said work problems?" she asked curiously…hesitantly. He was actually seeming to invite comment.

"Well, I thought we just ruled out me," he said. "Is it me? I mean, honestly, you can tell me. Is it something I'm doing? Besides not telling you often enough that you're doing a good job? You've got to let a guy know these things. It's all about communication."

She sighed this time, sinking into the chair. "It's not just your lack of appreciation, really. It's a combination of things. It's hard—you have this streak of perfectionism that's absolutely impossible to live up to. And I think that leads to your strangely intense desire to micromanage."

As soon as the words were out of her mouth, she gasped. She had never spoken that way to a boss. Good grief, she'd never even spoken that way to a co-worker. What had happened to her?

Sean. Surfing. Both had "happened" to her.

Frank spluttered and coughed. His eyes bulged out. "Remind me never to have a heart-to-heart with you again."

"Well, you *asked,*" she muttered, realizing immediately that he'd just asked to show he was a good manager, not because he actually expected her to say anything negative whatsoever, since he was perfect.

"I didn't ask you to rip out my heart with a salad fork!"

"You're a tough guy, you can take it," she said, trying desperately for a note of humor. "I don't think it's that bad. It's just...I've been really stressed, Frank. And doing this stuff over and over again, when there's really nothing wrong with it, is not helping my mental state one bit."

"I see," he said, still obviously ruffled. "So you're feeling a little put out because I want things just right?"

"You might call it 'just right,'" she said gently. "But I think a jury of my peers would say it's starting to cross into cruel and unusual."

He scrunched down into his chair. "What, did you get a refill on your prescription of honesty pills or something?"

She sat silently, miserable.

"Well," he said, and he coughed for a second. "Have you always felt this way?"

"Honestly, Frank, I don't know," she admitted. And slowly, in fits and starts, she admitted everything. The anxiety attacks, the doctor's orders. She left out the bits with Sean, the private stuff, but everything else got thrown into the mix.

He grew pale as her story continued. Finally, he rubbed his hands over his face. "Allison, why didn't you tell me you were cracking up?" He sounded more than unhappy...he sounded angry.

"Would you have told *your* boss?" she shot back.

"Listen...I'm sorry you're going through this," he said, and to his credit, his voice did sound sincere. "But...you know how important this account is," he said.

"Yes, I—"

"So you know why I'm going to have to take you off of it," he said. "I just need to see if Peter or Kate can take over. Thank God you had them working on your team."

"Wait a minute!" she said. "Listen, I told you what I've been doing. I told you that I can handle this. I—"

"No, you've just proven to me that you can't handle this," he said sharply. "I can't afford to screw this up. Sure, it's an account sup job for you...but this is a vice presidency for me, Allison. And much as I like you personally..." He shrugged. "Well. This isn't personal and I have to think about the bottom line."

"So. I'm off the account?"

"As of right now," he said. "Hey, you've got New Year's coming up. Might as well take a day or two off."

"Take a day or two off," she said woodenly. So she could

think about the fact that, in her honesty, she had just thrown away everything that she had worked toward in her whole career in advertising. Just focus on that.

"You could even go home early today, if you wanted," Frank added. Like this was some sort of added incentive.

She got up, feeling numb. There was no way she was going home. It was two o'clock in the afternoon.

The only place she could go where she might feel better did occur to her.

"SEAN?"

Sean stood up. "Yes?"

The guy, Gabe's head of marketing or something, was wearing a blue shirt and khakis. He looked like the poster child for business casual. He seemed nice enough. Sean wondered if he'd bumped into the guy surfing—he seemed vaguely familiar, Sean thought as they shook hands.

"I have to say up front, I learned how to surf and got all my gear at Tubes, back in the day," the guy said.

Sean narrowed his eyes. "I'm sorry. What's your name, again?"

The guy laughed. "Wouldn't surprise me that you don't remember me. Steve…Steve Milton."

"Stevie?" Sean goggled. "Didn't you just graduate from high school?"

Steve laughed a little ruefully as he looked around. "Uh, it's Steve now," he said, and Sean immediately felt bad for blurting out the guy's childhood nickname. But Stevie—Steve—had to be about twenty-four. If that. Sean remembered selling him his first board, with his dad.

Good grief. Am I that old? Sean felt completely awkward

as he walked into Steve's office. "Sorry," he reiterated as Steve shut the door. "I guess it's just been a while."

"Yeah. You've been at Tubes forever. I was actually pretty surprised when Gabe told me you wanted to come work here," Steve said, sitting down at his desk. Despite the corporate casual and the desk, Sean still couldn't help superimposing the mental picture of the twelve-year-old over the man who might be his boss.

This was going to go badly. Sean could just tell.

"So. Mind if I ask why?"

Sean forced himself to focus. "Why what, exactly?"

"Why do you want to come work for Lone Shark?" Steve definitely sounded older...and on the ball. He crossed his arms. "It's a lot different than retail. Not to say that the experience won't translate over. Just...well, I'll let you do the talking."

Do you have to? Sean squirmed internally. "I just feel like it's time for a change," he said, wishing he'd taken Gabe up on his offer to coach him for the interview. "I think I can offer a lot to Lone Shark."

"Like what, exactly?"

Steve wasn't trying to grill him...it sounded like a perfectly innocuous question. So when Sean started sweating, he wondered if maybe he was blowing things just a smidge out of proportion.

Get a grip, Gilroy!

He felt a nervous bubble of laughter. "Well, let's see. I have been a surfer around here since I was maybe eight. I've worked at Tubes since I was sixteen. So I'm offering a lot of job loyalty. And I know surf gear...so Gabe thought that I'd work out well in helping with your distribution. I know surf stores and what works for them, like the back of my hand."

Steve nodded thoughtfully. "This would require a lot of travel. Are you okay with that?"

"Uh…" Unbidden, a mental picture of Allison snapped into his mind before he could dispel it. "I suppose so."

"Okay. You wouldn't really be in marketing, you'd be more in sales."

"So, I need to provide my own checked jacket and get a personality transplant?"

Steve did not look amused. Sean cleared his throat, embarrassed.

"It's not like that," Steve said, just this side of prim. Mrs. Tilson would be duly impressed, Sean noted. "We don't really have anything in marketing, and besides, you've been working in sales for the past sixteen years, basically. It'd be much better for you to learn the ropes that way." He sounded faintly snide. "I mean, I know I'm young, but I do represent the sales force for Southern Cal."

"How long have you been working at this?" Sean asked, crossing his arms. He'd sold this kid his first wet suit. He didn't need to be talked to like he was an moron!

Steve frowned. "I don't see that it's that important. The important thing is, Gabe's trusting me to build a sales team. And that's what you'd be a part of."

Sean was pretty sure that Gabe was just pitying him at this point…and the really pathetic thing was, working for this punk kid, driving around to different surf shops, *malls,* would probably pay a hell of a lot more than he was getting paid now.

The thing was, he liked what he did now. He liked helping people get the right gear. He liked talking to surfers. And while most of the people who owned surf shops were surfers, he didn't want to talk selling points or anything like that. He wanted to talk to real people.

"So, what do you think I'd be best suited to doing?" Sean asked, a little challenge in his voice.

The kid looked thoughtful for a moment. "Well, you'd have a small territory to start. Then we'd see how you did."

Would we, now? Sean felt a spurt of irritation. "Well."

"So. How about I let you know sometime after the first of the year? And just so you know, there'd have to be a trial period before anything became permanent."

Sean sighed. Thought of his apartment, his decrepit truck.

Thought of Allison, again.

"Sure," he said, although it was like talking through a mouthful of overcooked oatmeal. "Why not?"

Steve looked a little taken aback by Sean's distinct lack of enthusiasm. "Well then. I look forward to it."

Sean shook his head and ignored the clamoring of his gut. He needed this, he reminded himself as Steve went through the company's mission statement, key objectives and expectations for all employees, prospective and otherwise, the whole nine yards.

"You'll be fine," Steve assured him.

Sean thanked him, then headed out to his pickup. He suddenly, abruptly, felt the need to go out into the surf. If only to feel clean again.

ALLISON TOOK A DEEP BREATH as she surveyed the surf. She'd already checked her handy tide table—she was back at the easy part of the beach, where the waves weren't so harsh. She was wearing her wet suit and had her board out. The beach was relatively deserted.

She was ready, and she couldn't seem to move.

Well, there's something therapeutic about just sitting and watching the waves.

She shook her head. She was making excuses, she realized. In a nutshell, she was "punking." Oh, how far the mighty had fallen.

Just because Sean isn't here doesn't mean you can't get out into the water.

Although Sean always did tell her to be careful. She could always rely on that, she said. She ought to be careful. Maybe she should wait until later that afternoon, when they had their rescheduled lesson.

Chicken.

She was about to get up and walk back to her car, when she saw three boys, all junior high in age. They looked adorable in their wet suits, carrying their boards. They were relatively long boards, so at least she felt a little better…they weren't experts.

"Are you gonna surf?"

The first boy to speak to her had short blond hair…more like peach fuzz, cropped so close that you could see the tanned skin beneath it. And the kid was tanned. Even though it was winter, his light green eyes stared out in sharp relief against the darkness of his skin. She wondered what he looked like in the summertime.

"I was thinking about it," she said, feeling like a complete and utter coward.

The other two boys were taller than the first, and had dark brown hair…one cut short and spiky, the other long, collar length. They looked at her warily…not just an adult on their beach, but a female, at that.

"Well," the first boy said, as if making a decision. "It's pretty cold. Don't know if you want to go out there."

She felt her chin go up a little, as if challenged. "I've got my wet suit."

"Okay, then," one of the dark-haired boys said.

The boys stared at her expectantly.

"I'm Allison," she offered.

They shrugged.

So much for introductions. "And your names are...?"

They looked at each other, then at the blond boy. He was obviously their de facto leader. "Toby," the blond boy said, giving her the hey-there head nod.

"Mark," the dark-haired boy who'd spoken to her said.

"Jake," the other said. "Mark's my brother."

She'd guessed as much, but didn't say anything.

The trio stood there a moment longer, then did the group shrug. They dumped their towels, and then headed with purpose toward the surf.

She wondered if kids this young should be surfing alone, even if they did know what they were doing. Still, she decided it might not be a bad idea if she went out with them.

She got up, taking a deep breath, and headed out into the ocean. It was only her intense desire not to look like a complete wuss in front of her new friends that kept her from yelping painfully as her toes went numb from the cold.

The boys hooted as they got soaked, diving into the first wave possible. They looked at her expectantly again.

She had always been the inch-in-slowly type of swimmer, but apparently they'd done this before—a lot, so she took a deep breath, steadied her board, and then plowed headfirst into a wave.

Whoosh. The icy sensation was like a hard wake-up call, and her heart started pumping double time. She felt ultra-awake, like she'd just had a triple-espresso shot. "Whoo-hoo!" she shouted, then realized that the boys were laughing at her.

She didn't care. She laughed right with them.

The boys were like otters…slick-wet and playful. She was careful to watch their hand signals, so she wouldn't steal one of their waves. In the meantime, she wasn't really doing much in the way of surfing. Still, she was floating companionably, and watching the boys while she was belly-riding her board was fun.

Toby paddled over to where she was, sitting astride his board and studying her. "You don't really know what you're doing, do you?" he said in the artless way that only ten-year-old boys seem to master.

She shrugged. "Not really. But I just started surfing a few weeks ago."

"Why?" Now the other two otters had paddled up, wondering what the conference in the water was all about.

"Because I was stressed out, and I thought surfing would help."

"Oh." The boy looked at her, then shrugged. "Weird."

"Yeah, weird," Mark agreed.

"So, how do you guys know how to pick a wave?" she asked, partially because they seemed to know, but also because it was kind of nice to talk to somebody about something other than work.

The boys' eyes lit up. "Really?"

Suddenly, she was surrounded by experts. "Well," Mark said with the air of a college professor, "what you want to do is…"

She was suddenly alert as the three boys threw instructions at her. Finally Mark, in a fit of impatience, told her that they'd point out the waves, and she should try for them.

She stood at the ready, holding on to her board the way Sean had shown her.

"Now!" Mark yelled. "Start paddling!"

"Paddle now!" Toby yelled even louder, his thin chest distended with the effort. The third boy just hooted loudly.

She got on the board, thankful for a brief second that she managed to stay on without humiliating herself, and then started paddling for her life. The action was unnatural, and she was breathing hard, but she felt the water swell beneath her and heard the increased hooting from the boys, so she paddled even faster.

"Now get up!" Toby shrieked.

"Up! Up!" Mark chanted.

She gritted her teeth…and then, just like she'd practiced countless times on the beach and on her carpet, she jumped up.

Don't look down. She could hear Sean's words in her head, just as if he was standing behind her. The tacky surf wax on her board held her feet in place, and she felt her equilibrium slowly shifting.

Suddenly, like the beauty of a symphony, everything fell into place. She found her sweet spot. She barely registered the triumphant shouts of the boys as she realized in a rush that she was standing, she was surfing, she was actually *riding* the board…

"I did it!" she screamed with wonder, feeling a rush of adrenaline so strong it threatened to make her head explode. "I did it!"

She looked out, down the wave…and then glanced at the beach, wishing that somebody she knew could be witnessing this historic event. She wished that somebody would take a picture. She hadn't been this proud in her life.

There was somebody on the beach…a man, a surfer.

Sean.

"I did it!" she yelled to him around a big smile.

He waved.

She waved back…and just as abruptly lost her balance, plunging into the water hard.

CHAPTER TWELVE

SEAN HAD ONLY STOPPED back at his apartment briefly enough to strip out of his interview clothes and throw on his wet suit. He'd never felt like he needed the sedating power of the waves as much as he did today. He knew it was a good opportunity that he'd probably all but thrown away. He knew that the surf shop was closing, and he couldn't just drift around like kelp for the rest of his life—his very kind landlady and drinking buddy Mrs. Tilson would probably have some choice words to say on that matter if he tried. So he'd gone to the ocean, feeling despondent, knowing that the ocean would, as usual, make him feel better.

Of course, he wondered how long that would last, since he'd be in close proximity to Allison…and after that searing kiss in her office, he wasn't sure just how much surfing he was going to be able to coach her on, and how hands-off he was going to be able to be.

So he was surprised when he got to the beach and found Allison already there, looking like a true surf girl in her black-and-red winter wet suit. She was with a few of the neighborhood boys—he thought he recognized them, but at this distance, it was hard to be sure. They were yelling at her like loons, and sure enough, she was focusing all her laser-like attention on their instructions. He just sat on the beach, next to his short board, watching her as she paddled and, miracle of miracles, actually laughed.

He was so engrossed in what he was watching though, that he barely noticed what was going on. The water had gone calm. If he'd actually been in it, if he'd been in the zone and water conscious, he would've immediately realized what was happening.

Ninety percent of all rescues happen just after a lull.

That fact registered just seconds before she stood on the board, and the tidbit of information was washed away by a massive wave of pride…a sensation that quickly turned to a lump of cold fear in his stomach as his mind finally put together what his subconscious had been yelling at him for the past ten minutes.

Riptide.

She wasn't coming up, he thought with panic. She should've surfaced by now.

He grabbed his board and rushed out into the water, yelling for the boys to come into shore as he headed out for her. He should've been paying more attention. He didn't notice the cold of the water, didn't notice anything beyond the spot of ocean where Allison had disappeared.

Before he could get there, her board popped up like a cork, and she was a few seconds behind it. She took a deep gulping breath and immediately coughed.

"Allison! Allison!" He paddled up to her, grabbing her, helping her onto her board. The boys had taken his shouted instructions to heart and were already safely on the beach. "Are you all right?" he asked, desperate for her answer.

"I got rolled," she said. "Scraped the bottom a bit, and that wave hit me like a sledgehammer." She giggled a little.

"The tide's coming in heavy," he said. "We need to go in now."

"No problem," she said gamely, still with a smile, and started to paddle.

It took him twice as long as it would normally, partially because he was trying to make sure that Allison got in all right, and partially because his muscles had turned to jelly at the sheer relief that the panic his mind had goaded him into was at least somewhat unfounded. When they got to the shallows, he ran to shore, untethering his board and throwing it onto the sand. He then went back and grabbed her, all but carrying her to shore.

"Sean! Put me down!" she croaked as he slung her over one shoulder and tucked her board under his arm. "I'm fine, Sean! I'm fine!"

It was as if he couldn't hear her. Instead, he dumped her board on the sand next to his, and placed her on her feet. Then he stared her down. "What did I tell you when I started classes?"

"That you're a kook?" she said, her eyes gleaming.

"You don't surf alone." His words could've pounded rocks to powder. He kept a grip on his temper, but his eyes kept searching her over, as if to reassure him that she was, indeed, safe. "There was a riptide starting. You could've been carried out."

He looked over to where the boys were standing, drying off. He finally recognized them. "Mark? That you?"

"Hey, Sean." Mark nodded, smiling slightly. "She's one of your students, huh?"

"You know you should be careful out here," he warned instead.

"Yeah. Shoulda seen that lull coming," Mark replied with the supreme confidence of a twelve-year-old who is convinced nothing bad can happen.

"You'll be more careful next time," Sean said in a calm voice.

The kids all looked shamefaced, and nodded glumly.

He turned back to Allison. "Don't even try to be mad at me on this one," he warned.

"Did you see me?" she countered, obviously neither hearing nor heeding his warning. "I did it! I jumped up, just like I'd practiced! I found my sweet spot and everything. *I rode that wave!*" Her eyes snapped. "And I have had one of the worst days on record. Don't even—"

He couldn't help it. He grabbed her, dragged her up against him and kissed her with all the pent-up fear and relief warring inside him.

She was obviously surprised for a second, then she responded with a passion of her own that hit him like a Hawaiian giant. Her arms tugged his head down to hers, and he crushed her against him. She opened her mouth, and the kiss turned hungry.

It must've been a long time, because only slowly did he register the kids' hoots and whistles. He finally released her, resting his forehead against hers.

"I was scared," he said finally. "I was so damn scared that something bad would happen to you."

"I see that now," she said softly. "But something great happened to me."

"I know," he said. "You really did it…you rode that wave."

"No," she said. "I found you."

And she kissed him again, slowly, full of promise.

Suddenly, the interview, the surf shop, everything that he was supposed to sort out, all seemed unimportant. The only important thing in his life was getting as close to this woman as humanly possible…and never, ever letting go.

"You're not getting a surf lesson today," he said against her lips.

"Mmm," she agreed, tugging him toward the car.

They were halfway there when Mark yelled out, "Yo! How about your surfboards?" And one of the other kids said, "Sheesh. Get a *room.*" Which was the point.

They somehow managed to gather their boards and get into his truck, leaving her Jag at the beach. "Your place okay?" he asked, thinking of privacy.

"Perfect," she said. "Just *hurry.*"

Oh, yeah. They were definitely on the same page. He drove as fast as his ancient pickup would allow, but it still seemed like a million years before they got to her town house. He grabbed their boards, but she led the way.

The second they were in the town house, he propped the boards up against the wall while she locked the door. And then they catapulted into each other's arms.

It was times like this that wet suits were particularly awkward, and she laughed breathlessly as he unzipped her. "I was a real surfer today," she proudly stated.

As the zipper lowered, he saw her petite but full breasts pressed against the neoprene. His body, already hard, seemed to tense to the breaking point. "Holy crow," he muttered. "You are…beautiful. Unbelievable."

She led him to the bedroom, a room he'd never been in.

He couldn't have named a single detail if he tried. All he was aware of was her. She tugged awkwardly at her wet suit, laughing with frustration as it caught on her skin. He peeled off his wet suit with some difficulty, too…partially because his skin was still dry, but mostly because he was clumsy with desire for this woman. He stripped down to the waist, feeling another rush as she paused in her own undressing to stare at him. "You're pretty amazing, there, yourself," she murmured.

He couldn't help it. He leaned over and kissed her…then tugged the wet suit off her shoulders, not even looking as he slipped it off of her arms. When his hands came in contact with her smooth, slightly damp skin, he shuddered slightly. When her bare chest pressed against his, he groaned.

"Sean," she whispered against his throat, pressing tiny, maddening kisses. *"Please."*

She pulled away and tugged at her wet suit hard enough to think she'd tear the neoprene in half. He sat on the bed, wiggling off his wet suit, then looked up to find her naked, and staring at him, desire and nerves warring in her heart-shaped face.

He took in the look of her, her slight but perfectly proportioned figure, her hair tumbling in wet waves around her shoulders. The flush of cold and passion on her barely sun-kissed skin.

"You're perfect," he breathed.

She smiled, like the sun burning off clouds. Then she walked over to him, taking a deep breath. He opened his arms, and she stepped into them, like the last piece of a puzzle.

He just held her for a moment, warming her, feeling her shiver against him and causing his already sensitive skin to go haywire. But he swore he'd remember this moment forever, breathing in the smell of her—girlish perfume and the intoxicating scent of saltwater and sea air. He tilted his head back, kissing her chin…kissing her lips.

She sighed, and then pushed him over onto the bed.

He laughed in surprise, but only for a second. Passion quickly burned everything away but the pure need for her.

She was, as always, unstoppable. Her delicate hands smoothed along his skin as she responded to his kisses with an ardor that almost knocked him out. The feel of her, sliding along the length of him made something snap in his mind. He wanted her. He had to have her.

And now, he actually could.

He tore his mouth away. "Condom," he said. "I don't…I want to make sure you're okay."

She smiled, then rolled away for the briefest of seconds, pulling open a drawer and producing a foil packet. "You know, I used to think it was dumb to have these around when I never used them," she said, her eyes glinting mischievously.

He rolled one on with haste, laughing to himself about her remark in the dressing room: *I have a whole new respect for people who have to put on condoms.* Then he paused. "You're sure?"

She leaned back against the bed, holding her arms out. "More sure than I've ever been about absolutely anything," she breathed.

He was a man who didn't need to be told more. Still, he wasn't rushing. He kissed every inch of her, reveling in the taste of her, the feel, until she was begging for him in an incoherent nonlanguage of sighs and moans. Finally, he slid on top of her, gently, carefully. She wrapped her legs around him, her eyes full of trust, her hands clutching at his shoulders.

"Now, *now,*" she insisted.

But she wasn't quite ready, and he moved slowly, entering her carefully, gauging her reaction, taking his time to be gentle even as the effort practically killed him. She was pressing against him, her breathing uneven, urging him.

Suddenly, it was just like catching a wave—the rush, the feeling of being embraced and pushed. She cried out his name, kissing him feverishly, and he started to move, their bodies moving together, matching perfectly, melding in a perfect dance of passion in motion.

She let out a rippling sound as her body contracted around him, and that was it. With a groan, he pressed against her, sensation exploding around him. When he could get his wits back, he rolled over, carrying her with him, resting her on top of him.

She let out a long, sighing breath. "That was…wow."

"Wow," he repeated. "You're as amazing as I knew you'd be."

She smiled. "So…when can we do that again?"

He laughed, wrapping his arms around her as warmth that had nothing to do with the adrenaline and passion in his system seeped through his body. "Make that even more amazing."

RRRRRING! RRRRING!

Allison's first instinct was to hit the alarm with a groan, but as she rolled over and reached, she realized she couldn't quite move…that there was a large, warm male body curled around hers, his arm just beneath her breasts.

Sean, she thought. They'd made love until two o'clock in the morning, and then had fallen asleep, entwined, as if they couldn't bear to be separated even then.

She still felt that way, she thought abruptly.

She then glanced at the clock. It wasn't her alarm—she hadn't set it. That annoying ringing noise was her phone.

"I have to get that," she said to him, and with a reluctant groan he released her, much to her body's disappointment. She sprang out of bed naked, grabbing the cordless phone and wandering out into her hallway. "Yes?" she said impatiently.

"Where the heck are you?"

She grimaced. It was Gary. "I'm at home, obviously," she said in a hushed voice. Then she remembered…yesterday. Getting taken off the account. "I'm sorry. I'm staying home today. I should've left you a note or something. I left in kind of a hurry."

"What happened? There are all kinds of rumors going on, and when I didn't hear from you, I tried calling your cell phone…."

"I shut it off," she admitted with a wince. "What kind of rumors?"

"You had some kind of nutty episode and told off Frank and now he's kicked you out of the office."

She sighed. "Yeah. That sounds about right."

There was a pause on Gary's end of the line. "You're not kidding."

"Apparently not." It still didn't quite seem real. Of course, after the past twenty-four hours, nothing did. "He said that I could stay home until the presentation. Kate and Peter will take over, I'd imagine."

"Yeah, well, we'll see about that," Gary said ominously. "But here's the thing—they've been by every five minutes, asking when you're coming in. Kate's even asked me for your home phone number, and I imagine she'll raid HR to find it if she has to. It's just a matter of time."

"Oy," Allison said, rubbing a hand over her face.

"So I think they're going to want you to come in, is my point," Gary said. "Frank will realize they can't handle the account any minute now. I'm sure he'll reconsider."

She knew that he probably would. Then she walked to the bedroom, and saw Sean, sleeping. His sandy brown hair was tousled around his closed eyes, and what she could see of his torso…

"Allison? Hello, Allison?"

She snapped back to attention. "Sorry," she muttered. "Got distracted."

"So? You going to come in, or what?"

She thought about it. "No," she said in a low voice. "I've got…other things I want to do today."

Another pause. "Why are you talking so softly?"

She blushed. Even though she couldn't see it, she could feel it in the heat of her skin. She retreated toward the living room, grateful the blinds were drawn. "I'm not talking softly," she said in a more normal voice, clearing her throat.

"You got lucky!" Gary's voice was low enough to be secretive, and tinged with incredulous laughter.

"That's so inappropriate," she said, a giggle escaping.

"I'm not just your assistant, I'm your friend…and I've been working with you long enough to know that you have no life," he pointed out. "So forgive me for commenting on the obvious and add a big *hoorah.* It was that guy from yesterday, wasn't it? The tall guy?"

She threw a glance over her shoulder at the bedroom door. "Not telling."

"That's why you're not coming in?" He let out a low whistle. "Wow. He must be something if you're going to blow off something this big to spend the day with him."

She bit her lip. Gary had a point. She had been working all her life toward this…not toward a few sex-drenched days with her surf instructor.

But Sean's not just my surf instructor…and this isn't just sex.

She wasn't sure what prompted her internal voice to chime in with those observations, but once she'd recognized them, she knew that they weren't going to go away.

"It wasn't my idea," she said instead. "Frank sent me home. If they want to manage the account without me, then that's his call."

"If you say so," Gary said dubiously. "Still, I wouldn't be surprised if Kate drove by your house. She's starting to look a little crispy around the edges."

Allison made a mental note to unplug her phone. "Thanks for the warning. I'll see you on the thirty-first."

"So you're still coming to the presentation?"

"It's my presentation." She might be dealing with a bunch of stuff with Sean, but that was one thing she wasn't missing. "Somebody else might be delivering it, but I'll be there."

"All right." There was an evil, mischievous chuckle in Gary's voice. "You have fun today, boss."

"I plan to," she retorted, then hung up on him. Then she unplugged the phone from the jack.

"Everything okay?"

She looked up…and then caught her breath.

Wrapped up in one of her Egyptian-cotton sheets, his hair rumpled, his eyes slumberous, Sean Gilroy was possibly the most gorgeous thing she had ever seen. From the expression on his face, one of sleepy hunger, she felt her body stir.

"Nothing. Nothing important, anyway," she said. She walked up to him, tentatively, disbelief still hovering in her system. "Good morning," she whispered.

He smiled…then reached out and pulled her to him, nuzzling her neck as her body turned into jelly. Then, with casual strength, he picked her up and carried her back to the bedroom. She laughed as she bounced on her bed.

"That was work, wasn't it?" he asked, stroking the hair out of her face.

She tensed slightly. "Yeah."

"You going in?"

She shook her head, biting her lip. "Said I had other things to do," she replied in a soft voice.

He smiled, slowly, wickedly. "Please tell me I'm one of those things."

"Actually," she said, stretching out in invitation, "you're the entire list."

She watched his hazel eyes glow, and she thought the happiness she was feeling at that second was going to knock her out. She couldn't remember ever feeling this way, in her entire life.

"Well," he said, leaning down and kissing her shoulder, then her neck, then her jawline. "If I'm all you have to do today, I guess I'd better make sure I'm worth it."

She closed her eyes, letting him work that same silken

web of pleasure over her, and before rational thought fled completely, she felt a flash of clarity.

She'd tossed everything else in her life out the window for this man. Not for a lifetime—she had no idea what his plans were. Not for any promises—he hadn't made any.

She'd thrown everything away for basically one day, maybe a week. However long she had with him.

Guess I'd better make sure I'm worth it.

She kissed him with all the passion she possessed. She couldn't figure out any other way to tell him without scaring him.

Sean, you already are worth it.

She just wished she'd be able to hold on to that thought forever, and gave in to enjoying her day.

"HEY SEAN," Oz said, a smudge of dust on his face the only thing marring his look of relief. "Glad you could make it."

Sean nodded in greeting. He didn't want to be there. It was hard enough to leave Allison, all warm and sleepy in her bed. Knowing he was coming here to close up the shop forever made him drive even slower. He felt heavy, like he was walking out in high tide, everything pushing against him.

"I figure I'll need to take a complete inventory," Oz said. Now that Sean was there, he sounded all business. But Oz no longer met Sean's gaze, instead stayed riveted on the surfboards and other materials like he'd never seen it before.

I just have to get through today, and it'll be all over.

Sean took a deep breath. "It shouldn't be too bad," he said. "There wasn't a whole lot of movement in December, and I've been keeping track of it in the slow time. The records are all behind the counter."

"Really?" Oz sighed. "You always were better at this than I was."

Sean didn't respond to that, just walked behind the counter and pulled out his inventory binder. "You were always a better surfer than you were a businessman," he said.

"Don't remind me," Oz groaned.

"That's actually meant to be a compliment," Sean said with a small smile, especially as he thought of Stevie and his interview at Lone Shark. "I mean, you may not be a multi-millionaire or anything, but you've got to admit, you've had a hell of a lot of fun."

Oz chuckled, rubbing his hand over the back of his neck. "Yeah. It has been fun, huh?"

Sean handed him the binder, and Oz took it blindly, flipping through the pages. "Whoa. Have you been this anal all the time I've known you?"

Sean laughed, even though he felt a sinking sensation in his chest. "Well, I had to do something."

Oz finally looked at him—his face had gone melancholy, and Sean gritted his teeth. "You're really going to go places, kid. And about time, too."

Sean took a deep breath. "It wasn't like it sucked to work here," he said.

"Yeah, but it wasn't much of anything," Oz said, his voice mournful and downright maudlin.

"You're kidding me with this, right?" Sean said. "You keep this up, and I'm going to have to go into the back room and break into the emergency beer. And it's only ten in the morning."

Oz didn't laugh. "I'm fifty-two years old," he said instead, "and all I have to show for it is this place."

Sean sighed. Apparently he wasn't the only one feeling lousy about the end of an era that this day represented, and frankly, he wasn't sure if he could handle holding Oz's hand through it, either. "Have you decided what you're going to do?" Sean said, trying to change the subject.

Oz sighed. "I still need to talk it over with my accountant and lawyer and stuff, but I think I may travel just a bit. And…I don't know. Maybe I'll try to find something else, maybe get some hobbies."

So why are you in such a hurry to get rid of this place? Sean wanted to yell at him. But they'd had the conversation twice now. "Sounds…" He bit back on the term *boring* and said instead, "…okay."

"Yeah, well, I guess. I might meet somebody," he said, perking up a little.

Sean thought immediately of Allison, and smiled. "You might, indeed."

"Hear you've got yourself a girl," Oz said, his voice slightly sly.

"Working on it," Sean dodged.

"And maybe a job?"

Sean's merry mood dissipated. "Working on it," he repeated with less enthusiasm.

"You do that, Sean. You get a nice steady job, get married…settle down. You don't want to be my age and figure out you're all alone and married to a money pit."

Sean shook his head. "Oz, you're my friend. So I have to say—would you shut up about Tubes already? It's not like it's bleeding you dry. Almost all of the South Bay has been through these doors at one point or another. You've surfed in South America and Thailand and England, for God's sake.

You've carved the Pipeline in Hawaii. You've met some of the best shapers in the business. And the thing that let you do that was this damn store! So I know you're going through some midlife crisis or something…"

"Late for midlife," Oz said, and then shut up when Sean glared at him.

"But basically, you've had a life most people would love to have. And hearing you moan about it this way? Frankly, it stinks!"

Oz's mouth fell open. "Uh…wow. I don't think I've ever seen you lose your temper." His eyes widened. "I don't even think I knew you had a temper."

"Yeah, well, I do," Sean said bitterly. It was as if a pressure valve had been snapped open, and nothing was going to be able to shut it until everything he was feeling was released. "I know you've got your reasons for getting out of the business, and all of that, and I sure didn't expect you to stay in it because of me. But I've spent the best years of my life in this store. I've taught most of the surfers under the age of twenty in the Los Angeles area. We've been *the best,* man. And you're going to tell me that I've just been killing time? That Tubes has just been some kind of parasite and my life has been a big waste?"

Oz looked shocked. "I didn't mean you!"

"Yeah, well, how the hell did you think that was going to work?" Sean said.

"I meant it was just like that for me," Oz snapped.

Sean leaned forward, feeling anger rise in him like lava. *"This store was my life!"*

Oz stared at him as if he'd never seen him before. "I…I know. I guess I just wasn't thinking about you when I was saying all that."

"That's the problem, Oz. You weren't thinking about me." Sean shook his head. "And you didn't need to…it's your store. But I thought you ought to know."

He headed for the door.

"Where are you going?" Oz said. "I thought you were going to go over the inventory, get me all ready to sell!"

"It's all right there," Sean said tiredly. "And I can't go through this again."

"Sean?"

Sean paused, the door half-open. "Yeah?"

"I couldn't have lived the way I did without you," he said. "I was really upset when your mom just left you here…you know. Back when."

"I wasn't too thrilled, myself," Sean said, with dry humor, pushing back the memory…sixteen years old, with a teenage sister to look after. "And you thought of us then. Gave us a place to stay."

"The store might've been a bad idea for somebody like me," Oz said quietly. "But you kids were the best thing to ever come into my life."

Sean closed his eyes against the emotion hitting him. The ocean and this store were the best things in his life.

"The full inventory's all there, and you've still got all the notes I gave you," Sean said instead, sidestepping the whole issue completely. "Just…call if you need help."

CHAPTER THIRTEEN

ALLISON PUTTERED AROUND her house, humming to herself as she cleaned up the breakfast dishes. Sean had to go to the store to help Oz close up, he'd said the night before. She'd felt his kiss this morning, when he left her early to go back to his apartment and change. It was nice, to be kissed goodbye.

She was rather looking forward to seeing how it felt to be kissed hello when he got back.

What the heck are you doing?

She kept humming, something goofy and pop-influenced. Probably something about love.

She didn't know what she was doing, but she did know what she wasn't doing. She wasn't worrying about the presentation that was going on tomorrow.

Sure, at odd moments, she'd remember that it was happening and feel a quick, sharp stab of panic. But for the past thirty-six hours or so, she'd been with Sean, and it was amazing just how calming that was. She'd never been around a friend, much less a lover, when she was in the throes of career stress. And with Sean, it was as if he could sense when she tensed about something. Before she even became cognizant of the fact that she was stressed, there he was, stroking her shoulders, kissing her neck, hugging her gently in that amazingly comforting way of his, as if he never wanted to let her go. She'd never felt anything quite like it.

It was a little unnerving, actually, how quickly and thoroughly he was able to read her. It was even more unnerving to realize just how addictive that kind of on-call emotional support was quickly becoming.

Today, he was going to come back and the two of them were going to go surfing. Another addictive thing that he had introduced her to, and if he left tomorrow, she'd still love it. She could thank him for that.

She quickly loaded the rest of the dishes in the dishwasher and grabbed a diet soda. She wasn't going to think about him leaving. Not now. Not when so much else in her life was going haywire.

The doorbell rang. She wondered if Sean had gotten out early—she hadn't given him a key. She smiled quickly as a rush of anticipation tightened her entire body. She threw the door open. "Hey, you," she purred.

Her brother, Rod, stared at her aghast. "Um, hello to you, too, sis."

She felt as if she'd just slipped and fallen into the Arctic Ocean. "Ugh. What are you doing here?"

"I'm your brother. What, I can't visit?"

"Not when you scare two years off my life, you can't," she snapped under her breath as he stepped into the town house, a frown etched into his face.

"You haven't been answering your phone. Not your home phone, not your cell," he chastised.

"I had things to do," she said, then remembered when she'd mentioned it to Gary…and why. A sexy little smile crossed her face, but she quickly quelled it before Rod turned back to her. Then she paused, her heart stopping for a second. "What are you doing away from your job? And in the morning?" Her heart started back up at double speed. "Is something wrong with Dad? Another heart attack? Is Mom okay?"

"They're fine," he said. "Mom's just worried about you, that's all. She wanted to make sure you were going to go to the New Year's party. You know. The usual." He frowned.

"So she sent out her crack sibling squad to make sure I RSVP'd?" Allison asked, incredulous.

Rod scowled at her. "Were you always this sarcastic, and I just never noticed?"

"That's ridiculous," she said, then grinned. "You've noticed before."

He was her older brother, only two and a half years apart, but lately it had seemed like decades. She blamed his job. "This is serious. You're dodging the parents, you're not at your job…oh, and you'll want to talk to that snippy assistant of yours," Rod said sternly. "The guy was no help whatsoever."

"He'll be promoted by the end of next week," she said. "So, if everyone's healthy and you've delivered your party invitation…"

He sat down on her love seat, and she sighed. This wasn't a check-in, she could just tell.

"Mom and Dad have been asking about you," he said with all the solemnity of Al Pacino in *The Godfather*.

She sat down across from him on the couch. She couldn't quite believe she was having this conversation. "Why are they worried, exactly?" She supposed it was petty to point out that they hadn't worried when, say, she actually lived there, or when she was cracking up in college. That kind of thing she really should've let go of by now.

His frown deepened. "You've just been acting really strange," he said, making a nebulous sort of motion with his hand.

"Anything specific?"

"What's all this about you surfing, for example?"

She closed her eyes, and let out a deep breath that she hadn't realized she was holding. "This is all because of the surfing crack I made at Christmas, isn't it?" She felt a little relief, even though she realized she was still tense "Don't worry. I'm being very careful, and I'm taking lessons from a really good instructor." *You don't know how good,* she thought, and carefully schooled her face to remain impassive. Rod was sharp about reading people—it was part of what made him such a great businessman. "You know how thorough I am, anyway. When has one of us not been a great student?"

Rod looked as if he was weighing her words, and she held her breath again. "Is that all there is to this?"

Now she felt anger start to spark through her system. "Exactly when did we fall into some kind of Jane Austen period piece, where the older brother lectures the flighty younger sister on her behavior?"

"When my younger sister started flaking out on the job promotion she's been talking about for months," he said bluntly. "Listen. I know I haven't been there much for you, but Mom and Dad really think that something's going on. And you have to admit, you've been acting pretty odd. Normally I could set my watch by your routine."

She winced at the obvious truth in his words. *Damn, but I'm boring.*

"My life is changing," she admitted. "I don't know what that means. But I do know that Mom and Dad really don't need to worry about it." She paused, and smiled at him. "And neither do you, Rod."

He scowled.

"But," she added with a smile in her voice, "I'm kind of glad that you are worried."

Rod looked startled at this admission, then shrugged, even as she saw some of the tension leave his face. "Yeah. Well…you know."

"Yeah," she said. "I know."

It was probably the closest her brother had ever come to admitting he loved her. As far as she was concerned, it was close enough.

"So, what's going on with the job?" he said, trying to get back to territory where he felt comfortable.

She sighed. "I got taken off the account."

He now looked appalled. So much for closeness, she thought, wishing abruptly that Sean was there for a hug. "What did you do?"

"I sort of told my boss he was a vicious micromanager," she admitted.

"Good grief. Then what? Did you insult his mother?" Rod shook his head. "What in the world possessed you to do something so completely…"

He trailed off, and she smirked. "Dumb?"

"To say the least!"

She flopped back against the cushions of the couch. Raised in their family, of course she realized just how rash her actions were. "I was in a weird place," she said, then noticed Rod's puzzled expression. "Haven't you just ever wondered why the hell you're going through all of it? All the stress? All the pressure? Haven't you ever sat down and asked yourself, is any of this worth it?"

"Hell, no," he said with obvious revulsion.

Of course he hadn't. She had to be the freak of the gene pool. She rubbed her eyes. "Okay, let me put this a different way. Have you ever asked yourself how you ever got this lucky?"

"It's not luck," he said immediately. "I work hard for everything I have."

"Yeah, but have you ever thought how glad you are to have it?"

"Sure," he said, but he sounded a lot less certain.

"Really?" she pressed. "You've actually thought about how happy you are in your life?"

"Well, I don't sit around like some self-help nutcase," he said, sounding insulted. "I don't *dwell* on it or anything."

"I'm not happy," she said. "Or at least…I haven't been happy. I think I'm finally figuring that out."

"We can't be happy all the time," he said in that maddening I'm-older-and-know-better voice of his that she loathed.

"I'm not asking for all the time," she said, and even as she said it, she realized—*you're pretty much happy all the time around Sean.* "Anyway, I also realize that I can do something about it. I've got a plan."

"As long as this plan doesn't include throwing your career away," Rod warned. "You've worked too hard to toss it all down the toilet just because you're a little unhappy."

She sighed. He was never going to get it. "Don't you have

a meeting or conference call or something else important that you have to rush off to?"

He stood up. "I can see I've worn out my welcome," he said with a smirk. "Still, don't forget what I said. And check in with Mom. She's a little frantic, and that's unusual for her. At least, when she's not under deadline."

"Will do," Allison said, opening the front door and resisting the urge to kick him out of it. But before he could step out, Sean stepped in…and kissed her, long and hard.

Her mind spun, the way it always did when his lips touched hers, and for a flash of a second, she forgot that Rod was standing in her foyer. She just leaned in and enjoyed the taste of Sean, the feel of him.

"Something you neglected to mention, sis?" Rod's voice was utterly unamused, and much louder than usual.

She pulled back, then the two of them looked over at Rod. His eyes, brown like hers, looked hard as stone.

"Uh…this is Sean. Sean Gilroy."

Sean sized up Rod, then held out a hand. "Nice to meet you."

Rod didn't return the pleasantry, and paused, meaningfully, before shaking Sean's hand. "It's obvious you know my sister," Rod said, each word staccato. "Are you her boyfriend?"

Sean looked at Allison, startled. "Well…"

"Or are you just sleeping with her?"

Now Sean's eyes flashed. "I'm not 'just' anything with her," Sean said sharply, and Allison quickly jumped in before violence broke out.

"Rod," she said sharply, "you've said what you needed to say. I'll call Mom tomorrow at work. I promise. Now, why don't you go."

Rod sent one last menacing look to Sean, before staring at Allison. "I hope you know what the hell you're doing."

Sean took a protective step in front of Allison, looking angrier than she had ever seen him. When Rod disappeared down the street, Sean shut the door, then enveloped Allison in a strong hug.

"Whoa," she said, surprised…but melted into the hug nonetheless. "Well. How was your morning?"

"Not great, but I get the feeling yours was worse," Sean said, and his words warmed her like a bonfire. "So. That was your older brother, and I assume he was giving you grief?"

"It's an older brother's prerogative," she said with a shaky laugh, even as she felt her brother's glare in absentia.

Sean leaned down and kissed her softly on the temple. "I guess I can't blame him for being protective," he said philosophically. "But I have to say, any guy takes that tone of voice with you, and I instantly have the overwhelming urge to beat on him."

"Really?" She didn't know why that pleased her, but absurdly, she felt comforted. "I don't think that'll be necessary, but it's nice of you to say." Then she remembered the beginning of his sentence. "What happened this morning? You said you had a bad day."

"I don't want to talk about it," he said, stroking her cheek. "I just want to get out on the ocean, with you, and put this whole morning behind us."

She leaned against him. Simple words. She had a lot to think about—the presentation tomorrow, her mom, her dad…her brother's warning.

But that was tomorrow.

"Let's go," she said, and kissed him.

SEAN WALKED HIS BOARD out into the swells, looking over to where Allison was doing the same thing. He dived into a wave headfirst, getting his hair wet, and surfaced, a bubble of pure joy expanding in his chest. He was surfing, which he loved. And he was with Allison, whom he also…

He stopped himself abruptly, bobbing over a wave.

Actually, he wasn't sure how he felt about Allison.

Are you her boyfriend…or are you just sleeping with her?

Just the memory of her brother's irate question was enough to make his heart start pounding with rage. He didn't just sleep with Allison. Having said that—he'd like to be Allison's boyfriend. That is, if being her "boyfriend" meant going to sleep with her compact little body against his, waking every day to that mind-blowing smile of hers, spending every single day thinking of how to make her feel better, and sharing the best parts of his life with her.

Yeah, he supposed he wanted to be her "boyfriend" then. He guessed that they could "date."

"Sean!" she called out, smiling broadly at him as she paddled. "How'm I doing?"

"Beautiful," he said, meaning it on a couple of levels. She was actually getting pretty proficient, for somebody just at it a few weeks. She was still a rank beginner, but she had something that other beginners didn't have. She genuinely loved surfing. You could tell the difference in how she concentrated—in her fearlessness. In her dedication.

He wondered if she'd bring the same level of commitment to being a girlfriend…and if she considered herself his.

Dangerous thoughts, Gilroy.

He got on his board, gauging the waves. It was a pretty

low set, not a lull, but nothing to write home about, and there were hardly any other surfers out. Perfect for Allison to practice on, but not much for him to work with, nothing challenging. He signaled, got on his board, carved a little, switching back as best he could on the small crest.

"Whoo!" Allison called, admiration clear in her voice.

With all the grace of someone who had been surfing for more than twenty years, he skimmed over the top of the diminishing wave and dropped back down onto his board. "Now you try… The next one looks pretty good," he called out encouragingly.

Allison got that look of determination, and she paddled out, catching the wave as it started to crest. She popped up, bobbled, and fell in. "Grrr!" she yelped when she surfaced, but she was laughing, not angry like she was the first time they'd gone out in the water.

She never gave up, he thought. She always kept doggedly pursuing…only now, he saw that she was also genuinely appreciating and truly enjoying.

God, she's beautiful when she's happy.

She got back on her board and paddled up to him. "I'm still not getting it. Think you can help me?"

She had a dangerous glint in her eyes. His body responded with its characteristic tightening. He felt like a teenager, a randy one at that, and he was glad that Mark and the guys weren't around to witness this. The other surfers were packing it in, driving away. It was just the two of them.

"I'll be right back," he said, and with the speed of a sprinter, he rode a wave back to the beach, left his board and swam back out to where she was lying on her board. "Now. Where were we?"

"I need your help," she said with a suggestive pout. "I'm still not quite getting the hang of this."

"It takes a while," he said, even though he was fairly certain at this point that "this" had nothing to do with surfing. "You'll get it."

"Why don't you get on the board and help me out?" she said. "Show me where I'm going wrong."

He looked at her board. It was a long board, so it was slow, and it could, in theory, accommodate two people, even though he hadn't surfed double in forever. "I guess," he said. "Climb on. I'll get on behind you."

There it was again—that glint, and that devilish smile that suggested that riding tandem was just what she had in mind. She straddled the board, and the look of invitation she shot over her shoulder was unmistakable. He smirked, then climbed on the board behind her, scooting up so his body fit hers. She sighed, leaning back against him, making sure her backside rubbed against him. If it weren't for the wet suit, they'd be in real trouble here, he thought, holding her hips and pulling her against him. They just sat there for a second as he kissed her neck, his hands smoothing over her front as she moaned. They bobbed in the water, the swells nudging them. It was calm, the sound of the seagulls crying countered by the constant crash…the sun shining brightly.

It was, in a word, perfect.

He sighed raggedly. He was lucky. He was so incredibly lucky for this moment. For this girl.

"If we stay out here another minute, I'm going to take you," he said. "And then we're going to drown."

"Well, nobody wants that," she said with a shivery little

laugh. "So why don't we go back in, head back to my place and…"

She wiggled suggestively. She didn't have to say another word.

"Okay," he said, looking back and gauging the waves. There was one wave, bigger than the others… The tide was starting to come in. This one would be a mini barrel.

"Scoot up toward the front of the board and kneel," he said, still watching the wave. She was giggling, but she did as he suggested, an edge of excitement in her laughter. He paddled, anticipating…leading the wave. Then he hit the right spot, popped up and rode the wave.

She screamed with delight as they picked up speed, dancing across the water like a sandpiper. He grinned broadly.

Perfect. No matter what else happened, he had today.

ALLISON WALKED INTO WORK early on the thirty-first. New Year's Eve. She didn't really celebrate New Year's, as a general rule, other than her enforced presence at her parents' annual party.

But today, she was a strange mix of feelings. She was dreading the presentation, the final nail in the coffin of her career here at Flashpoint Advertising. She knew that some part of her was going to hate watching all of her hard work being rattled off by Kate and Peter, and Frank would probably do what he could to make her feel shut out. She knew that, on any other day, she would be near tears. She'd probably be breathing in a paper bag as Gary set up a coffee-drip IV. She would normally be on the razor's edge of keeping her grip.

She smiled, stroking a sea-smoothed pebble that she'd picked up on her last beach outing with Sean.

There was nothing normal or usual about her anymore, she thought. Not since surfing. Not since Sean.

I think I'm in love with him.

Gary peeked his head in. "It's been two days," he said. He looked haggard, and there were circles under his eyes. "And it's been pure hell."

"Oh, yikes," she said immediately as he walked in and closed the door. He handed her a large coffee, then sat down in one of her chairs and took a large swig from his own coffee. "That bad, huh?"

"I thought Kate was going to beat Peter to death with a stapler," Gary said. "And after last night, I would've handed one to her. They've been nuts."

"How is Frank letting this happen?" Allison marveled. "He's usually so on top of things."

"He's been trying to see which one of them was going to survive," Gary replied. "That, and he's used to working with you. Kate's got a temper, and Peter's passive-aggressive. Frank's been going progressively balder from tearing his hair out."

Allison grinned. She knew it was probably uncharitable, but some small part of her relished the image. She knew she probably shouldn't have mentioned all his shortcomings, but at least she got the vindication of seeing him find out just how hard she'd worked, and what a good worker she was, all on his own. "Guess we're in for a show this afternoon, then," she said.

Gary stared at her for a second. "You know," he said reflectively, "I don't think I've seen you this relaxed ever, in the whole time I've known you."

She smiled back. "Thanks. I don't think I've ever felt—"

The door burst open. Frank was standing there, his hair sticking up comically, his tie askew. He was wearing his "big-boy suit," the black pinstripe Hugo Boss that he only wore to the most important client meetings. His eyes looked bloodshot and his expression was harried.

"Allison," he said, and it was a plea for mercy. "*Where* have you been?"

She clamped down on a smirk. It wasn't nice, she reminded herself, even if it was funny. "You told me to stay home for a couple of days," she said with a small shrug. "So I stayed home."

"It's been pandemonium!" He looked as if he'd just been chased into her office by villagers carrying pitchforks. "Peter's threatening to quit. Kate's locked herself in the women's bathroom. I've got clients coming in just over two hours. What are we going to do?"

Allison blinked as she processed that bit of information. She knew that she was an important part of the team, but she hadn't anticipated this kind of delirium. It was flattering, and not a bit scary.

"Wow," she murmured, looking at Gary, who was rolling his eyes because Frank couldn't see it. She grinned, tongue in cheek. "I go surfing for a couple of days, and all hell breaks loose."

At that, Frank grimaced. "What, you want me to grovel? Okay. I'm groveling. I need you to take over this presentation. I need you to get this back on track. I need you to…do what you do best!"

"Which would be what, exactly?" she asked sweetly.

"Save our collective ass," he announced. "So. Will you do it?"

She paused. This was what she wanted—and in a better position than she'd anticipated. "Of course," she said slowly.

"Good," Frank said, relief crossing his face. Then he scowled. "You know how big this is. If you do anything, you know, just because you're mad at me…"

At that, she gasped. "Are you kidding? If you think that I could—" her glare could have flash-frozen fish "—you don't know me at all."

Frank looked satisfied at that. "Okay. I'll see if I can get somebody to pry Kate out of the bathroom."

Allison nodded. Then, she leaned back in her chair, closing her eyes.

She wasn't quite ready. She wasn't expecting this. She had two hours. She could make it work. Then they'd have the presentation, and one way or another, she'd know that at least she'd done her best.

Of course, if her best included a promotion…

Sighing, she opened her eyes…and discovered Gary studying her quizzically behind the sheen of his wire-rimmed glasses. "What?" she asked.

"I could see it," he marveled. "You went from completely relaxed to tensed like a catapult in under sixty seconds. Weird."

The words startled her.

Gary didn't notice her sudden discomfiture. "So, boss, what's the game plan? What do we need to do?"

She was still adjusting, so she bit her lip, her mind suddenly racing. This was what she wanted, right? So it was just a matter of a game plan.

"First, have one of the women tell Kate that I'm taking over. If anything will get her out of the bathroom, it'd be that," Allison said slowly.

"Why? Because she doesn't want you to give the presentation, or because she's glad the pressure's off?"

"Doesn't matter why. It'll look bad for the clients to come here and find out we've got an ad exec building a barricade in the restroom," Allison said. "The slides are all taken care of, the presentation's a lock. I just need a final walk-through…but unless Frank and the crew have made any changes, I could probably breeze through that."

"Of course Frank made changes," Gary said.

Allison closed her eyes. "Of course he did." She thought about it. "So we're going to just use my slides."

Gary's eyes widened. "You mean…just toss what Frank wanted?"

She nodded, feeling her heart start to race ever so slightly. "Yup. If he's in such a jam, we're going to do this my way."

"Wow," Gary said, his voice dry and sardonic. "Somebody came in wearing her big-girl panties."

"Apparently somebody did," she joked back, even as her palms began to sweat.

Sean, I wish you were here.

TWO HOURS LATER, she was standing in the conference room. Kate was sitting at the table, looking both disgruntled and relieved. Peter was there, too…but he was sitting with three people separating him from Kate. Apparently the stapler death threat was still in effect. Frank had finally settled in a chair—she thought he was going to wear a hole in the carpet from his incessant pacing. The Kibble Tidbits people seemed unaware of the high-nerve situation that pervaded the agency. Allison felt jumpy from the adrenaline, and her heart was still pounding a bit hard. Still, she'd made sure that she got them in the big conference room, for one reason: it had a view of the ocean. She had told Frank that was so she could impress the clients, who were from Denver. The real reason was the calming flashes of blue-green water.

They were all settled expectantly. They reminded her to a certain extent of her parents on Christmas morning, looking over the gifts of their various children.

Wrong image. For a flash of a second, she thought, *I can't do this. I can't possibly, possibly do this.* She just wanted to run outside, gulp air, crawl into her car. Drive away.

She stood up instead, straightening her back.

She thought of her board. Thought of paddling through the water. Thought, as always, of Sean, a talisman.

Then she smiled.

"I'm glad you could make it today," she said. "We've got some ideas that I think your company will find very interesting… Please feel free to ask questions at any time."

And just like that, she launched into her presentation. She barely registered Frank's surprise and disapproval when she veered from his changes and stuck with her own presentation—but he couldn't say anything, not without showing a divided front to the clients. She bobbled a little when she saw his frown, but then thought of the otters, as she called the boys who went surfing with her. *It's just a lull,* she told herself. Any grom worth her salt could keep an eye on the weather.

The clients sat there impassively, not helping her demeanor a whole lot. With little fanfare, she tied up her presentation. They hadn't asked a single question.

That normally wasn't a good sign.

She took a little breath, gripping her hands together

behind her back and keeping her smile bright. "So. Any comments? Anything?"

The head client, a pretty woman in her forties, looked at the other two, then looked at Allison. "Are you nervous at all?"

Allison laughed, wondering what exactly she'd done to tip them off...and thinking abruptly that she must've screwed up somewhere along the line. "Well, yes."

Frank closed his eyes, and she could've sworn she saw him muttering.

"Well, it doesn't show at all," the woman said, admiration clear in her voice. "In fact, that's the most relaxed presentation we've sat through this week—and believe me, we've sat through a couple."

"Uh, thanks," Allison said, nonplussed.

"We're going to need to discuss this," the woman said with a knowing smile to her colleagues, "but, well, I think it's safe to say we feel good about this one." She paused. "Can I assume that you'd be heading the team if Flashpoint won the business?"

Allison shot a quick, questioning glance at Frank.

Frank stood up, his chest puffed out. "Definitely," he said with feeling. "She would be the account supervisor for the Kibble Tidbits account, you can count on that."

Allison felt a wave of relief rush over her, and her knees felt weak. She leaned as subtly as she could against the table she was standing next to.

The woman nodded. "Excellent. That would have made a difference," she mused. "You'll be hearing from us soon. Oh...and Happy New Year."

With that, the lot of them shook hands all around and filed

out, leaving the building. The team looked at each other, then started to laugh triumphantly.

"You got us the business, damn it," Frank said, clapping Allison hard on the back. "You did it!"

"Congratulations," Peter said, holding out his hand. Kate did the same, although she looked a little crestfallen.

"Normally, I'd say don't count your chickens, but I know this one's a lock," Frank said expansively. "Let's hit the bar. Drinks are on me."

"I can't," Allison said. "I've got a party to go to. Two, actually."

And for the first time, she was actually looking forward to going to her parents' party. For the first time in a long time, things had worked out perfectly. And then she was going to collect a kiss at midnight, starting the year off right. After all, it was only thanks to Sean and her surf lessons that she had any of this at all.

"Well, party it up," Frank said with a grin. "We get this account, and all your butts are mine for the long haul. We'll have a lot of work to do!"

There was a ragged cheer.

"Yay, us," Allison said, grinning…then looked out at the water.

CHAPTER FOURTEEN

SEAN LOOKED AROUND his apartment. He hadn't spent more than five minutes there in the past forty-eight hours, it seemed.... Already, Allison's place was feeling more like home. Probably because he felt at home wherever Allison was, he thought.

Man, he was turning into a sentimental idiot.

He glanced at his answering machine. It blinked with three messages. He felt a little knot of tension in his stomach. He got the feeling he knew what at least one of those messages was.

Just suck it up and get it over with.

He pressed play. The first message was from Ryan.

"Sean! Don't forget you're on *cerveza* patrol with me. Two cases of Corona—I'll pick up the keg. See you at Gabe and Charlotte's house."

Sean smiled at that one. He'd already given Allison directions to the annual party, and she said she'd be there after a brief command performance at her parents' place. He felt torn about that one...about the fact that she hadn't invited him, and didn't seem to even think of it.

The next message was a bit more painful—from Oz. "Listen," Oz's voice said, crackling with static, "about yesterday. That was bad. It wasn't how I meant for you to leave at all. Do me a favor—could you call me, or stop by my house, or something? Thanks."

Sean deleted that message with a tinge of remorse. It hadn't ended the way he'd hoped, either. Still, he wasn't sure what reopening those wounds was going to do to help matters any.

Finally, the third message. Sean took a deep breath as he recognized the voice.

"Sean? Hey, it's Steve, over at Lone Shark."

Sean immediately tensed. This. This was the one he was waiting for.

So just how badly did I botch that interview?

"I know that the interview didn't go all that well. Frankly, I'm just being honest here, but I had serious doubts about whether or not you could make it as one of our sales reps."

Braced for bad news or not, Sean still winced at that statement. He had really screwed that one up royally.

"But Gabe felt really strongly about you as a candidate," Steve persisted.

Sean's feelings of discomfort tripled. Oh, *man,* if he was going to get a pity job offer just because Gabe was twisting this guy's arm, he was going to call Gabe up and call the whole thing off right here. He never should've taken that interview.

"So I wound up talking to several of the surf-shop owners in the Los Angeles area," Steve continued. "Turns out you're a bit of a legend, even outside of the South Bay. People say you could've turned pro and hit the tournament-surfing circuit if you'd wanted to. And even though nobody's surprised that Tubes is going under, all of them said that it would've gone under years ago if it weren't for you."

Sean stood next to the counter, his jaw gone slack at that little tidbit.

"Nobody knows gear or surfing like you. They would all trust you in a heartbeat," Steve said, and his prerecorded voice laughed. "I wouldn't be surprised if you got a few other job offers this week, actually."

Now Sean was officially gobsmacked.

"So, before I get beaten to the punch, I'd like to officially extend an offer—forget that trial period. We'd like you to come work here at Lone Shark immediately. Just give me a call." He left his number, but Sean was still too stunned to jot it down. "I know it's New Year's Eve and all, but that number's my cell, and I'll answer it all day. Looking forward to hearing from you."

With that, Sean's message machine shut off with a click.

Feeling a little shaky, Sean sat down on the futon.

He'd been bracing himself for a change-of-heart speech from Steve, he realized. Gabe would probably have some choice words about his lack of self-esteem, or believing in himself, or some similar attaboy locker room–type pep talk. But it occurred to Sean that his nerves, and his disbelief, had nothing to do with any of that.

I don't want the job.

He'd done everything he could to sabotage it, and get himself out without disappointing Gabe. He'd thought he could go through with it if he had to—he thought it was the only way he could get into a relationship with Allison, by settling his life down. But he *had* Allison now. There wasn't any other reason to go on with the charade.

So now he knew what he felt.

The only question was, what did he do next?

ALLISON GLANCED at her watch. Eleven o'clock. It was late, especially for her parents, who had been surrounded by people all night long. Still, she knew her presence here was a command performance—she had to be here because her parents had asked to speak to her.

She felt a tap on her shoulder and turned around.

"Haven't gotten your turn yet, huh?"

It was her older brother. She smiled weakly, still wary from her last meeting with Rod. "You just getting here?"

"Just left the office," he said with a shrug. "And, no, that's not one-upmanship... We had a New Year's party to celebrate rolling out the new product line, that's all."

Her grin was bitter. "Gotta give the troops something, huh?"

He looked at her quizzically. "I don't follow."

"Nothing. Glad to hear you were getting your groove on with your direct reports." She glanced at her watch again.

If her parents didn't acknowledge her in the next fifteen minutes, she was leaving. That would give her about forty-five minutes to get to Sean. And once she got to him, she'd have a few seconds to do something she'd never done in her life.

She was going to ring in the new year by kissing her boyfriend. She was going to kiss him from one year straight into the other...and then some.

She smiled just thinking about it, and checked her watch one more time, in case her rather prurient daydream had lasted, say, fifteen minutes.

"You've got another party you're going to, I take it," Rod said, his voice dry and sarcastic. "Either that, or maybe Beth got you a watch for Christmas, too, that I didn't know about, and you're just admiring it."

She shrugged. "Mom and Dad said that they wanted to talk to me, and I really did want to talk to them, but they're busy tonight, so I may have to table it," she said with exaggerated casualness. As if being put on hold by them didn't hurt. As if the thought of walking out despite the fact that they'd asked for her wasn't pulling a coup of some sort.

Rod's eyebrows jumped up toward his hairline. "They'll talk to you, of course. They want to talk to you."

"How do you know…hey!" she protested as he grabbed her by the elbow and started walking toward their father, who was surrounded by a knot of his business cronies.

"So I think we're not going to be able to wait until the second quarter to start pursuing that opportunity…. Oh, hi, Rod," he said, blinking as Rod tapped him on the shoulder. "You all remember my son and my daughter, don't you?"

Allison watched as her brother sent a business-friendly smile to the group, then whispered something in his father's ear. Her father's gaze then shot to her, and she felt uncomfortable for no good reason. Glanced at her watch: 11:05.

Should've left when I had the chance.

"I need to take care of something—family related, you understand," her father said, excusing himself from his circle. Then he and Rod both flanked her, practically frog-marching her to her mother's study.

Oh, hell. This is not going to be good.

Of course, she had good news, but she got the feeling that unless she mentioned she was promoted to queen of the Netherlands or CEO of the biggest company in the world, she wasn't going to be getting a lot of traction tonight.

Damn it! She was going to get kissed at midnight tonight or somebody was damn well going to pay for it.

Her mother was talking to her editor and her agent.

"So I've got some new ideas for my next book project," her mother was saying, until she was startled by Allison's father and brother, and the sudden appearance of her taken-prisoner daughter. "What is it, dear? Is something wrong?"

"Allison was going to leave," her father said, and though he was wearing a polite smile for the sake of her mother's professional guests, he looked disturbed just saying it aloud.

"But we need to talk to her!" her mother said, sending a surprised glance over at Allison.

"I know, Mom, but you guys have been so busy," Allison said, feeling all of twelve years old and being forced to interrupt one of her parents' fancy dinner parties. She hated that feeling. "Also, I have another party I need to go to." And that need was building with every passing minute.

"You know this is important, or we wouldn't have asked you," her mother said, her tone faintly reproving.

"But not so important that you couldn't stop and talk to me when I first got here," Allison said…and then shut her mouth as the shock of her own words hit her.

Allison's mother reddened, and she turned to her guests, who were already getting up of their own accord. "Won't you excuse us?"

They were already whispering murmured assurances even as they beat their feet toward the door, which Rod shut behind them.

"Allison, I am shocked," her mother said without preamble.

"I know, that was rude and I'm sorry," Allison said. "But you guys did keep me waiting for over three hours."

"That was business," her father chided, his voice sharp.

She stood up to her full five foot one inch. "And I'm your daughter," she said in a voice of challenge.

If Rod's eyes widened much more, she thought, they'd pop right out of his head.

"If it were that vital, you could've talked to me over the phone, and if you can keep me waiting while you talk business, then it's not life threatening. We could've discussed it tomorrow over lunch or something," Allison said, her voice only very barely conciliatory.

Her parents stared at her. Then, to her surprise, they both turned as one to Rod.

"You're right," her mother said to Rod, not even glancing at Allison. "I wouldn't have believed it, but she's changed completely."

"What?" Allison said, floored.

"How long have you been seeing this young man?" her father demanded.

She blinked. "This? This is what you have to talk to me about? *Sean?*"

She would've laughed if she weren't so incredibly mad.

"Rod mentioned that you were seeing a surfer," her mother said, standing up and crossing her arms. "You're a grown woman, obviously, and ordinarily we wouldn't want to intrude on your life, but we have noticed that you've been, well, not yourself. We noticed it at Christmas, but we didn't want to say anything until we'd gathered more data."

"And now that you've got one week's worth of observations, Mom? What's the conclusion?"

"Well, you've never been quite this cross before," her mother replied tartly. "You don't seem to care about your work anymore, you're curt to your family. Rod said you practically bit his head off...."

She looked at Rod. "You always were a nark," she said.

His answering glare and shrug really did transform them, her back to twelve, him to fifteen. "I just saw that you were losing it. You're obviously not interested in what I think, but I thought you'd listen to Mom and Dad. Although you didn't seem this far gone the other day."

"What is supposed to be wrong with me, anyway?" Allison's voice went up belligerently. To her shock, it actually felt good to yell. To be bitchy. Hell, it was the holidays. She had a perfect right to let loose, didn't she?

She took a deep breath. No, she didn't. She wasn't that person.

"I'm sorry," she said, and this time, she meant it. "But this doesn't have to do with Sean. I care a great deal about him," she said, and her voice trembled a little. She took a deep breath, and found herself saying, "I may even love him. I don't know yet. But I do know one thing...I love who I am when I'm with him. And I like myself a whole lot better than I did earlier this year."

Her mother looked puzzled, and not surprisingly, she picked up a pad of paper and a pen. It was how her mother coped with things, Allison remembered. "The two of you are from completely different worlds," she finally said in a "be reasonable" voice. "There's no way he can possibly understand..."

Her father walked over to the cut-crystal decanter of Hennessy and poured himself a drink. Ah, yes. Her father's coping method jumping to the fore. "This makes absolutely no sense," he said, taking a long swallow and then coughing slightly, the experienced drinker's cough. "How do you know this isn't some surf bum, out for what he can get? If he's just using you? You'll get all wrapped up with him and next thing you know, that career of yours is in the toilet with these shenanigans!"

"I'll have you know, my career is going just fine, thanks," Allison said, suppressing the desire to stick her tongue out at Rod. Or, say, key his car. "In fact, if you guys hadn't been so bent on shining a light in my eyes and asking me how my sex life was ruining my social skills, I could've told you—I got promoted. We landed the account. You're looking at one of the youngest account supervisors at our ad agency, working on one of the largest accounts we've ever landed." Now she crossed her arms. "So yay, me."

"Well, we're proud of you, of course, but do you really think you're in any position to handle this," her mother asked, her voice full of concern, "in your current state?"

Allison stared at her, slack-jawed. "You're kidding me, right? You have to be kidding me!"

Her father looked at her. "Don't take that tone with your mother!"

"I just told you I got promoted. So there aren't really any *concerns* if that's what you're really worried about," Allison yelled. Yes, yelled. "And you don't have any right to all but ignore me and then take the time to call me up on the carpet for something that is absolutely none of your business. That goes for you, too, Rod," she said tightly, turning.

"Where do you think you're going!" her father roared.

"I could be polite and say I'm going to another party," she said over her shoulder, "but I know what you'd be thinking.

You think I'm rushing off to go sleep with my new boyfriend, the one that's apparently making me psychotic and is somehow going to be responsible for the downfall of western civilization in general and our family in particular. And you know what? *You'd be right!*"

It was about then that she realized her voice was echoing in her parents' cathedral-ceiling living room…for the edification of their various guests.

She felt the blush boil in her cheeks as she cleared her throat. "Um, happy New Year, everybody," she said.

And then fled.

All I can say is, this kiss had better be worth it.

"SO WHERE'S YOUR GIRL?" Gabe asked.

Sean frowned. "She was supposed to go to her parents'…some family thing," he said, feeling a little uneasy. Here it was, quarter to midnight, and she still wasn't there.

He hoped nothing had gone wrong. He hadn't talked to her since she'd gone off to work this morning, and he knew that it was going to be a stressful day.

"Are you okay?" Gabe asked. "I swear, for a guy who's supposedly Mr. Zen Surfer, you're starting to look pretty freaked out."

Sean sighed.

"It's the new job, isn't it?" Now Sean looked over at him and felt his stomach drop. "Heard, huh?"

"I think Steve wanted to make sure that I knew," Gabe said. "He's a good kid, but kind of a go-getter. Have you decided when you're going to start? Is that part of what's got you so spun out?"

Sean glanced around. Gabe and Charlotte's house was

milling with people, all having a good time, dancing, talking, laughing, listening to music. It was just the kind of scene he loved, with people he loved.

But this was going to be bad.

"Can't hear myself think in here," Sean said. "Come on."

He and Gabe walked out to the front porch of Gabe's house, a large, three-story Victorian. He could hear the muted sounds of the party inside, but underneath that, he could hear the sounds of the surf, some three blocks away, faint but reassuring.

"Gabe…" he started slowly. "You know, I…"

"Oh, no." Gabe shook his head in disbelief. "You're turning the job down."

This was the problem with having friends who'd known you since junior high. They could practically read your mind. "Yeah. I haven't called Steve yet, but that's the plan."

Gabe crossed his arms, leaning against the house. "Why?"

"The surf shop…"

"The surf shop's over, Sean." Gabe's voice was sharp with impatience. "I know how much it meant to you, and I know you'll need time to get over it. But come on, buddy…you've got to move on. You've got to get a job, right? You've got to pay your rent—you've got to make sure you're taken care of!"

"I'm not a complete idiot," Sean said, letting a little anger edge his own voice. "But I know that I'm not going to be happy working sales…not that way, don't get started. What do I care if a bunch of stores order ten more units of winter suits or…or women's hoodies, for God's sake? It's not just the store, damn it. I love teaching surfing, I love helping all the neighborhood kids get started. It's…I don't know. Being a part of the community. It's like being a part of you guys, you know? Grown men with a goofy surf-crew name. But we have a hell of a good time, and we're always there for each other."

Gabe smiled a little at that one. "Yeah. Guess we do."

"I know the surf shop's closing—I can't stop that." Sean's voice was pleading. "But I just…I can't just say 'forget it' and move on to a desk job that, as much as I believe in your products and know you guys mean well, I will be miserable in. I'll *hate* it, Gabe."

Gabe sighed heavily. "So…what's your option? What are you going to do instead?"

Sean shrugged. "Haven't figured that part out yet. But I know something will turn up." He laughed, with very little humor. "Apparently other surf shops out there are hiring."

"Sean," Gabe said, "I know it's your life. But you're thirty-one. You could be doing so much more with your life."

"I could," Sean said. "But it's my choice. I'd rather do something I love than make tons of money doing something I hate."

Gabe stared at him. Then he nodded, putting a hand out to give Sean a one-armed hug. "You know I'm just looking out for you, man."

"I appreciate that." And the thing was, he really did. He knew that Gabe wasn't just busting his chops.

"So. Does that lady of yours know about your decision?"

"Today was going to be kind of a tough day for her," Sean said. "I thought I'd see how that went first, before I told her."

Now Gabe smirked. "Okay…gotta call you a big chicken on that one."

Sean was surprised into a laugh. "I'm a little nervous, but no kidding—today was going to be difficult. Her job…it's been making her nuts. I get the feeling her family's probably the reason why," Sean said. "She's got issues. My stuff is bush league, comparatively speaking. So I'll let her process what she needs to tonight, and then I'll tell her when she's feeling a little better."

"Do you think it'll bother her?"

Sean paused before answering that one. It was something else he'd been worrying about, a little bit, since he made the decision to turn down the job offer. He wanted to be settled, to know that he had a job and a place to live, before he got seriously involved with Allison. But they'd sort of jumped the gun on those plans, and now he realized that all his talk of needing to be settled and have his life in order was just that, talk.

Not a lot in his life made sense right now, but he knew one thing. His life made a lot more sense with her in it. And considering all her recent experiences with hating her job, with the stress around her family…he had to think that she would understand.

He prayed that she would understand.

"Come on in, have a beer," Gabe said. "I'll stay off your back until you ask for help, I promise."

"No worries," Sean said, wishing that were true. "I think I'm going to just hang out here in the quiet for a few minutes."

"You got it." Gabe retreated back into the house, leaving Sean alone with the dark and the sounds of the ocean at night.

She has to understand.

CHAPTER FIFTEEN

ALLISON WOKE UP with Sean's arm around her, feeling a little cramped and a little sore. Not from the night's activities…although she did feel pleasantly exercised, she remembered with a grin. No, the sore muscles were from sleeping on Sean's futon. She was spoiled by her own mattress at home.

"Next time, we sleep at my place," she said in a soft voice, turning over and kissing him on the chin.

"Like the sound of that," he said, blinking like an owl. "Good morning, beautiful."

"Morning," she said, feeling happy, peaceful. Relieved, now that the whole thing was behind her.

"What did you feel like doing today?"

"Surfing," she said. "And you."

"I think we can put both of those on the agenda," he answered with a chuckle, nuzzling her neck. "I need to look at the tides, though."

"Whatever the tides are like, I want to get in as much surfing as I possibly can," she said. "And whenever I can't surf, I want to spend as much time as possible with you. If that's all right."

He looked at her, those blue eyes of his dreamy—but wary. "So…are we going to talk at all?" he asked.

She remembered her edict from last night, after talking to

her parents. In the light of a new year, it seemed sort of moot, but she still sighed. "Sure."

"Bad news, huh?" he said, stroking her back consolingly.

"Not exactly," she said. "Actually…it's good news. We got the account."

He blinked, smiling with obvious surprise. "Hell. That doesn't sound that bad at all. Were you upset because you weren't involved?" He sounded puzzled but still sympathetic. "I mean, because your boss cut you out, and all."

"No. Actually, the other two account execs had meltdowns, and I wound up pinch hitting," she said slowly.

Sean waited. Obviously things weren't computing, and she couldn't blame him for not following. It still seemed pretty disjointed and hard to believe for her. "So…but they wouldn't give you what you wanted because they were afraid *you'd* melt down, right?"

"No," she said. "Actually…actually, I got promoted."

He sat straight up. "Really? That's great, then!" His smile was like the sun, and she wondered why she'd ever been worried in the first place. Of course he'd be supportive—why wouldn't he be? "So you got everything you wanted. That's wonderful, Ally." He paused. "I guess…your parents didn't react quite the way you wanted?"

Not about that, she thought. "I think they're proud of me. They said they were proud of me."

He sat silent for a minute. "Okay, I'm an idiot. I still don't get it. Why, exactly, were you so upset?"

She laughed ruefully. "Well…well." She swallowed, then shrugged. "They were a little concerned. About you."

The smile slipped off his face, and she immediately bit her tongue. "I'm sorry," she said immediately.

"Why...no. I bet I don't want to know what their problem with me is," he said with a ragged little sigh. After a second, his jaw clenched. "No, I guess I do. Considering that they've never met me and you and I have only started having this relationship, exactly what sort of problem would they have with me?"

"That's the thing," she said, hoping to repair the damage immediately. "They don't know you. They're just concerned that I..."

She tried to figure out how to word it, and his frown deepened. "That you what?" he prompted.

"That, after all this hard work," she said thoughtfully, "I'm going to get sidetracked. That's all. That I'm going to let my career slide."

Now he was getting that Zen-surfer look...one that looked both concerned and deep. "Ally, do they know what your career was doing to you?"

"It wasn't that bad," she demurred.

Now he blinked. "Not that bad. Do you remember how you met me?"

"Sure I do," she said, laughing to try to lessen the tension that was increasing with every passing second. What had happened to surfers being laid-back? "I was coercing you into teaching me how to surf."

"And it only took a trip to the ER to get you there," he said softly. "Don't suppose they know about that."

She stiffened, and pulled imperceptibly away from him. "Not in so many words, anyway. But they do know that work was stressing me out."

"Well, as long as we're on that subject," he said, and he pulled away a little, too. "What about this promotion of yours? How's that going to work? I mean, I know it was tough to get. Does this mean that the hard part's over?"

She wanted to say yes, but she knew she'd be lying. What's worse, even after this short period of time, she got the feeling he'd know she was lying, too. "It's a new account, Sean," she said, hating how conciliatory her voice was sounding. "It'll just be for a while. I mean, it'll just be stressful for a while. Then it'll get better."

"Really?" Now his voice took on an edge she'd never heard before. "I'm sorry, but what in the entire history of this career of yours convinces you that at some point, it's going to actually *get better?*"

She blinked at him, pulling the sheet around herself as some sort of protection. "Why are you so angry?" she said. "This isn't like you."

"I thought…I don't know what I thought."

"You knew what I was like when you got involved with me," she said slowly, thinking reluctantly of her parents' words. *The two of you are from completely different worlds. There's no way he'll possibly understand.*

The problem was, he always had understood, in the past. What had changed?

"I know what you're like, Allison, and I…I care about you for who you are," he said, and his voice was slow and careful, too, and a distinct counterpoint to the flames in his eyes. "But I thought that you were figuring it out."

"Figuring…what out, exactly?"

"You told off your boss," he said. "You stood up for yourself. You drew boundaries. You decided that you wanted your life back," he declared, his voice shaking with passion.

"So after all that, you get the promotion and you're going to keep running yourself into the ground?"

"But things are different now," she assured him.

"How?" he said with obvious frustration.

Because now I have you!

She shook her head. Love, a man, was never the answer. Hadn't her parents all but…

No. She wasn't dragging their arguments into this.

"Because now I know how to control my stressors and my responses," she said. "I haven't had a panic attack since. It was rough going, but I've finally learned how to manage my anxiety. I just have to think of the ocean…or think of you."

"So, you're going to make sure you have time to spend with me, and time to do stuff you love," he said, and he sounded approving. "You're still keeping boundaries."

"Pretty much," she said, biting her lip quickly.

His gaze bore into her like a power drill, and she sighed.

"Sean, the first few months are going to be tough," she admitted. "I mean, it's going to mean some juggling, timewise, and I don't know how much I'm going to be able to surf. That's why I wanted to do as much as I can this weekend."

"With surfing…and with me." The bitterness in his voice was overwhelming. "So, you'll work until you hit the breaking point, and then you'll grab your board or grab your boyfriend until the feeling passes, is that it?"

She gasped, and actually stood up, her heart pounding. "You can't be serious with this. What, did I stumble into a daytime soap opera and not realize it? Is this *As the Surf Turns* or something?"

"You tell me, Allison," he said, standing up, as well. He

didn't bother with a sheet, though, so she was momentarily sidetracked by the cut of his swimmer's physique. His eyes were raging with pain and anger, and his jaw could've been carved out of marble. He looked angrier than she'd ever seen him. "You tell me. Where, exactly, do I stand in this picture of yours? Because when I'm in a relationship, I make it first priority. And I don't make my job my life."

"You're going to be busy, too, aren't you?" She tried a new tack. "I know you don't think that the job is that important, but you're going to be starting that new job with your friend's company. There's going to be a learning curve with that. Sure, it won't be as stressful because you won't let it be, but I know you. You love what you do. I don't see you just slacking off because you've got a girlfriend."

"If the girlfriend is you," he said, and the intensity in his eyes almost drove her to her knees, "then there's no way I put clocking in before you. No way in hell."

She felt small. He didn't understand. He absolutely didn't understand. "So, what do you want me to do, Sean? Do you want me to quit, just so I can be your girlfriend? Is that it?" *Please, please don't say that!*

"Of course it isn't," he said. "Give me a little credit."

"Well, I just don't see where the problem is!"

"I'm not saying you have to put me before your job," he said. "What I'm saying is...you have to put *you* before your job, damn it. I'm not going to put everything on hold just so I can watch the woman I'm falling in love with self-destruct!"

"Aren't we being just a little—"

"No," he said, stepping up to her and taking her into his arms. "No, we're *not*. And the scary thing here is, I see it, and you don't."

"So what would you do?" she said. "You're taking a job you don't like. Sacrifices have to be made sometimes. That's just part of life."

He sighed. "I didn't take the job, Allison."

For a second, nothing computed. "You…didn't?"

"They offered it to me," he said, his voice heavy. "But I just couldn't. It wasn't *right.*"

"So…how are you going to live?" she found herself asking. The words jumped out of her mouth before she could stop herself.

"I'll have to figure it out, and fairly soon," he said. "But I know that I will."

She stood silent for a second, digesting that fact.

Surf bum. Out for what he can get. Just using you.

And here he was, accusing her of just using him.

She didn't like the way this was going. Not at all.

"You're going to have to figure out something," she repeated.

"I know that," Sean said, and he was the one who released her, running his hands through his hair and looking stressed. "I'm not a complete loser, Allison. Although I'll bet you anything that's what your parents were trying to point out."

It had come full circle. It was so far from how they'd started, but they were back at each other's throats… She, the type-A overachiever. He, the stereotypical surf bum.

How in the world can this work?

"What are you thinking?" Sean said. "I can see it in your eyes, on your face. What's wrong?"

"Can't you tell?" She laughed a little, only it sounded more like a low sob. "I thought… I didn't know how this was going to work out, but I really, really wanted it to. And all that's hitting me this morning is, we don't really know each other at all. We're from completely different worlds. There's just no way that this can work, is there?"

Now Sean looked sad. "I…I don't know."

She was a problem solver. She was dedicated. When she had wanted something, absolutely nothing had stopped her.

Until now.

She got up, got dressed. Looked at him.

"Where are you going?" he said, sitting on the edge of the bed with the comforter around him.

"Home," she said. "I've got a full week coming up."

"We should talk about this," he said, even though he still looked troubled.

"What else is there to say?" She really wanted to know, but he didn't seem to have an answer to that.

"Allison…we should talk."

"Do you think we can work it out?"

"I told you, I don't know."

And that was the deciding factor. She grabbed her purse. She could problem solve, she could fight, she could believe in love overcoming all the odds. But here he was, a man who waited for answers to come to him. Who waited for things to be handed to him. Who wanted her to be like that.

I can believe in love, she thought.

But I can't believe in it enough for the two of us.

SEAN WAS STILL MULLING over the way Allison left one week later. It wasn't even as if they'd broken up, he supposed—you had to be actually in a relationship to break up, didn't you?

Don't kid yourself. You were definitely in a relationship. It might've been brief, it might have been confusing, but it was definitely a relationship. One of the most intense he'd ever been in, if it came to that.

Which made him wonder how long it would take to get over her.

He was out at the beach. He had been out here a lot, when he wasn't on the phone with surf shops. He'd been given several offers, and even though he knew that the pay they were offering was at the high end of the scale, as far as retail jobs went, he still couldn't help feeling dissatisfied. He knew several of the owners, and even liked many of them. But Tubes had been special, on several levels.

So not only had he turned down a good-paying job because he loved working for a surf shop, it couldn't be just any surf shop.

Have you ever considered the fact that maybe you're a loser who just doesn't want to work, period?

He dove out into the waves, letting the cold water numb him temporarily from the sting of that thought. It wasn't what Allison said, but he'd read between the lines. He'd realized that much, at least.

Probably because, on some level, he agreed with her.

He paddled out half a mile, before turning back to catch a few waves. He caught a few big ones in on the way to shore. As he got closer, he saw people…some surfers, guys he knew. He waved, and they nodded companionably.

"Heard Tubes closed," one of the guys, Edgar, said without a greeting. "That true?"

"Yeah," Sean said, feeling the melancholy hit him.

One of the other surfers, Daniel, shook his head. "That sucks. That was one of the last good surf shops in the South Bay, you know?"

There was a general muttering of assent at that remark. Sean felt a little better—he wasn't getting overly sentimental about the store. Other people recognized it was special.

"What I want to know is," Edgar continued as Daniel grabbed a wave and sped off, "how is it some of these slick, weak, lame stores stay in business when a store like Tubes can go under? It just isn't fair."

Sean didn't have an answer to that. Strangely enough, the guy to his right, a surly, relatively new surfer named Tom, did have an answer.

"It's easy," Tom said in his slight British accent. "Tubes didn't want it badly enough."

Sean immediately took offense. "The guy, the owner? He was having some money trouble. And he wasn't a businessman." He shot Tom a challenging look. "So it's easy to say he didn't want it. Even guys with MBAs can have businesses that fail."

"Whoa, whoa, easy," Tom said, holding a hand up. His scowl was still present, though. "Wasn't trying to insult your friend."

"So what were you saying?"

"I'm just saying—plenty of people with no business experience whatsoever become big successes. It's not just luck, either. It's just they want it more. If you want something badly enough, you figure out a way to get it."

Sean now had a matching scowl. He wanted to beat the guy up. What did he know? He didn't understand anything. This wasn't one of those "positive attitude" nonsense solutions. He might feel like a loser, but he knew that much.

"Listen, sorry I said anything," Tom said, even though from his expression, apology seemed like the furthest thing from his mind. "But look at me. Two years ago, I was just a disgruntled Welshman who was freezing his ass off, hating his job. Now…well, look at me." For the first time since Sean had seen the guy, he broke into a smile. "People say it's freezing when it gets down to sixty degrees, and my office stares out on the ocean. I'm not saying it was easy. I'm just saying…you want it badly enough, you can get it done."

With that, he signaled, grabbing the next wave and riding clumsily but happily down the shore, leaving Sean surprised, disgruntled…and determined.

TWO WEEKS AFTER the fateful New Year's Eve presentation to Kibble Tidbits, Allison sat at her desk. She'd been working late and coming in early, nothing really new there. She wasn't having anxiety attacks anymore, but she was continually exhausted. She was more than exhausted, if that was possible. She was having some trouble sleeping. She was running herself into the ground.

On the plus side, she was hardly thinking about Sean at all.

Oh, that is such a lie.

Gary knocked on her door frame. "I'm all packed up," he said, taking off his glasses and wiping them on the edge of his shirt. "I can't thank you enough, Allison."

She grinned, feeling at least an infinitesimal relief. She'd managed to get one thing done in the limbo since they started waiting for the account. Gary's promotion had gone through. "You deserved it," she said. "Do you have your cubicle all set up?"

He nodded. "And they've given me one of our accounts to focus on anyway, one you had me helping you out with, so I should be hitting the ground running." He shifted his weight from foot to foot. "I'm just sorry that this leaves you in the lurch, without an assistant."

"I'll hire somebody. We'll post the position any day now." She stood up, and gave him a hug, which surprised both of them. "Good luck, Gary. You deserve it."

He looked as if his eyes were misting. "Gotta go," he said, and fled for his new cubicle, almost knocking into Frank, who was headed Allison's way. He didn't look amused by the near run-in. In fact, he looked angry, which was unusual since he'd been in a jovial mood for the past two weeks—something of a record for her high-strung and often angry supervisor.

"Whoa. What happened to you?" she asked when he swept into her office.

"Shut the door," he said instead, and she immediately felt the usual sensation—her stomach clenching, her temperature rising.

I am sick of feeling this wave.

"What happened, Frank?" she repeated, sitting down at her desk and forcing herself to focus.

"The account. The damn account," he bit out.

"We didn't get it," she said, feeling numb. No, not numb. *Relieved.*

"They're trying to lowball us. Can you believe it?" he asked. "They said it's a tie between us and McMurtan and Lowe! They want us to come up with a tiebreaker…and of course they want us to sweeten the deal with tons of extras and…"

He kept on talking, and this time, she barely heard him. Sean had told her that she had to take care of herself. The relief that she'd felt at the idea of the account going away was acute. She had never thought of what her life would be like if she *didn't* get the account. What would happen if they lost?

Her parents would be disappointed. They were finally starting to respect her. Her reputation would probably take a beating here at Flashpoint, and she'd have to take a different job at another company if she even hoped to have a stab at the big promotion, which would mean more hours, yet again, and more proving herself.

Or would it?

"Allison, are you even listening to me?" Frank snapped. "Of all the times for you to have one of your little episodes, this is the worst. So *focus,* damn it!"

She stared at him. "Excuse me?"

A new emotion started to well up in her, one that had nothing to do with fear or anxiety.

She was suddenly and overwhelmingly well and truly past this.

Something must've shown on her face, because for the first time, she saw Frank surprised…and hesitant. "I just mean I need you to stay focused on this," he half muttered.

"If I recall correctly, I was the only one who did focus on this. When I was gone, people were running around screaming in a state of mass hysteria," she said, her voice shaking with the rage she was feeling. "So now you're saying that because we're in the lurch, I need to snap out of it? Because you need me to?"

"It's important to the company—"

"When, exactly, has this company ever been concerned about me?"

He blinked at that statement.

Sean might be a lot of things, but he hadn't given her an ultimatum because he wanted to see her fail, she realized immediately. Even if she wasn't going to be with him, he cared about her. Her. Her health, her well-being. Herself.

It was about time that she cared about herself, she thought.

"You can handle the account on your own," she said firmly. "I'm leaving."

Now Frank got his mental footing, and stood up, starting his blustery windup. "What, are you going to go surfing again? I've been pretty tolerant up to this point, Allison, and yeah, I could've probably handled it better, but how many times do I have to tell you how important this account is? We can't just blow it off because you're having some kind of personal crisis. Go to the doctor, get some pills or something, and then I swear, I'll give you a week's vacation when the deal's sealed. How about that?"

"A whole week?" Like he was conferring some kind of honor on her. The irony of it actually made her smile.

He smiled back, misinterpreting. "Well, for you, sure. It'll take at least a week for the initial paperwork to come over anyway, and you wouldn't start working the account for another week on top of that."

"I quit," she said, still smiling.

"It might be a month before we...what?" he said as her words finally sank in. "You're *quitting?*"

"Yup," she said, grabbing her bag. "Right now, as a matter of fact."

"You can't do this to me!"

"I'm not doing this 'to' anyone," she said reasonably, feeling her heart beat fast but her stomach relax. "I'm doing this 'for' me, Frank."

"You're throwing away your career. You know this," Frank threatened.

"It'll be worth it."

"Think this through," he insisted. "What could possibly be worth throwing away everything you've worked so hard for? Huh?"

She paused. "I am."

With that, she walked out the door, into the sunshine.

CHAPTER SIXTEEN

ALLISON STOOD OUT in the surf, staring at it for a second. School was back in session, so her boys, the "otters," were nowhere to be seen. There were a few other surfers out there, men and women, from what she could see. They nodded at her. She nodded back, feeling completely at home.

No reason why she shouldn't, she thought. After all, she was a surfer now.

She paddled out. She'd been practicing and the bracing cold still hit her, but she could enjoy it now. Besides, ever since she'd broken up with Sean, she'd gotten used to a sort of cool numbness. With the stress of the job out of the way, she felt a sort of dead serenity. That probably wasn't the best term to use, but it was how she felt.

She went out past the immediate crashing surf into the swells. The sounds of the ocean, the music of it, enveloped her.

Despite feeling miserable whenever she thought of Sean, she had to say that this was the most peace she had felt in a really long time.

She had savings put away…she was too organized not to. And for the first time in her life, she was not worried about what was going to happen next.

She saw the swell coming, paddled out to catch it, and stood. The only thing on her mind was her equilibrium. In that moment, stretched out between the impossible blue of the Southern Cal sky and the sandy blue-green of the Pacific, all she thought about was the ride.

She was, strangely, perfectly content.

It was only when she was off the board—in her now too-empty town house, say, or driving her car—that she found herself thinking upsetting thoughts. And they were almost always about Sean.

She paddled back out, caught another couple of waves. She deliberately avoided staring at the sand. Partially because Sean had taught her not to look at the beach—you looked where you wanted to go, not at your board, not at your feet, not at the sand. You stared at the wave. You kept looking ahead.

For a guy who couldn't seem to look at his wave, when it came to relationships, he seemed to have really good advice.

The irony was so thick you could cut it with a knife.

She looked out on the beach, against her own admonishments…just hoping, as always, that he might be there. That he might somehow get it together, decide he wanted her back. Decide he wanted *her.*

Instead, she saw four people who looked as if they had absolutely no business on the beach at all.

As per usual, she lost her sweet spot, spilling into the water. It was a bit of a relief, actually. The darkness and silence underwater gave her a moment to balance…a moment to process the scene she had just witnessed.

That's my family out there.

She came up, took a deep breath, pushed her hair out of

her eyes. Then, slowly, methodically, she made her way back to shore.

They were staring at her warily, as if she might explode at any minute. "Allison," her mother said, her eyes entreating.

"Hi, Mom," Allison said, wringing water out of her hair. "Wow. Weird to see all of you here."

Her little sister at least had kicked off her shoes. Her brother was frowning in such a way that Alison felt sure he was regretting that he'd left his expensive Italian wingtips on. The man no doubt had sand in his shoes and his socks.

Allison grinned.

Her father grinned back a little. "We were just a touch concerned," he said with no preamble. "Claire Tilson said that you were almost always at the beach."

"I had no idea that you'd grown so close to Claire," her mother added, sounding a little…

Jealous? Allison blinked. No, that wasn't right. Her mother barely tuned in to Allison's life. That wasn't a judgment…that was just a statement of fact.

"We thought that maybe you should try a different hobby," her father said. "Surfing is too dangerous!"

"Surfing," Allison said sternly, "is probably the healthiest thing in my life right now," she said, unstrapping the Velcro band that tethered her board to her ankle. "I know you guys don't understand it, and that's okay. You don't need to. But I will ask you to respect my choices."

Her mother bit her lip, looking at Rod. Rod cleared his throat.

"You snapped, sis," he said. "We understand that."

"No, I don't think you do," Allison said. "Because if you

did, you'd realize how close each of you are to the same thing. Dad, you work, what, ninety hours a week? Mom, you're always on one promotional tour or another, or locked up in your study working on a book. Rod, your girlfriend's just about ready to leave you. And Beth…hell, you're a poster child for pre–neighborhood ax murderer."

Beth jumped up as if goosed. "That is *so* not true!"

"Okay, I'm exaggerating a little," Allison said, with a small smile. "But the fact is, we're a family of workaholics."

"That's sort of a facile generalization," her father grumped.

"Call it what you like. The bottom line is, I don't want to be that anymore. I want to have a marriage and kids. I want to have fun. I want to have a life." She took a deep breath, staring at each one in turn. "I want to *surf*."

They stared back at her, bewildered.

"I know you didn't understand what I had with Sean, either," Allison said quietly. "But he understood me. And he understood this…living, enjoying every single moment that you're given. The idea of stressing out about a stupid dog-food commercial finally stands out in sharp relief. Nothing's more important than loving people and enjoying every single moment you're given. Nothing."

Her mother walked next to her, and to Allison's surprise, gave her a small hug. "You're absolutely right, of course," she said. "You know…I think I'd like to write a book about your findings. I've considered tackling the subject of work-aholism for a few years now."

Allison sighed, shaking her head. Not that she should've expected her mom to get it, but…

"You know…I think I'd like you to help me with it," her

mother asked tentatively. "You've got a great perspective." She paused. "And...we could spend some time together."

Allison's mouth fell open as the size of her mother's olive branch suddenly became apparent to her.

"I could help with that, too, you know," Beth protested, then blushed. "Apparently, I'm on the razor's edge of a psychotic break."

"We could all help," Rod agreed, and Allison's shock redoubled when he put a companionable arm around Beth, squeezing her. "You don't corner the market on stress, you know."

"Dork," she said, hitting his shoulder. And for a moment, they seemed...close. As picture perfect as a family as dysfunctional as theirs was going to get.

Allison hugged her mother and her father, who was looking a little shell-shocked. "I'd love to help," Allison said with a broad smile.

Her father stared at the board. "You know, the guys at the office would be impressed as all hell if I learned how to surf," he mused. "Especially at my age."

She laughed. "Well, you'll need to start from scratch and take it easy."

"Could I take lessons from you?"

She thought of how Sean taught her...

"Well, I can't really teach you everything, but I can show you the basics," she offered, closing her eyes and thinking of Sean. "But I learned from the best."

Standing there, surrounded by her family, she felt some of the bruise that had haunted her heart recede, just a bit. If only for Sean, it would've been perfect.

"YOU MIGHT BE WONDERING why I called you all here today."

Sean stood in his living room, surrounded by all of his

friends, a bunch of chart pads and several cases of beer. He had no intention of drinking the beer. Still, he didn't know how long he'd be keeping everyone, so he figured better safe than sorry. They were staring at him like he'd gone out of his mind.

"What, exactly, are we talking about here, Sean?" Ryan was the first to ask.

"I didn't take the job at Lone Shark," Sean started a bit obliquely. "I thought I was going to take it. I thought it was what I was supposed to do. I mean, hell, I'm thirty-one. I need to grow up, get a real job, right?"

"It's not so much that," Charlotte protested. "It's just you're capable of so much…."

"I know that." At least, he knew that now. Thanks to Allison, and her belief in him. "But the thing is, it wasn't what I wanted to do. It might make sense—"

"And a lot more money," Mike pointed out.

"Yeah, but the thing is, I love the surf shop. I know all the surfers, of all ages, in Redondo Beach. I've sold 'em their boards. I've taught the kids. I've competed with the guys. I've made great friends. The shop isn't just someplace I go to make a living…it's been the center of my *life*."

The group assembled nodded, and Gabe sighed heavily.

"I know," Gabe said. "But be that as it may…Oz is still selling the shop. Your realization isn't going to change that."

There was a knock on the door. Since most of the Hoodlums were already assembled, he figured it was the only person missing…Jack Landor. He got the door.

It was Jack, all right, with Mrs. Tilson in tow. "You didn't tell me you were having a party," Mrs. Tilson reproved.

"Wasn't really," Sean said, pecking her cheek, gratified

when she smiled in response. “It was more of a brainstorming session than a party.”

“Hey, but now that *you're* here, Mrs. T…” Ryan added, grinning wickedly.

She shot him a look that would've frozen pond water, and Ryan looked repentant for all of about two seconds. “Brainstorming? For what?” She sat down on the couch, next to Charlotte and Bella.

“We're trying to help Sean figure out what to do with the rest of his life,” Bella said helpfully, trying to bring Mrs. T up to speed.

“No, we're not,” Sean corrected. “I know what I want to do with the rest of my life.”

“No, you know what you want in your life,” Gabe corrected. “You want to work in the surf shop, but that's not going to happen.”

“Not the way it stands now,” Sean countered.

“I don't see what you're getting at.”

Sean took a deep breath. “What I'm getting at is…I want to *buy* the surf shop.”

The sheer audacity of the idea stunned the group into silence…all except for Mrs. Tilson, who nodded with satisfaction.

“Now we're talking,” she said with relish. “It's what I thought you should do all along, my dear boy.”

“Really?” Sean gaped at her.

“Of course. You obviously love the establishment, and I have to say, from what I saw, you're obviously the one running it. So why shouldn't you buy it?”

“Uh…for one thing, I'm not exactly rich,” he pointed out.

“That's what investors are for,” Mrs. Tilson said with a

negligent shrug. "Good grief. You don't think that big businessmen purchase all their real estate in cash and their franchises on their own credit, do you?"

"You know, she has a point," Jack mused. "I've been dabbling in real estate, and getting a collective together…actually, the building itself's a great investment."

"I know that, too," Mrs. Tilson said. "I did some research."

Now the entire room stared at her.

"I'm seventy-eight and I don't exactly have a life," she said with a sort of formal asperity. "Now, kindly quit staring. I'll be more than happy to let you all in on the investment opportunity."

"I'm in," Gabe said immediately, looking at Charlotte.

"Correction. We're in," she said, putting her hand over his and smiling when he kissed her.

"Hey, I'm in, too," Jack said, his movie-star smile broad.

"We're in," Mike and Ryan said, giving each other a high five.

Sean felt the tension, the creeping fear, that had been building since the idea had crept into his head. It intensified. "I can't guarantee anything," he said, unable to bear the idea of misleading his friends. "You're all saying this now, but Oz has been having a hard time. I can't guarantee that you'll make any kind of profit. For all I know, the business will go under, and you'll all lose money. This is a huge risk."

"Yeah, I guess," Gabe said, clapping him on the shoulder. "But we believe in you."

Sean felt a lump in his throat. He hadn't believed in himself. Not until he'd met Allison, and started to think beyond what he was doing. Think about why he was doing what he was doing. Dream of something more.

Dream, in short, of a life with the most amazing woman he'd ever known.

"Okay, I'm glad we got that out of the way," he said, clearing his throat of the huskiness caused by his emotions. "On to brainstorming my second problem. I call this Operation Win Allison Back."

Charlotte, Bella and Mrs. Tilson grinned at each other. "Now we're really talking," Charlotte said, and everyone laughed.

ALLISON LOOKED DOWN at the store-opening invitation in her hand, ignoring the wave of pain that being in front of this particular building inevitably brought. It had been eight weeks since she'd been anywhere near it. Obviously, the new owners had bought a mailing list of Oz's prior customers, because the invitation was addressed to "local surfer," and the only people who knew that about her could be counted on one hand. This new store was slick, vibrant, totally revamped.

It was also no longer Tubes.

She glanced up. The familiar faded sign had been replaced with a new sign. Seventh Wave, it read, with a stylized wave design that she had to admit looked pretty sharp—not too sharp, though. It was simple and looked good. The whole place looked nice, but not too nice. It looked surf friendly.

She hated it.

On the other hand, she had a coupon in her hand, she needed a few hoodies and some surf wax…and she had to admit, she wanted to see the thing that had forced Sean out of business and into her life.

You just can't let it go, can you? After two months, you still can't let him go...

She focused on the store instead. It had a huge selection of surfboards, not just for sale, but a few hanging suspended from the ceiling. Vintage boards, she could tell. There was a good selection of wet suits for people of all shapes and sizes. There was even a large selection of surf videos and magazines. It looked gorgeous, and the prices weren't even that unreasonable.

She felt her anger ebbing as regret and sadness slowly seeped in to take its place. She saw a counter in the back, separate from the sales registers. It was dedicated to sign-ups for surf lessons, surf tours and volunteer sign-ups for surfershealing.org, a charity she'd heard of, where surfers volunteered to take autistic kids out on surfboards, with really amazing results. There was a community bulletin board. There were pictures of the local kids, including the otters, she noticed, all grinning and giving the thumbs-up to the camera. Apparently, Seventh Wave was sponsoring the junior-high surf team.

Sean would have loved this, she thought with a stab of regret. She hoped that in time, the feeling would lessen, even if it didn't seem as if it would any time soon.

"Allison," she heard a voice say behind her. "You made it."

It was Sean's friend Gabe, flanked by the whole surf crew. It was then that she realized of course that Sean would be working here.

Oh, because just what I needed right now was irony, she thought just before she was hit with a harsher one.

He's here. Now.

At which point, the only thought that was left in her head was to run away. Fast.

"I'm really sorry," she said quickly, and was already turning before she even finished her sentence. "I have to… I was just stopping in for a second… I'll come back later."

She turned, not even listening to his protests in her urgent desire to escape. Which is probably how she didn't notice another person sidling up beside her. She walked smack into his chest with a soft *oof.*

The familiar scent of him overwhelmed her, and a sense of longing rolled over her, drowning her. She looked up into his eyes, her own vision edged with tears.

"Hi, Sean," she murmured.

He smiled, then took her arm. " I've been waiting for you," he said, his voice raspy. "Come on."

They left Gabe and the Hoodlums standing there as he led her through the crowd, past the counters and through the back office. It was as she suspected. He *was* working there now. And he no longer seemed angry with her.

She felt the tiniest glimmer of hope.

Of course, the fact that he was angry with you wasn't really the problem.

He took her up a flight of stairs, and it got quieter as they got farther away from the grand-opening bash. Only moonlight illuminated the unfinished and now-empty apartment. The apartment, she realized, where he had lived when she met him. Before she crashed into his life.

She cleared her throat, needing to say something, anything. "Won't the owner mind you taking me up here?" she asked.

Then she could've kicked herself. *The man you're in love*

with gets you alone, you can barely breathe for wanting him...and you bring up getting in trouble with his boss.

No wonder she was still single.

In the dim light, she could make out Sean's look of surprise. "Don't worry," he finally said, and she could've sworn there was a small grin on his face. "The owners are pretty cool."

They stood there for a second, staring at each other.

I can't take it, Allison thought. I just can't take it.

Then, almost imperceptibly, Sean held out his arms.

She moved into his embrace with a low sob, and his arms closed around her like steel bands. "I'm sorry. I'm so sorry," she said, her voice breaking. "I didn't... I was so hung up on where I thought I had to go, and I just didn't know how to get past it. I didn't mean what I said to you. I had already fallen in love with you, and I was scared...."

"Shhh," he soothed, stroking her hair, then kissing her temple. "Baby, you weren't wrong. I was so into not changing myself that I didn't realize I was hung up on what I thought my life had to be like. I didn't look at any other option—it was just win or lose. And I wound up losing you. And that just didn't work for me."

"I quit," she said, stroking her cheek against his chest. "I was just trying to prove something to my family. To other people. It wasn't worth it."

"I was just running," Sean countered. "So I stopped running. And I bought this store."

"Hello. What?" She pulled away, her eyes wide. "You...you're the owner?"

"One of 'em, anyway," he said. "I've got investors backing me. Your godmother being one of them, bless her."

"Aunt Claire is...part owner of a surf shop," she marveled. "That's sort of perfect. In a twisted sort of way."

"So are you, you know," he said. "Perfect for me, anyway. You showed me that if I didn't want to do something that I hated, then I had to go all out going after the things that I really loved." He paused, then framed her face with his hands. "And I really love you."

Her heart filled with the joy of it. "Guess we both made the right decision, then. Because I really love you, too, Sean Gilroy." She smiled widely. "And I always get what I want."

"And I'm genuinely thankful for that," he answered, and kissed her.

Everything you love about romance...
and more!

Please turn the page for Signature Select™ Bonus Features.

surf girl SCHOOL

Author Interview:
A conversation with
CATHY YARDLEY

Are you a surf girl?

No, actually—I'm much more of a land girl. But I spent my junior high and high school days in Encinitas, California...one of the best "surf" towns in the country. I knew a lot of kids who surfed, and went to school with Rob Machado, one of the top ranked surfers in the world. To top it all off, my mom is a surf girl, or at least, she's starting to be; at age fifty-seven, she's been surfing for a year now and it's changed her life!

What's the one thing you don't have enough of?

Time! There's so much I want to do, see or write, and I think I let myself get spun thinking "how am I going to fit all this in and still sleep?"

What part of being a writer do you enjoy the most? The least?

I love coming up with story ideas, seeing how characters are going to develop and how the whole thing is going to pull together. The part I enjoy the least: actually making it work out the way I've seen it in my head.

Do you have a writing routine?
I write a couple of hours a night, and a couple of hours in the morning when I don't have a day job to go to or other things scheduled. It's not set in stone, but I do know that early afternoon is the absolute worst time for me to write. They schedule siesta there for a reason, in my opinion.

When you're not writing, what do you love to do?
I hang out with my boyfriend or my friends. I love watching movies, and listening to music is a huge passion of mine.

How do you de-stress?
I meditate, or exercise. I like walking, especially on the hiking trails around San Diego. And I have to say, spending time with Angel, my boyfriend's black Labrador, is amazing as far as reducing stress levels.

Is there one book that changed your life somehow?
There are too many books to list! I've loved reading since I was a very young child, and I've been reading at an adult level since the second grade. I can't pick just one.

What are your top five favorite books?
Strangers, by Dean Koontz
It, by Stephen King
Bet Me, by Jennifer Crusie
Last Chance Saloon, by Marian Keyes
The Moon is a Harsh Mistress,
by Robert A. Heinlein

Keep in mind...this list changes all the time!

What matters most in life?
I think accepting who you are and being happy with it, knowing what all your strong points are and recognizing (and embracing) your faults are the most important things in life.

What are you writing at the moment?
Right now, I'm finishing up my next Red Dress Ink novel, *Turning Japanese.* It's about a woman who moves from the United States to Japan, to become a manga illustrator—someone who draws the Japanese comic books that are so popular right now. I can't wait to finish it. The research has been incredibly fun!

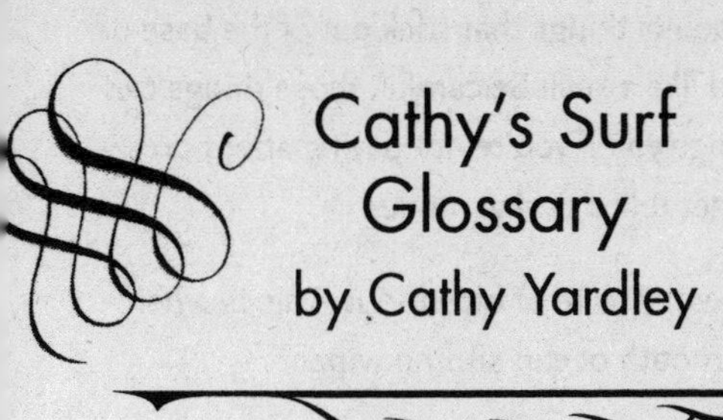

Cathy's Surf Glossary

by Cathy Yardley

Barrel: That's the tubelike part of the wave.

Barreled: To be inside the tubelike part, with the wave closing around you. As long as you're not submerged, that's a good thing. *"Man! It was beautiful. I love getting barreled."*

Blown-out: A bad surf, because the wind makes the waves all churned up and impossible to ride on.

Deck: The top surface of a surfboard.

Drop: When you head down from the top of the wave to the base...the first part of the ride.

Duck dive: You'll see this all the time. Instead of fighting against the waves (and getting pushed back a lot), a surfer will take the board and dive straight into the face of a wave, going through and coming out on the other side of the break.

Face: The unbroken surface of a wave.

Fins: The pointy things that stick out of the base of a surfboard like a keel. Be careful, those things can really damage you if you're not paying attention when you get rolled and go under.

Glassy: The opposite of blown-out. This is when there's a smooth ocean and no wind.

Gnarly: Slang for really powerful, intense or possibly scary or disgusting. A wave you're dying to take on could be gnarly. Then again, so could the nasty guy who's trying to pick you up at a local surf dive.

Grommet: Little kid. (See also *weed.*)

Haole: From the Hawaiian for *mainlander.* Basically means anybody who isn't local.

Lineup: Where the group of surfers hang, just behind the wave breaks. Generally one surfer tags in at a time, or else there's an etiquette problem (and much yelling ensues).

Localism: Surfers can be very turf-protective. (Or surf-protective, if you like!) Be wary that these hyper-defensive people don't mess with you for being a *haole.*

Pounded: What you don't want. When you get thrown from your board, pulled under by the wave and then get the crap...well, pounded out of you, between the water and the sand.

Rolled: What you also don't want. Getting rolled by a wave often results in losing a sense of which way is up.... Keep in mind, surfers can stay underwater for a long time once they're off the board.

Stoked: Thrilled, ecstatic. As in *"Man! I'm stoked!"*

Weed: Little kid, or little surfer.
(See also *grommet.*)

Wipe out: What you really, really don't want. Just because the song's cute doesn't mean the verb is.

Cathy's Guide to California
by Cathy Yardley

California has a reputation for three things: great weather, great beaches and weird people. Since I moved to California when I was eleven, I've enjoyed the first two and become the third. (Although my family argues I was weird to begin with, so I rather neatly blended right in!) I'm not a true native...there are some people here who have never left the state. I mean, ever. But I've lived up and down the Coast, and I've driven from one border to the other, so I consider the entire coastline home. If you want to hit "Cali" like a local, then here are my recommendations for the absolute must-hits in the Golden State.

A few basics:

Keep in mind, California is really more like two states: Northern Cal and Southern Cal. Northern Cal is usually typified by slightly colder and wetter weather. (Mark Twain is noted for saying, "The coldest winter I ever spent was a summer in San

Francisco.") Northern Cal is also noted for trees. For those of you who live in states with forests, that might not seem like that big a deal, but once you head south and the only trees you see are pine and eucalyptus, you'll realize what you're missing in a hurry. Northern Cal is more "granola," more environmentally conscious, more likely to have the remnants of old hippie communes. Northern Cal is old architecture built by old money. Oh, and one last thing...Northern Cal hates Southern Cal with a passion that defies reason. They think that everyone from Southern Cal is vapid, vain and superficial.

The funny thing is that Southern Cal is vaguely aware that there is life north of Bakersfield. They're just not all that interested in it! If you've seen the Rose Parade, then you've seen Southern California in its winter glory: skies that are impossibly blue, weather ranging somewhere in the seventies and glassy waves crashing against pretty beaches while palm trees wave gently in the distance. (Of course, the Rose Parade is in Pasadena, which is nowhere near the beach. But they usually like to show a beach scene at some point, just to show people who are hip deep in snow what they're missing.)

There are three main cities that I've lived in or near, and they're the three major cities of

California. Here are the tips and must-sees that I think any visit to California ought to include.

San Francisco

One of the most beautiful cities on earth, no question. I've set two books there already! First: *Don't drive if you can avoid it.* The one-way streets alone make even the most sedate drivers curse like sailors with Tourette's syndrome. Then there's the fun roller-coaster effect of forty-five-degree sloped hills. (Here's hoping you've got a good emergency brake!) San Francisco is built for public transportation. Their BART, the train system, is very simple, and their bus/subway system, the MUNI, is very comprehensive. Just ask a local at the bus stop about where you're trying to go...the people are friendly and helpful. Or take a cable car, which gets you where you want to go, lets you sightsee and is fun.

For fashion-conscious girlie-girls: For those who need a heavy dose of retail therapy, Union Square can fill your shopping prescription and then some. All the top shops, like BCBG, Max Mara, Benetton, are all found in a few square blocks. Catch a Vera Wang trunk show at Nordstrom, check out the funkier boutiques and the FCUK store. If you've got any money left over, hop over to

Bix for a martini and stare at beautiful young professionals while you crow over your fashion stash.

For granola girls: One word—*Berkeley.* This isn't actually in San Francisco, it's over on the "mainland," but it's worth seeing for those of you who always wondered about the sixties but never got to experience it. It's full of university students and hippies who never woke up enough to leave, you can get a tie-dyed *anything* and hear the yelling protestors and various "street prophets" in Sproul Plaza. The café culture in Berkeley is like intellectual turf wars: if you like foreign culture, hit the café at I-House at the top of Bancroft or Café Milano. Have you always had a thing for German Expressionists and the movie *The Big Lebowski?* Try Café Utrecht. And Thalassa is a great pool hall, right on Shattuck Ave. You can buy almost any album under the sun, new and used, at Amoeba or Rasputin Music on the infamous Telegraph Avenue, or hit Moe's, one of the oldest and most eclectic bookstores in the state. (You can see it shown briefly in the movie *The Graduate.*) Finish off your tour with a T-shirt saying you visited the "People's Republic of Berkeley."

Los Angeles

L.A. is a huge, sprawling set of mini-cities, rather than just one metropolitan area. Saying you're going to L.A. is like saying you're going to Europe—completely true, but not really specific. From the hinterlands of the Valley (of "Valley girl" slang fame) to the posh spots of Beverly Hills to the funky sphere of Santa Monica and Venice, it's the best of all possible worlds for those people who have a good chunk of cash and a short attention span.

For beach bunnies: Head West, young woman! Start at Malibu for sheer scenic value (and possible star sightings—lots of celebrities live up in the canyons), then head south to Santa Monica's pier and the Third Street Promenade (prime shopping and lots of street performers). After that is Manhattan Beach, where the wealthy buy Victorian houses to view the surf. And just south of that is Redondo, which has every kind of water sport rental imaginable.

For fashionistas: You remember the series, now experience the street: Melrose Place, baby! Bring your savings! From big-named stores to small boutiques, it's practically a guarantee that you'll go from fashion victim to almost famous in a matter of hours (if you can afford it). Be sure to hit the vintage stores for a truly L.A. look. Or you can buy one fabulous outfit and hit Sunset Boulevard, where you can get drinks at the Viper Room, hit the Whisky and head to the Hollywood sign to celebrate your star-quality experience.

San Diego

As you head south, the pace slows down from the hyper-reality of Tinseltown to a nice, leisurely stroll. San Diego is growing, but it's still one of the most tranquil and beautiful cities on the Coast, or in the country for that matter. Other than wondering what gods we've angered when it (very rarely) rains, the weather is so uniformly perfect, you'd think you were trapped in a time warp. And you'll wonder how you got so lucky.

For surfer girls: Encinitas Surfboards is a local tradition in the North County. Get yourself outfitted, and take classes from Linda Benson at her SurfHER classes at Moonlight Beach. Or get coaching and surfer-girl sexy clothes at Surf Divas in La Jolla. Just want to check out the ocean? Hit Swami's, a Leucadia landmark. It's a religious center, but it's got a garden on the cliff that's open to all. Spend some tranquil time in a thicket of hydrangea, on a stone bench overlooking wave after wave, as a babbling brook stirs up the koi in a pond behind you. You'll be surf-Zen in no time.

For coffee addicts and music fans: Welcome to a thriving coffee culture, fellow caffeine-istas! From Hill Street Café and the Motorcycle Café in Oceanside, to the Pannikin on the Pacific Coast Highway and E-Street Cybercafe in Encinitas, they've got the perfect blend anytime you need a fix. Love live local music? Lestat's in Normal Heights is a showcase for local acoustic music. If you love a louder brand of music, the Belly-Up Tavern is a legendary institution which has some decent bands every single week. If you want to bring some music home, hit Lou's Records, also on the Coast Highway. It's got one of the most amazing vinyl collections you'll ever see.

I love California...every funky nook and cranny of it. Pack your sunscreen, and grab a visit. You'll be glad you did!

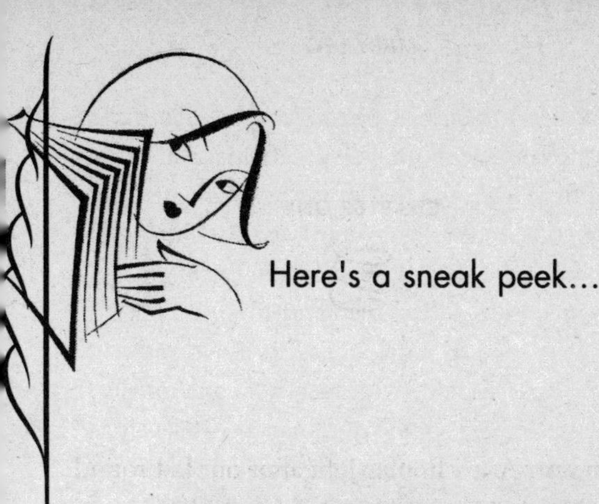

Here's a sneak peek...

BREWING UP TROUBLE

by

Mary Leo

Story #2 in the WRITE IT UP! collection

in bookstores January 2006.

When you're dating to a deadline...

It started simply enough. The editor of TESS *magazine demanded an article about dating practices for the urban set. Something fun. Something sexy. Something that the three women working on the assignment—Julie, Samantha and Abby—could research and* really *get into.*

CHAPTER ONE

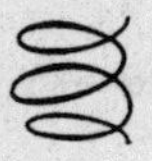

I HAD SENT ANDY home right after our last round of orgasmic bliss. We'd had three, which wasn't unusual considering he was leaving for Atlanta in the morning and I wouldn't see him again for months.

I liked to store up orgasms like squirrels stored up acorns and dig one up from my memory during those harsh winter months when the land is barren and comfort can only be had from something mechanical.

Andy had wanted to spend the night and take me out to breakfast in the morning, but I'd insisted he return to his hotel and order room service. I argued that he'd be far too busy in the morning with cab rides, valets and airport schedules to think about what kind of eggs to order.

I didn't have to argue long—he was practically asleep during the debate. Three times can really take a toll on a guy. I put the spent libido soldier in a cab around midnight and cheerfully sent him on his way.

Actually, I wasn't a morning-after kind of girl. Breakfast scared me. All that sunlight and bacon was enough to give me heart palpitations and sweaty palms, not to mention the added calories. Breakfast meant starting the day together. Planning an event for that afternoon. It was a symbol of a new beginning. A new start. An actual relationship. A from-this-moment-on type of thing. The whole scenario smacked of romance and commitment, both of which I wasn't up for, especially not with someone who lived in another state.

Not that it wouldn't be great to someday share a side of hash browns or a fruit cup with a guy I was all gaga over, but Andy just wasn't the gaga type. At least not for me. So, I sent him packing and told him to consider finding someone closer to home. I wasn't ready for the breakfast commitment.

After that, I couldn't sleep. Not really. I tried, but it just wouldn't happen, and according to the digital clock on my nightstand it was now 3:38…3:39 and I was completely wide-awake.

3:40.

Again.

But what was the big deal about sleep, anyway? Who said a person needed eight hours of the stuff? Where did that magic number come from? Was there something wrong with six hours, or in my case, none? Why was it absolutely necessary to actually sleep?

My boss, Tess, a chronically observant woman, claimed that lately I'd been looking like the walking dead. I'd made the case that I simply wasn't wearing my usual amount of makeup, but she didn't go for it. In reality, lately, that was exactly what I'd been feeling like. A flatliner, walking.

Perhaps it was the age thing that had finally taken hold. Like some midlifer in a crisis. Never

mind that I was only twenty-seven. Other girls my age had already written and produced their own plays, made an important documentary, run a couple marathons, a couple companies and discovered a cure for some exotic disease. And most of them had done it all before they took their first legal drink. I was losing and hadn't even made it to the right game.

I tossed off my blanket thinking I should get up and do something, write something or learn something to keep my edge. Keep my advantage. Keep my job before Tess gave it to the next eighteen-year-old who walked through the door with an idea.

But wait. I had ideas. Great ideas! I just couldn't think of any at that exact moment.

Coffee. I needed coffee to spin my mind back into greatness. I was stimulant deprived and my body was rebelling. Perhaps my new walking-dead look was simply the result of my caffeine intake, which I'd substantially cut down due to shaking hands and those pesky heart flutters.

Not that I had any medical reason to back off. It wasn't as if I was on the verge of some major heart crisis. At least I didn't think I was. I'd actually been trying to clean up my act. I mean, thirty was just around the proverbial corner and I had already grown a couple wrinkles that my latest peel wouldn't remove. My facial therapist blamed it on my obsession with coffee and cigarettes, so I stuck a patch to my ass and cut down the caffeine to eight hits a day.

Big mistake.

I needed coffee, a whole pot of coffee and about a thousand cigarettes. Perhaps the combination would lull me back to sleep.

Could happen.

Better still, I remembered the coffee in my orange mug behind my clock. It couldn't be that old. I'd just poured it that morning...or was that yesterday morning?

It didn't matter. Coffee's coffee and these were desperate times.

After gulping down the remainder of the French roast with slightly sour milk, and lighting up a vanilla-flavored cigarette, I decided to jump on the Web and learn Chinese or at the very least, do some research on sleep deprivation, while still in bed, of course. I was hoping that simply by remaining in bed for at least another four hours, it would somehow count toward my eight, and with the coffee and cigarettes I'd feel and look like my old self again.

I was thinking that part of my sleep deprivation research should include an in-depth interview with my friend Nico, a brilliant cosmetic chemist. The man probably knew everything there was to know on the subject of sleep problems and facial deterioration.

The vision of my deteriorating face was enough to make me go screaming into the night. However, I wasn't adequately dressed for the occasion, so instead I pulled my laptop up from the foot of my bed to begin my research.

I was never too far from my laptop just in case I needed to look something up or write something down. More importantly, I had a deadline looming on "Alternative Dating in the Twenty-

First Century" for *TESS* magazine where I worked, but for some reason I couldn't get an angle on it. My story centered around finding love at your local coffeehouse, an idea that Tess herself had whipped up. "We're going to show women the quickest, hippest way to find a mate, a rich mate," she'd said.

The piece was divided up between three of us: Abby, Julia and myself. Abby's assignment centered around women who found lovers for their ex-boyfriends, Julia had to cover speed dating and I was assigned coffeehouse dating. Patrons provide their personal stats and a photo for a matchmaking binder that the barista managed. Personally, I thought Tess used these assignments as her own matchmaking service. She wanted each of us to find true love, or at least someone who could pay part of our bills.

Actually, it wasn't as if I was totally opposed to finding love, I just didn't want one now. And certainly not with Atlanta Andy. Not when I was working on my career and had to keep up with the eighteen-year-olds. No, I believed the best thing that could happen from all of this was I wouldn't have to dig up those orgasmic memories. Instead, I might make some new ones.

The thought of all that sex gave me an idea.

Sex, Coffee And A Dating Service

I leaned back and stared at the title. I liked the way it read, at least for the moment.

The glare from my bedroom light bounced off the screen causing my eyes to sting. An odd sensation considering I slept with the lights on every night—the lights and the TV. Always. Constantly: 24/7.

I had this thing about quiet and darkness. Didn't like either one. It was my mom's fault. She had insisted we live over our bakery in Hoboken. My two sisters and I shared the front bedroom, the bedroom with the bakery's neon sign hanging directly underneath our windows that illuminated our room all night long. Where the street noise was nonstop. The continuous chatter of the TV somehow reminded me of that time and also of my older sisters, who've both moved to Maryland, married doctors and had two kids each. I didn't really know what kind of sex lives they had with their husbands because they didn't like to talk about it, especially Natalie, the oldest.

Although, it was curious about the doctors' connection....

My laptop chimed and a message popped up.

Nico: samantha, you should be sleeping

I swear the man had a sixth sense. Every time I wanted to talk to him, he was right there.

Samantha: i am

I hit the enter key and my answer zoomed across the ocean to Milan, Italy. Home to Michelangelo's David and Nico Bertuzzi. Somehow, I pictured Nico with the same attributes.

Nico: how can that be? you are on your computer

He simply didn't understand.

Samantha: i know, but I'm in bed

Nico: what does this mean?

Samantha: i have a new theory about sleep. as long as i'm in bed it counts toward my eight hours. what do you think of my new theory?

Nico: fascinating! can i join you?

I immediately conjured up a vision of myself and Nico lying in bed together. Naked. Sweaty. In the afterglow. My head resting on his David-like chest…but we were just friends. Distant friends. So I threw the vision aside and dreamed up something much more soothing: window shopping at Bloomingdale's. I'd had enough sex for one night, thank you very much.

Samantha: not tonight, honey. i want to sleep. BTW, i broke up with alex

Nico: i thought you liked him?

Samantha: he wanted to go out for breakfast

Nico: some men never learn

Samantha: but now i can't sleep. you think you can help?

He didn't answer. My clock clicked off a minute. A whole entire minute and nothing. Another minute passed. Then another, and still nothing.

The whole thing with Nico had started several months ago when I was researching an article on perfume. I couldn't exactly remember how I'd gotten his name, probably from Tess. The woman had an endless contact list. She seemed to know everybody who was anybody on the entire planet. No six degrees of separation with Tess—only one degree and she was the one.

Anyway, I phoned Nico for a brief interview and we ended up becoming friends and setting up instant messaging.

Nico: are you lying down?

I crushed out my tasty little cigarette and lay down, eager to start our late-night tryst.

Samantha: yes

Nico: mmmm...bella! are you comfortable? a woman should be comfortable when she wants to sleep

Oh, God was I ever. I scooted up on the bed.

Samantha: yes

Nico: but you must turn off the lights

A reasonable request, but I didn't think I could honor it. The question was, should I lie to the man or should I tell him the truth? I pondered this for a moment, reluctant to give up the security of Thomas Edison. I had to opt for truth or my nose would grow and I'd end up like Pinocchio.... I tended to base most of my ethics on kids' stories. It just made my life easier.

Samantha: you know i can't when i'm alone...at night

Nico: but you are not alone. i am there with you. you can feel safe with me. safe enough to turn off the lights

I clapped my hands and my light went off, but the TV remained on in a low mummer. I couldn't have it totally dark, or I'd freak. As soon as I got comfortable again, I let out a great big yawn, grabbed my down pillow and hung on.

At one point, I had genuinely thought our friendship might have turned into something more. That was my reasoning behind wanting that internship Tess had offered. It was in Milan at our sister magazine. I should have gotten it, but Tess gave it to Abby, my sometime friend. She hadn't exactly known how much I'd wanted to go, so I couldn't legitimately blame her, but still, she should have asked me.

Okay, so it was my own fault and I shouldn't take it out on Abby. I had opened my big mouth and made a pact with Tess to help her quit smoking. So how could she possibly have sent me all the way to Milan during our pact? Of course, neither one of us has actually quit smoking, so the whole thing was a complete bust. And now all Abby ever talked about was her time in Milan. As if anybody cares!

But wait. Perhaps it wasn't the pact. Perhaps it was Abby's age. Tess sent Abby because she was younger than me, and I'm an old hag.

Argh!

I made a mental note never to use the word *old* when referring to myself. Better still, I needed to strike that barbarous word from my vocabulary.

I pulled up the blanket and tucked it in all around me, leaving one hand out to do the typing.

Samantha: okay. it's dark and i'm imagining that you're here with me

I hit Enter and closed my eyes for a moment, trying to release all the negative bullshit out of my head. I focused on my vision of Nico...and Bloomingdale's...Nico in a window at Bloomingdale's. After that little vision, I had to open my eyes.

Nico: i want you to relax and dream of a full moon in a sky filled with stars as we lie under it

Samantha: not good enough

Nico: then, you are watching a fashion show by your favorite designer…who is it?

He knew me too well.

Samantha: Dolce & Gabbana

Nico: you have superb fashion taste. i…well, we will save my story for another time. first we will concentrate on your sleeping. you are watching the models on the runway, one after another wearing fabulous creations

I closed my eyes and saw a flash of color, an endless parade of models wearing crazy blends of textures, styles and flair. They were all around me. Catwalks stacked up to the heavens. It was glorious.

Samantha: now you're talking

Nico: try not to think of anything else but this moment. relax. float on my words. breathe slowly, deeply

I turned over on my back, taking in slow, deep breaths, concentrating on his words, the moment. I suddenly felt light, lazy and ready to think of what it might be like to…

...NOT THE END...

COMING NEXT MONTH

Signature Select Spotlight
SUNDAYS ARE FOR MURDER by Marie Ferrarella
FBI agent Charlotte "Charley" Dow is on the hunt for her sister's murderer and finds herself frustrated, yet attracted to agent Nick Brannigan. Working together, Charley and Nick must battle the mind of a psychopath, as well as their own personal demons, to put the serial killer away.

Signature Select Collection
WRITE IT UP! by Elizabeth Bevarly, Tracy Kelleher and Mary Leo
In this collection of three new stories, three reporters for a national magazine are given a unique assignment to write about dating practices for the urban set. And when Julie, Samantha and Abby each get to work, love and mayhem result.

Signature Select Showcase
THE QUIET GENTLEMAN by Georgette Heyer
On becoming the new earl of Stanyon, Gervase Frant returns from abroad to take possession of his inheritance. However, he is greeted with open disdain by his half brother and stepmother. When Gervase becomes prey to a series of staged "accidents," it seems someone is intent on ridding the family of him...permanently.

Signature Select Saga
WEALTH BEYOND RICHES by Gina Wilkins
Brenda Prentiss lived a simple life—until she inherited over a million dollars from a stranger! Now several attempts have been made on her life and her benefactor's son, Ethan Blacklock, is the prime suspect. Ethan must prove to Brenda that he's not out to protect his money...he's protecting *her.*

Signature Select Miniseries
PATTON'S DAUGHTERS by Janice Kay Johnson
The people of Elk Springs, Oregon, thought Ed Patton was a good man, a good cop, a good father. But his daughters know the truth. Both police officers themselves, Renee and Meg have been estranged for years. Now the time has come for the Patton sisters to reconcile... and to let love back into their lives.

The Fortunes of Texas: Reunion
THE LAW OF ATTRACTION by Kristi Gold
Alisha Hart can't believe how arrogant fellow lawyers like Daniel Fortune can be, especially when he offers her a bet she can't refuse. Daniel can't wait long for victory, and soon their playful banter turns into passionate nights in the bedroom. But could this relationship with Alisha cost him the promotion to D.A.?